The Cove Cottage

JESSIE NEWTON
THE HAMPTONS
BOOK 3

ISBN-13: 978-1-63876-451-9

Chapter One

Mandie Kelton stood in the driveway of Charlie's parents' house, watching her dad, Charlie's step-dad, and her husband unpack their few belongings from the U-Haul. The late spring breeze carried the promise of a fresh start, and she closed her eyes for a moment, letting memories of growing up in Five Island Cove wash over her.

"Hey." Charlie appeared beside her, sliding an arm around her waist. "Mom's making your favorite chicken pot pie for dinner."

"Alice knows the way to my heart." Mandie leaned into him, grateful for his steady presence. They'd been married for almost seven years now, and sometimes she still couldn't believe how lucky she was.

"Arthur's already organizing the garage to make room for our boxes." Charlie kissed her temple. "You okay?"

"Yeah." She wasn't entirely sure that was true, but she didn't want to worry him. "Just thinking about everything we need to do before the project starts."

"I don't start at the hospital for another couple of weeks," he said.

"Right." She turned into him. "You have one job, though. Tell me what it is."

Charlie grinned at her and touched his lips to hers. "I'm going to find us somewhere to live."

She tucked herself into his arms and watched her dad take her suitcase down the front walk as he laughed with Arthur.

Her phone buzzed, and Mandie wanted to ignore it. There had been so many messages lately, and Mandie sometimes didn't want to get sucked into the flurry.

"They're probably just telling you they landed," Charlie said as he stepped away. "We're almost done, and then you can come make the bedroom what you want."

"I can't believe we're living with your parents," she said, but Charlie only grinned and went to finish with the unpacking. "It's temporary." She grumbled the words to herself and pulled out her phone.

Just landed! Suzie and I are getting our rental car. See you soon, and we can decide where to go for lunch.

Mandie typed out the address for where she'd be staying—not *living*—for the next couple of weeks. She sighed as she looked up, the loud, metallic rumbling of the back of the moving truck filling the neighborhood as her dad pulled it closed.

He turned and met her eyes, a grin sitting widely on his face. Mandie loved her family, and she and Charlie had been working to return to the cove for almost a year now. "Thanks, Dad."

He reached her and put his arm around her. "I'm so glad you're in the cove."

"Me too." She snuggled into his side as they went into the house. Alice had bought this house after she'd moved here from the Hamptons with Charlie and Ginny, her twins. They'd only been fourteen, and Mandie had met Charlie then. She glanced down the road, having driven here hundreds of times in high school.

Everything looked exactly the same—the trees with their bright green leaves, the normal houses set in a neat row—yet somehow different too.

Or maybe she was the one who'd changed. She had lived in the city now for almost a decade.

"I'm so glad Charlie got a job here," her dad said.

"Me too." Mandie flashed him a smile. "We didn't think it would happen, but here we are."

Charlie had been the second choice for the hospital pharmacy here in Five Island Cove, so the job had gone to someone else. He'd found a job in New York City, but when the medical director had called, Charlie had put in his two weeks, and they'd immediately made plans to make the move across the water to the cove.

Mandie hadn't even known there'd be a job here for her, as the Black Sand Bungalow had taken forever for Candace to close. Then, she'd started working on getting the proper permits and permissions to build and rebuild the house in the way she wanted.

She'd been required to turn in blueprints, a timeline, and a full budget, and the Five Island Cove Planning and Zoning Commission had taken their sweet beach time getting back to her.

At least you didn't have to quit, Mandie thought. She'd gone into the offices of PastForward one day, fully expecting to tell Candace that Charlie had gotten a job in Five Island Cove, and she'd be leaving in three weeks.

That day, Candace had announced that she needed a team for the Black Sand Bungalow, and she hadn't looked away from Mandie during the whole meeting.

No satellite office had been opened anywhere, and Mandie didn't think Candace would open one here in the cove. It didn't have the real estate to support that, the Black Sand Bungalow notwithstanding.

She also hadn't been able to get pregnant yet, and a squeeze of disappointment twinged through her whole body. Another sigh escaped her lips as she entered the living room behind her father.

"Hello, dear." Alice Kelton opened her arm to bring Mandie into her side, her smile so genuine. "It's good to see you."

"You too, Alice." Mandie hugged her back. "Thanks so much for letting us stay here."

"Of course," she said easily. "Those bedrooms upstairs never get used."

"Wait," Mandie said. "Ginny said she and Bob were here a couple of weeks ago."

Alice grinned. "Yes, and I'm headed there in another month, when she has the baby."

Mandie's smile felt etched on face. "I can't wait to see that baby." She loved Ginny like her sister, though she and Charlie didn't see his twin and her husband as often as Mandie would like. They lived in Boston, where Bob practiced law at a huge technology corporation. "Have they decided on a name?"

"Ginny's being very tight-lipped about it," Alice said.

"Last I heard, Ruby was their favorite, but that was a few months ago."

Mandie nodded, as she'd heard Ruby as well. Along with Leah, Lucy, and even Willow.

The doorbell rang, and Mandie turned toward it. "That's probably my friends." A quiet excitement built within her as she went down the short hallway to the door and pulled it open.

Alicia stood there, looking like she'd just stepped out of *Modern Businesswoman*, with Suzie at her side, dressed for a beach vacation in capri pants and a tank top. At the sight of them, Mandie forgot all her worries and disappointments.

"You're here." She stepped out onto the porch, opening her arms to receive both of them at the same time. They formed a three-way hug, and Mandie sure was glad she didn't have to work on this project with a new team.

"I can't believe you're really moving back here," Suzie said as she stepped back. "It's so beautiful."

"And so quiet," Alicia added. "I don't know how you'll survive without the city noise."

"I grew up here." Mandie laughed, then sobered as she turned back to the house. "Come see everyone." Her friends had met her parents before, as well as Charlie's, as they'd all attended his graduation and the following party afterward.

They wouldn't be in town for long—Mandie had moved here, but Suzie, Alicia, and Candace were only going to be here for a few days to go over their final plans. Alicia was getting married next weekend, and after a week away on her honeymoon, she'd come back to Five Island Cove and join the field team working on the Black Sand Bungalow.

After quick re-introductions to Charlie's parents and Mandie's father, Mandie tucked her hands in her pockets.

"My mom is busy with a bride this afternoon." She indicated the back patio and swimming pool, which hadn't been fixed up for the summer yet.

"Have you heard from Candace yet?" she asked as she led the way outside.

"Flint texted to say we were lucky we'd left when we did." Suzie pulled the door closed behind her.

"What does that mean?" Mandie sat down at the small, round table on the patio.

"She delayed her flight until Sunday night," Alicia said in the practical, professional way she possessed. "I guess there was some problem with the Zombie House."

"I'll tell you what," Mandie said, pointing at her friends. "We dodged a bullet with that house."

"I'm not upset we didn't get that one," Suzie agreed. "Though...I'm not sure this black sand beast will be any better."

"Black sand beast." Alicia giggled, and Mandie joined her.

"I call it the cove cottage," Mandie said, her grin more genuine now. "It's what I imagine it'll be once we're finished."

"I'm worried this might be the one we *don't* finish," Alicia said.

Suzie clapped her hands together and rubbed them. "I can't wait to get in there and start bulldozing."

Despite its terrible condition, the bungalow had presence. Character. Soul. Mandie couldn't wait to start working on it either, if only so all of her plans-on-paper could finally start to come to life. Sometimes there was such a thing as over-planning.

She just wanted to get to work.

"You know what we should do before Candace gets here?" Mandie asked.

"You have that look on your face," Suzie said. "The one I don't like."

Mandie switched her gaze to Alicia. "What look?"

"It's a bit predatory," Alicia said thoughtfully. "She's right."

Mandie shook her head, trying to tame her smile and failing. "We should go to the library."

"The library?" Suzie asked, almost horrified.

"I'll go myself," Mandie said. "I used to work there."

"We've heard." Alicia got to her feet. "I'm going to go see if there's something to drink here."

THE FIVE ISLAND COVE LIBRARY SAT EXACTLY where it always had, its red brick walls and white columns as familiar as her own reflection.

"Mandie Kelton." Tessa Martin looked up from the reference desk, her silver-streaked hair in its usual neat bun. "I heard you were coming back."

"News travels fast." Mandie hugged her mother's longtime friend and her former boss. "I need your help with something."

"Ooh, a mystery?" Tessa's eyes twinkled.

"I need to do some research on the real estate and construction market on Rocky Ridge." Mandie hitched her backpack up onto her shoulder. She and Charlie had never owned a car, and she'd had her husband drop her off this morning before he went to sign some paperwork at the hospital.

"We have some property records," Tessa said. "I haven't been through many of them, but I can get them for you."

"Microfiche?"

"We've digitized it all," Tessa said.

"Thank goodness." Mandie followed her out of her office and over to the research computers.

Tessa put her hands on the keyboard and signed in, quickly navigating Mandie to the archives she needed. "Good luck. Let me know if you need anything, and come say goodbye before you go." She gave Mandie a warm smile and moved away.

She pulled out the notebook she'd brought with her and unhooked the pen from the wire coil. She started poking into the history of Rocky Ridge and the owners of the homes there, jotting down the names of the homeowners up and down the western coast of the island.

Wheeler.

Prescott.

Helms.

Williams.

She paused there for a moment, leaning closer to the screen before she just made the font bigger. "Connor and Denise Williams."

She knew those names, but she wasn't sure why they sat in her brain. She jotted them down and underlined them twice.

Turner.

Lyman.

Adams.

Mandie wasn't sure what she was looking for. Candace did all the purchasing of properties, and this one had been abandoned decades ago.

She sighed and leaned back, pressing her eyes closed and covering them with one hand. Movement on her right made her turn and look, and her mother slid into the seat beside.

Mandie's heart lifted. "Mom."

"I thought I'd find you here." She grinned at Mandie with such love in her expression, and Mandie had always loved her mother. Her mom was also very, very good at loving her, and Mandie smiled back at her briefly.

"Yeah, sure." Mandie scoffed. "You texted Charlie."

She grinned and nudged her. "He did say you were coming here to look up information about the house." She peered at the notebook, and Mandie pulled back her hand.

"Connor and Denise are Alice's parents," Mom said.

"What?" Mandie dove back into the notebook. "No wonder I recognized their names."

"They own that house on Rocky Ridge," Mom said. "And have for decades."

Mandie wanted that kind of life. One house, in one place, for a long time. She knew not many people did that anymore, but it was the small, slow, island life she wanted.

"You know, Denise's family owned a house there too, but they didn't live there long."

Mandie scanned the names again. "Maybe I should go talk to Alice's dad." She'd met him before, at the wedding for sure, and perhaps she could get some insight on the history of homes on Rocky Ridge through him. No matter what, she'd like to talk to some of the residents near where they'd be working, as it was quite the lengthy process to take a house from abandoned and falling down to renewed and rebuilt.

"Here they are," Mom said. "Prescott."

Mandie looked at the name. "Prescott." She returned to the archives and found the names. "Priscilla and James."

After looking over to her mom, she asked, "Do you know which one they lived in?"

"I think it's the first one after you turn onto Alice's lane," she said. "Her brother owned a house there at one point too, but Scott sold it when he made the move to Virginia." Mom smiled fondly, her expression somewhere in the past. "We used to tease Alice that she'd own the whole island of Rocky Ridge. Oh, she hated that."

Mandie had heard the stories of how certain friends of her mother's had left Five Island Cove the very moment they could—and Alice had been one of them. She'd come back to her roots, though, and Mandie put a star next to the name Prescott, determined to find out more about them.

"Is it really the first one on that lane, Mom?"

"I think so, yes."

"That's the house we'll be working on." Mandie looked up from the list of names and met her mother's eyes. Her heart started to race, and she wasn't sure why.

All old houses had secrets, even those that had been abandoned for over sixty years—and Mandie couldn't wait to find out what the cove cottage had to tell her.

Chapter Two

Alicia Halverson stared at her reflection in the full-length mirror of the bridal suite, hardly recognizing herself in the vintage-inspired lace gown she'd fallen in love with months ago. The dress hugged her curves before flowing out into a subtle A-line, and tiny pearls dotted the bodice like morning dew on spider webs.

Her dark hair had been swept up into an elegant up-do, with a few tendrils framing her face. The stylist had woven baby's breath and tiny white rosebuds through her hair, making her feel like a fairy tale princess.

"Mama." Lily appeared beside her, resplendent in her flower girl dress of pale green tulle. "You look like an angel."

Alicia's eyes filled with tears, and she quickly blinked them back. No need to ruin her makeup before the ceremony even started. "Thank you, sweetheart." She smoothed her hands down the front of her dress, her engagement ring catching the light. "You are the cutest thing in the world."

Lily giggled and did a twirl, which sent her skirt out in a fan.

Suzie stepped forward with a tissue. "In case you need it later." She tucked it under the shoulder strap of Alicia's dress, and surprise flowed through her, rendering her still for a moment.

"I'm not crying today." But Alicia's voice wavered as Gray entered the suite in his little tuxedo, looking so grown up it made her heart ache.

"Mom, I saw Henry," he said as he came over.

Alicia wrapped him up in a hug, her pulse quickening at the mention of her soon-to-be husband. In less than an hour, she'd walk down the aisle and become Mrs. Henry Aldrich. "Did you? Is he ready for the wedding?"

"I don't know." Gray stepped back. "He seemed to be. He was talking to Daniel."

Alicia nodded and took in the purity in the bride's room. Everything came in tones of cream, white, and ivory. The wallpaper held texture, and as a restoration expert, Alicia felt right at home here. Her wedding dress matched the more ecru tones in the two-tone carpet, and she smoothed her hands over her hips again, admiring the subtle mermaid shape and how it fit her.

She'd chosen dusty rose, sage, and a warm beige for her colors, and with the help of an amazing wedding planner, she'd gotten every detail in place—just like she did while at work. Honestly, planning her wedding had felt a lot like managing and working on the Hampton House or the *Amaranth*, two of her favorite projects in the past couple of years.

"Everything's ready." Mandie turned from the doorway, where she'd been speaking with someone. She carried elegance in her shoulders, which held up a beautiful dusty rose bridesmaid gown. "Sherri says everything is set in the chapel. Flowers, ushers, and the bows hanging from the ceiling are perfection."

She smiled with so much energy that Alicia felt it way down in her heart.

"Okay." Alicia nodded, trying to focus on the present moment instead of the nervous, swirling thoughts about her future. She loved Henry with all her heart, but the idea of blending their lives together still felt daunting. She couldn't believe she was doing this *again*, after so much heartache when her first marriage had ended unexpectedly.

She, Henry, and the kids would be spending the summer in Five Island Cove while she worked on the Black Sand Bungalow project, then moving into Henry's house in Yonkers when school started. The kids would have to change schools, make new friends, adjust to a new routine...

She'd have to figure out how to get them to Ryan, their father, and how to work in the field two hours—and a huge body of water—away, because the abandoned house in Five Island Cove was going to take a lot longer than three months to complete.

"I know that look." Mandie took Alicia's hands in hers. "Suze, she's overthinking everything again."

Alicia glared at her. "I'm not—"

"You are." Mandie squeezed her fingers as Suzie arrived in their huddle. "Marriage is about compromise and trust. You and Henry will figure everything out together."

Alicia managed a smile, though her relationship with Henry wasn't at the top of her Things-I'm-Worried-About list. Mandie had no idea how everything changed when a baby came into a family. She and Charlie had moved to Five Island Cove. She wouldn't have to manage relationships and motherhood from hundreds of miles away.

But she said nothing, because today was her wedding day, and she and Henry had a plan for this next week in St. Maarten, and then for the next three months in Five Island Cove.

They'd rented a beautiful, if tiny, house right on the beach, and Henry had gotten permission to work remotely so he could be with the kids.

If only she could believe what her friends and mother had told her so many times.

Everything will work out.

It will be fine.

"...right?" Suzie moved closer, causing Alicia to blink back to the conversation. "You weren't even listening."

"I'm getting married in thirty minutes," Alicia said, a sudden flurry in her stomach. "I'm allowed to be distracted." She pulled her hands back and nudged Suzie gently with her elbow. "When is Daniel going to propose?"

Suzie's cheeks flushed pink. "I don't know," she mumbled.

"You do want to get married, though, right?" Mandie asked.

"Yes," Suzie said. "We've talked about it."

Alicia exchanged a glance with Mandie, and neither one of them jumped to say anything else. Suzie had fallen fast for Daniel—and he for her—but they'd then taken things slowly after that. She'd told them she probably wouldn't be able to have children due to her age, and weeks later, she'd confessed she didn't really think she was suited for motherhood anyway.

"So there's no real rush," she'd said.

Before Suzie could speak into the silence, the wedding

planner bustled in. "It's time for final touches, ladies. We start in twenty minutes."

Alicia's mother approached with the veil, and suddenly the room buzzed with activity. Mandie touched up Alicia's lipstick while Suzie fiddled with the train. Lily practiced her flower-tossing technique while Gray stood at attention, taking his ring bearer duties very seriously.

"I can't believe my baby's getting married again." Mom dabbed at her eyes with a tissue. "And to such a wonderful man."

"He is wonderful." Alicia smiled, thinking of how naturally Henry fit into their lives. How he'd won over her children with patience and genuine interest in their lives. How he made her feel safe and cherished and completely herself.

The wedding planner reappeared. "Five minutes, everyone. Let's all take our places." She smiled graciously as she collected Lily and Gray, and Alicia's mother went with them too.

Alicia's heart began to race as the room emptied. This was really happening, and everyone would be waiting for her, staring at her. "Wait." She grabbed Mandie's arm. "What if—?"

"No what-ifs," Mandie said firmly. "You love Henry. He loves you and your children. Everything else will work itself out."

"But the summer in Five Island Cove, and then moving to Yonkers, and what if the project takes longer than we think? I'll be working—" She fell silent as someone else appeared in the now-open doorway.

An imposing figure.

Her boss, Candace Ewing. She wore a navy blue dress studded with sequins, which had to cost more than Alicia made in a year. Still, something about Candace's smile reminded Alicia that the woman was a human being, with flesh that bled like everyone else.

"I just wanted to come say congratulations before things get crazy." She entered the room, her blue eyes sparkling with friendship. She smiled at Alicia. "You look beautiful."

"Thank you." Alicia took a deep breath, smoothing her hands down her dress one last time, and leaned in to hug Candace lightly. "Okay, I'm ready."

She did hard things every day at work. She had no idea from one moment to the next how to parent her children, but she did the best she could.

This was the same—she'd take one step at a time until she arrived at Henry's side. Then, she wouldn't be alone anymore.

Suzie and Mandie lined up in the hallway with Daniel and Charlie. Lily headed the procession with her basket of rose petals, then Gray with the rings, followed by the small wedding party, which included Henry's sister and her husband. Alicia's mother kissed her cheek before hurrying off, leaving Alicia alone with her father.

"You look radiant, sweetheart." Dad's eyes shone brightly as he offered his arm.

The wedding march began to play from in the chapel, and Alicia's breath caught in her throat. Lily would have to lead everyone down the stairs, and she suddenly worried her daughter might trip. "Thanks, Dad," she said just as Candace disappeared around the corner too.

When the wedding planner gestured her forward, Lily took the first step, seemingly without any trouble at all. Gray followed, his back straight and his steps measured, the ring pillow held carefully in front of him.

Henry's sister, Lenore, and her husband, Caleb, took their first steps forward, and Alicia's grip on her father's arm tightened.

Dad looked at her but said nothing. She'd been nervous right before her first wedding too, and when she'd said something, her dad had assured her and reassured her that Ryan loved her. He'd apologized for that once everything had come out—all the lies, all the troubles—and her husband had filed for divorce, and Alicia had told him it wasn't his fault.

But he offered no such reassurances today. Alicia took a breath and searched inside herself as Mandie and Charlie moved forward. Suzie and Daniel would go next, and Alicia had to make a decision.

Images of Henry with the children, with her family on holidays, out with their friends...he adored her, and she loved him. He'd already shown her over and over what he'd do for her, Gray, and Lily, and his loyalty and love had been proven.

"Ready?" her father asked, and Alicia blinked, realizing the hallway sat empty. Suzie and Daniel had gone.

She nodded, cleared her throat, and said, "Yes," in a sure voice. Alicia gripped her father's arm as they stepped down the hall and to the top of the steps.

Sunlight streamed through the stained glass windows at the other end of the chapel, casting rainbow patterns across the hardwood floors. Ivory roses and sage bows decorated the end of each row, with dusty pink ribbons draped elegantly between them.

But Alicia barely noticed any of it, because Henry stood at the altar, and the look on his face when he saw her made her heart stop.

Pure joy and love radiated from him, and suddenly all her worries about the future melted away. This man loved her.

He loved her children. She didn't need any assurances from anyone—she felt everything in her mind, heart, and gut.

She started down the steps, careful to land on her foot surely before moving. Henry's smile grew with each step she took, and she couldn't help smiling back. Finally, she reached the bottom of the steps, and everyone else in the wedding party had already walked down the aisle.

She paused, soaking up the sunshine, the beauty of the room before her, the smile on her mother's face, the way her friends and family filled the room with love and light.

In that moment, Daniel stepped forward and held up one hand. "I have something to say."

Alicia's pulse pranced through her veins; a murmur ran through the crowd. A few feet away, a legit growl came from Sherri's throat. Her heels clicked into the silence as heads continued to turn toward Daniel, and she hissed, "I will take care of this."

But Daniel had just pulled a black velvet ring box out of his pocket, and Alicia shook her head. "No, it's fine."

Daniel met her eyes, and Alicia nodded at him. That gave him permission to turn toward Suzie and say, "Can I get Suzette Paxman out here?"

"No," Suzie said loud enough for everyone to hear.

Mandie moved to her side and practically hauled her out of the bridesmaid line. She gave her a little push forward, and Suzie looked like a new fawn who'd never walked before as she stumbled toward Daniel.

She huffed and brushed her non-bouquet-holding hand down the front of her sage-green gown. Daniel dropped to one knee and held up the ring box. The entire congregation seemed to hold its breath as Daniel cleared his throat. Suzie, in true Suzie fashion, stood frozen, her bouquet of roses trembling in her hands as she stared down at Daniel.

"Suzette Paxman." His voice carried clearly through the chapel. "We first met for dinner, and I think I fell in love with you before the main course was served. I've been falling more and more in love with you every day since. You're all I've ever wanted, and you'd make me the happiest man throughout the ages if you'll be my wife. Will you marry me?"

Alicia switched her gaze to one of her best friends, expecting Suzie to exclaim, "Yes!" the crowd to clap, and her wedding to resume.

But Suzie just stood there, staring at Daniel silently.

Chapter Three

S uzette Paxman did not like the spotlight.

Daniel knew this, and yet, he'd turned on the brightest beam in the world and aimed it directly at her.

She stared down at Daniel, her heart hammering against her ribs like a caged bird desperate for escape. The entire chapel held its breath, waiting for her answer, and the weight of every single pair of eyes bored into her.

Daniel's face radiated hope and love, his dark eyes searching hers for the response he clearly expected. The ring box trembled slightly in his outstretched hand, the diamond catching the light streaming throughout this beautiful hall.

She opened her mouth, but no sound came out. The silence stretched on, becoming more awkward with each passing second. Someone in the congregation shifted uncomfortably, and she heard what sounded like Mandie's disgruntled sigh from somewhere behind her.

"Suzie?" Daniel's voice carried the faintest note of uncertainty now.

Heat crawled up her neck and spread across her cheeks.

This wasn't how proposals were supposed to go. She was supposed to cry happy tears and throw herself into his arms, not transform into a statue while everyone—strangers—witnessed her having a panic attack.

But the truth was, she'd never imagined herself getting married. Not really. She'd spent most of her adult life convinced she was too difficult, too blunt, too much of everything for anyone to want permanently. Even with Daniel, even knowing how much he loved her, some part of her kept waiting for him to realize he'd made a mistake.

And now he was asking her to marry him in front of all these people, at her best friend's wedding? She couldn't seem to form words.

Mandie's arm laced through hers and took the bouquet. "You tell that man yes, because you love him," she whispered. "And Alicia is still waiting at the end of the aisle."

Suzie moved her eyes to Mandie, who nodded decisively, took the bouquet, and faded into the background again.

She looked down at Daniel, the warmest wave on the planet washing over her. She had no other way to describe it except for love.

"Yes." The word finally escaped her lips, barely above a whisper. She cleared her throat and nodded.

Daniel's face broke into a grin. "Yes?"

"Yes," she said louder, a smile starting to spread across her face. "Yes, I'll marry you."

The chapel erupted in applause and cheers as Daniel slipped the ring onto her finger. He stood and pulled her into his arms, spinning her around as she laughed despite the knot of anxiety still twisted in her stomach.

When he set her down, she caught sight of Alicia's face—pure joy mixed with just a hint of exasperation at having her wedding interrupted. Mandie beamed at her from the brides-maid line, tears streaming down her cheeks.

"Sorry," Suzie called out to Alicia, holding up her left hand to show off the ring. "Your turn now."

The ceremony resumed, and Suzie tried to focus on her friend's beautiful moment, but her mind kept spinning. Engaged. She was *engaged*. The ring felt foreign on her finger, heavier than she'd expected, and she kept twisting it around and around.

"I do," Alicia said first, and Suzie managed to listen while the pastor asked Henry if he'd love, honor, and cherish Alicia. The man had been at her side relentlessly for the past couple of years, and Suzie found them to be one of the cutest couples ever.

"I do," Henry said, and Suzie sighed in bliss for her friend. While she was thinking about things she couldn't believe, she could add *having friends* to the list.

She'd come so far in such a short amount of time, and Suzie tipped her head back slightly and smiled up to the ceiling.

During the reception, it seemed like every single person —again, strangers; people she did not know—wanted to congratulate her and Daniel and ask about wedding plans. *When were they thinking? Had they set a date? Where would they have it? What kind of dress did she want?*

"We haven't really decided on specifics yet," she found herself saying over and over, Daniel's arm warm around her waist as he fielded questions with much more grace than she managed.

"We'll figure it out," he kept adding with that smile that made her heart flutter even as her anxiety spiked.

What kind of dress did she want? She had no idea. She'd

just bought her first dress in a decade to attend the unveiling gala for the *Amaranth*. She'd only been able to do that, because Mandie and Alicia had gone with her.

By the time Alicia and Henry cut the cake, Suzie's skin crawled and she wanted to scratch it all off. She loved Daniel —she one-hundred-percent did—but the sudden spotlight on their relationship, the expectations, the assumption that she'd transform overnight into someone who knew there were different kinds of dresses and register for china patterns, left her feeling like she couldn't get a decent breath.

"I need some air," she whispered to Daniel as Alicia and Henry moved onto the dance floor.

He switched his smile to her, his eyes turning concerned. "Too much excitement for one day?"

"Yes." She managed a smile as he pressed a kiss to her temple.

"Sorry, Suze. I should've known to propose to you in private."

"It's okay," she assured him as she stepped back. "Really. I'll just step outside for a minute."

"Want me to come with you?"

"No, stay. I just need five minutes." She slipped out of the ballroom and into the cool evening air, grateful for the quiet. The sun had set while they'd been inside, and the first stars pricked the darkness of the sky above the city.

Her phone buzzed with a text, but Suzie ignored it. She suspected it would be from Mandie, who never missed anything.

She drew in a deep breath, getting the saltiness of the sea, as Alicia and Henry had chosen a waterfront venue for their nuptials. "This is good," she told herself. Just because she hadn't imagined her life to be the one she was currently living didn't mean it wasn't exactly the life she deserved.

———

THREE DAYS LATER, SUZIE STOOD ON THE FERRY deck, watching Rocky Ridge grow larger as they approached the northern island. The spring morning air carried a chill that made her pull her jacket tighter, but the sun promised warmth later in the day.

She'd barely slept the night before, excitement buzzing through her veins like electricity. Alicia and Henry were somewhere in the Caribbean on their honeymoon, and Mandie had texted that morning to say she and Charlie were looking at a house on Pearl Island that had just come on the market.

Which meant Suzie had the Black Sand Bungalow all to herself today. Everything in Five Island Cove belonged to her, as she'd rented a small one-bedroom condo on Diamond Island for the duration of the project—nothing fancy, but it had a view of the harbor and came furnished. More importantly, it was hers alone, a sanctuary where she could decompress after long days of work and social interaction.

Daniel had a job in the city, but he could get here in a couple of hours, and they'd already planned for him to come to the cove this weekend. She still had her grandmother's house in the city too, and Suzie didn't want to get rid of that.

While she loved the cove, and she could see why Mandie wanted to relocate here permanently, Suzie felt a familial pull to the house she'd inherited but didn't currently live in.

"Perhaps Daniel and I..." She let the thought flow out of her mouth in a whisper, but she didn't dare complete it. She should probably tell him about the house before she made plans for them to start their life there.

The ferry docked with a gentle bump, and Suzie gathered her backpack and toolbox. The walk from the ferry station to the project site took twenty minutes, or she could get what they called a RideShare and be there in seven.

Today, she wanted to walk, because she wanted to center her thoughts, breathe in the freshest air of her life, and see the neighborhood from a new perspective.

The streets here reminded her of small-town America—a simple strip of asphalt without lines on the sides or down the middle. Nothing had been laid out in a grid, but followed the contours of the rocky island, with weathered shingle houses that boasted just-starting gardens. Rocky Ridge had a different feel from Diamond Island—quieter, more isolated, with fewer tourists and more year-round residents—most of them older folks—who nodded politely or lifted a garden-gloved hand as she went by.

The Black Sand Bungalow sat at the front end of a lane that kept going north along the sea cliff, surrounded by tall pitch pine trees that had grown wild in the decades since anyone had maintained the property.

Suzie saw a couple of towering black oaks, surprised they'd been able to grow so tall in this sandy soil and windy environment. The shadbush stood much shorter, and they'd just bloomed, so they looked like great big puffballs of pure white popcorn.

Suzie paused at the rusty gate, breathing in the flower-scented air and studying the house that would consume her life for the next several months. A certain giddiness flowed through her, because she loved taking things from completely neglected and dilapidated to functional, beautiful, and restored.

Honestly, the journey of the projects she worked on mirrored her own life. She'd felt as neglected as this house at one point in her life, and now she had a great career, meaningful friendships, and a loving fiancé.

"So what's next?" she wondered, and she didn't mean just for the house.

She pushed open the gate and stepped onto the property. Calling the structure a bungalow was generous. The house sagged like an old woman bent with age, its cedar shingles weathered to gray and many missing entirely. The front porch had partially collapsed, and several windows boasted plywood that had warped and split with time, harsh weather conditions, and the salty humidity in the air.

But Suzie saw past the decay to the bones underneath. The roofline had good proportions, and the stone foundation looked solid despite the ivy that had claimed it. This house had character, history, stories to tell.

Her soul yearned for such things, and Suzie let the magnificence and wonder of the past move through her as she approached the front door, fishing the key from her pocket. Candace had warned them that the interior was in rough shape, but Suzie preferred to form her own opinions.

The door stuck, swollen with decades of moisture, and she had to put her shoulder into it before it finally gave way with a protesting groan. The musty, damp smell hit her immediately, and it carried undertones of something she couldn't quite identify. Not decay exactly, but the scent of a place that had been closed up and forgotten.

Despite the sunlight outside, Suzie pulled out her phone and turned on the flashlight, sweeping the beam across the front room. Water damage had buckled the hardwood floors in several places, and ancient wallpaper peeled from the walls in long, curling strips. A stone fireplace dominated one wall, its hearth filled with debris and what looked like an old bird's nest.

But the windows were larger than they'd appeared from outside, and once she pried the boards off, natural light would flood the space. The crown molding was intact, and the built-in bookcases flanking the fireplace showed craftsmanship that modern construction rarely matched.

She moved through the house methodically, her excitement building with each room, though she couldn't go up to the second floor. Mandie had said the damage up there had soaked into the joists, and it wouldn't bear much weight.

The kitchen would need to be completely gutted—the cabinets had rotted through in places, and the doorway that led out the back held no door. But the dining room had beautiful wainscoting beneath layers of peeling paint, and the main bedroom featured a bay window that would be stunning once restored.

She simply peered out at the deck, as Mandie and Candace had already made a plethora of notes about the outdoor needs and landscaping problems. She moved into the last room on the first floor, a very small space—probably only ten-feet by ten-feet.

This room seemed to be in worse shape than the others, with a section of the exterior wall that had been pierced by a tree limb, probably during a winter storm that sent branches whipping. The plaster had fallen away in chunks, exposing the wooden lath underneath.

As Suzie examined the damage, something pink and pearly caught her eye. Behind a particularly large section of fallen plaster, set into the wall at about shoulder height, sat a small decorative tile. It was maybe four inches square, made of what looked like hand-painted ceramic. The colors had faded, but she could make out a design—a family crest or coat of arms, with symbols she didn't recognize.

Suzie pulled out her phone and snapped several photos, then carefully worked the tile free from its setting. It came away easily, as if it had been placed there deliberately rather than incorporated into the original construction. The back was smooth, with no mortar or adhesive residue.

She held it up to the light streaming through the damaged wall, studying the faded design. Why would someone hide a decorative tile inside a wall? And why this particular wall, in what had probably been a child's bedroom or a storage room?

The rational part of her mind suggested it could be nothing—maybe a repair job gone wrong, or a leftover piece from some long-ago renovation. Something blown here by the wind and embedded in the plaster with the tree limb.

But her instincts, honed by years of restoration work, told her this was something more. Something deliberately hidden.

She slipped the tile into her backpack, thinking, *Every old house has secrets.*

As she worked her way back through the house, making notes and taking measurements, Suzie found herself wondering about the families who had lived here. According to the property records Mandie had shared, the house had belonged to the Prescott family for decades before being abandoned. What had driven them to leave? And what had they left behind?

By the time she locked up and called for a ride, the sun

had risen to almost directly overhead, and Suzie tipped her face back to soak in the warm rays. "This is going to be a great summer," she told herself.

The ferry ride back to Diamond Island gave her time to think as she watched the water churn while Rocky Ridge receded behind them. She'd always been good at puzzles, at seeing patterns others missed. It was what made her valuable to PastForward—her ability to look at a damaged structure and envision not just what it had been, but what it could become.

Despite her natural inclination to work alone, Suzie found herself eager to share her discovery with Mandie and Alicia. They'd become more than colleagues over the past few years—they'd become the family she'd never thought she'd have. And families shared their secrets.

Her phone buzzed with a text from Daniel: *What are you doing today? Anything fun while you wait for your project to start?*

Suzie smiled as she typed back. *I went to the site today.*

She looked down at her engagement ring, catching the light as the ferry pulled into the station on Diamond Island. Maybe she was finally ready to stop waiting for the other shoe to drop. Maybe she was ready to believe that good things—love, friendship, a home, a future—could actually be hers.

She didn't have to expect heartbreak because it was all that existed in her past. She could build a completely different future for herself, one brick, board, or tile at a time.

Chapter Four

C andace Ewing stood at the edge of the Black Sand
Bungalow property, her designer ankle boots—the
only kind of boots she owned—sinking slightly into the
sandy soil just off the asphalt of the road. She surveyed the
controlled chaos unfolding before her, as a team of eight had
descended upon the house to begin the first day of
demolition.

The morning air carried the scent of salt and pine, mixed
with the dust already rising from the work that had begun at
dawn.

She'd arrived on the first Steamer from New York City,
her usual polished appearance intact despite how early she'd
had to leave. Navy blazer, cream silk blouse, and her signature
pearl earrings—armor for another day of commanding her
empire, even if today's battlefield was a crumbling house on a
remote island instead of her Long Island office.

"Careful with that section," Mandie called out to Bear,
one of the demolition crew members, as he approached a

particularly unstable section of the front porch. "We want to salvage those support columns if possible."

Candace watched her direct the team with quiet authority, unsure of why Candace hadn't liked Mandie in the beginning. She mentally scoffed.

You know why, she told herself, flashing the younger woman a tight smile when Mandie caught her standing there.

"You made it." Mandie smiled as she came toward Candace wearing proper footwear, blue jeans, and a long-sleeved T-shirt. Safety was paramount, and Candace had told everyone to cover up and protect themselves, especially during demo. They also had to contend with the sun in Five Island Cove, as so much of this project would happen outside.

"You were right," Candace said. "The Steamer was easy and fast."

Mandie had grown so much over the past few years, transforming from an eager but uncertain young woman into someone who could command respect from seasoned construction workers twice her age.

The transformation still surprised Candace, because she'd never expected to care about any employee's growth the way she found herself caring about this team's development. She'd attended Alicia's wedding, for crying out loud. Candace had never attended a personal function for an employee before that.

"The structural engineer's report was spot-on," Alicia said, also approaching Candace with a tablet in hand. "The foundation is solid, but we'll need to replace most of the first-floor joists and all of the second-floor framing."

Candace nodded, studying the numbers on the screen. Alicia had returned from her honeymoon three days ago, glowing with happiness but immediately focused on the project at hand. Her ability to compartmentalize personal and professional life reminded Candace of herself, though Alicia managed it with far more grace and warmth.

"You get twenty weeks," Candace said, determined to be firm on the deadline for this house. "That puts us at the third week of September."

"Ambitious but doable," Alicia replied without missing a beat. "Assuming we don't hit any major surprises."

"There are always surprises." Candace's gaze moved to where Suzie stood photographing architectural details before the demo crew removed them. "That's why I'm leaving you three in charge."

The words came out more easily than she'd expected. A year ago, she would have micromanaged every aspect of this project, demanding daily reports and flying out for surprise inspections. But something had shifted in her—a recognition that her obsessive control hadn't just been about maintaining standards. It had been about fear.

Fear of failure. Fear of vulnerability. Fear of trusting anyone else with something that mattered to her.

"You're really not staying?" Mandie looked away from where she watched Casper, the lead demolition specialist, talking to his team.

"I have other projects that need attention," Candace said, which was true but not the whole truth. The whole truth was that she'd discovered she actually enjoyed watching her team succeed without her constant oversight. "Consider yourselves a fully functioning satellite office. Mandie, you're the project manager. Full authority for decisions and budget allocation within the parameters we've discussed."

She caught the look that passed between Mandie and

Alicia—surprise mixed with something that might have been pride. When had she started caring about earning their respect instead of simply demanding it?

"What about approvals for major changes?" Suzie asked, joining their huddle.

"Use your judgment. If it's something that affects the overall vision or budget by more than ten percent, call me. Otherwise, I trust you three to make the right decisions."

The word *trust* felt foreign on her tongue, but not unpleasant. When had she ever trusted anyone?

Maybe Lana, she thought. Her biological daughter certainly hadn't given Candace a reason *not* to trust her.

"Hey, boss." Flint approached with his camera equipment, already documenting the demolition process for the project archive. They always launched a new house with before-and-after shots too, and Flint was the best videographer at PastForward. "Should I set up the time-lapse camera on the eastern corner?"

"I think that's the best place," Mandie said before Candace could respond. Oh. He'd been calling *her* the boss.

"We'll want to capture the full transformation over time." Mandie stepped away from Candace to keep instructing Flint. "And that's the most sheltered corner from the wind."

Candace smiled at the easy way Mandie had stepped into her authority. Leadership suited her, and Candace found herself wondering who else she'd been holding back all these years by insisting on maintaining such tight control.

The sound of splintering wood drew her attention back to the house, where more demo crew members, Alex and Felicia, were carefully removing sections of the damaged porch railing. Each piece would be catalogued and assessed for restoration potential—a painstaking process that separated PastForward from less meticulous renovation companies.

"The tile you found recently," Candace said, remembering the photos that had been texted to her as she turned to face Suzie. "Any theories about its significance?"

"Not yet." Suzie squinted at the demo happening before her. "But I have a feeling it's not the only thing hidden in this house."

Something in Suzie's tone made Candace study her face more carefully. There was an excitement there, the kind that came from sensing a mystery worth solving. It was the same expression Candace had seen on her own face years ago, when she'd first started restoration work and every old building held the promise of secrets waiting to be uncovered.

"Document everything," she said, though a sense of weariness moved through her. She'd had enough secrets for a lifetime. "Even things that seem insignificant. Old houses tell stories, and sometimes those stories matter more than we initially realize."

Her phone buzzed with a text, and Candace glanced down to see Lana's name on the screen. *Lunch tomorrow? I found something I want to show you!*

The simple message sent a complex mix of emotions through her chest. A year ago, she hadn't even known her daughter's name. Now they had regular lunch dates, growing closer with each meeting. Lana had her father's curiosity and her own analytical mind, and their conversations had become one of the highlights of Candace's weeks.

But things with Bradley remained complicated. He'd been patient, understanding, even grateful when she'd finally told him about Lana. But twenty-one years of secrets had created a chasm between them that couldn't be bridged with a few awkward dinners and stilted phone calls.

She typed back: *Of course. Same place?*

Actually, I was hoping we could meet at your office. I want to see it.

Candace stared at the message, her throat tightening unexpectedly. Lana wanted to see her world, to understand the life her mother had built. It felt like another step forward in their careful dance toward a real relationship.

"Everything okay?" Alicia's voice was gentle, concerned.

"Yeah, just...family," Candace said, then realized she'd never used that word in connection with herself before. Not in front of her employees, anyway. "My daughter wants to visit the office."

She caught the surprised look that passed between Suzie and Alicia. They knew about Lana now—the whole story had come out during the *Amaranth* project—but hearing Candace refer to her as "my daughter" still seemed to catch them off guard.

"That's wonderful," Alicia said warmly. "She'll love seeing all the project boards and the archive room."

"Will she?" Candace found herself genuinely wondering. She'd spent so many years building PastForward into something impressive, but she'd never considered whether it would matter to anyone but her.

Another crash from the house interrupted her thoughts as a section of interior wall came down, revealing the skeleton of the structure beneath. Dust billowed out through the windows, and she could hear Bear calling out measurements to Felicia.

"The bones are good," Casper announced, emerging from the house with debris in his hair. "This place was built to last. Someone knew what they were doing when they put her up."

"Built in 1888," Alicia said. "It has a sturdy rock foundation."

Candace nodded, making a mental note to review whatever historical information they'd gathered. Understanding a building's past often provided crucial insights for its restoration—not just the architectural details, but the emotional resonance that would guide their design choices.

"But no family ties?" she asked.

"I'm still looking into the family crest on the tile," Suzie said.

"See what you can find," Candace said. "Quickly. We'll need to be making design choices before long." By the beginning of next week, actually, but Candace knew Mandie could handle the timeline. She'd boasted about the tradesmen and services in Five Island Cove, and Candace wanted to see things every step of the way but not be the one in charge of them.

An alarm on her phone went off, and Mandie turned back to them as Flint went to film whatever she'd asked of him. "I should go," Candace said, silencing the alarm. "It's so many boat rides here."

Mandie grinned at her as she joined them up on the road. "That's life in the cove."

For the first time in years, Candace found herself reluctant to leave a job site. Not because she doubted her team's abilities, but because she was genuinely interested in seeing how this particular story would unfold.

"Remember, we're going for beach vibes," she said. "Within the framework of history."

"We'll send daily updates," Mandie said, nodding. "Photos, progress reports, any issues that come up."

"I know you will." Candace surprised herself by reaching out to squeeze Mandie's shoulder. "You've got this."

She called goodbye to the demolition crew and told herself again it was time to leave, but she couldn't help pausing for one last look at the house. The front porch and deck were gone. Piles of wood and debris sat in the jungle of a yard.

Trees had been cut back, so she could see the structure better, and as she watched, Bear and Felicia removed the front window and brought it to a tarp that had been laid out for such purposes.

In just a few hours, it had already begun its transformation from abandoned relic to work in progress. By the time she returned—and she would return, she realized, probably sooner than necessary—it would be unrecognizable in the best way possible.

Watching her team grow and succeed, seeing the genuine affection they had for each other and—surprisingly—for her, had taught her something she'd never expected to learn: that strength could come from connection, not just from control.

As Rocky Ridge and the Black Sand Bungalow grew smaller behind her, she pulled out her phone and scrolled through the photos Flint had already uploaded to the project folder.

Her team was good. Better than good; they were exceptional, and they'd earned the right to prove it without her looking over their shoulders every step of the way.

For the first time in her professional life, Candace Ewing was learning to let go, and despite every instinct that told her this was dangerous, it felt like the most natural thing in the world.

She typed a quick message to Lana. *I'd love to show you the office. How about one o'clock?*

Then she leaned back in her seat and watched the city skyline grow larger, already planning which projects she'd show her daughter first. Maybe it was time to start thinking about what kind of legacy she wanted to leave—not just in buildings restored and profits earned, but in relationships built and trust freely given.

The Black Sand Bungalow would be her team's triumph. But perhaps, in learning to step back and let them succeed, she was finally building something even more valuable—a life that included people, not just projects.

Chapter Five

Mandie sat at the table, eating a bowl of cereal and watching Charlie adjust his tie for the third time in his reflection of the hallway mirror. Her heart swelled with pride and anticipation as she took in the sight of her husband preparing for his first day at Five Island Cove Regional Hospital.

"This tie," he muttered as he returned to the kitchen.

"You look perfect," she said, unable to keep the pride from her voice. "Very professional pharmacist-y."

Charlie came back around the corner with that crooked smile that had captured her heart in high school. "Pharmacist-y isn't a word."

"It is now." She stood and crossed to him, smoothed down his collar, and breathed in the familiar scent of his aftershave. "This is really happening." She brushed his hand away from his tie. "The tie is perfect."

She'd bought it for him for this very day, and the deep blue brought out the color in his eyes. "Leave it."

"I'm just nervous," he admitted, his hands finding her

45

waist. "What if they realize they made a mistake by hiring me?"

"Impossible." Mandie stood on her tiptoes to kiss him softly. "You're going to be amazing. The patients are going to love you, and the staff will wonder how they ever managed without you."

His smile grew more confident. "What are your plans for today?"

"Final demolition inspection at the house." She tried to keep her tone light, but anxiety crept in anyway. The project timeline felt impossibly tight, and every day mattered. "Flint's coming by for final before-shots, and then we won't see him again for a month. We need to make sure everything's ready for the rebuild to start next week."

"And house hunting after work?"

Mandie's stomach tightened, but she nodded anyway. They'd looked at six houses in the past couple of weeks, and each one had been either too expensive, too small, or in need of more work than they could handle. Mandie knew a lot about restoration, but that sometimes cost more than something that was already done.

The rental market was just as expensive in Five Island Cove, and she and Charlie figured for the same price, they might as well try to buy.

"Maybe." She forced a measure of optimism into her voice. "There's a new listing on Bell Island that your mom mentioned. Maybe you could call and see if we could go at like, seven?"

Charlie studied her face with the perceptive gaze that meant he saw right through her cheerful facade. "Seven? There's no way you'll make it from Rocky Ridge to Bell by seven."

"Eight, then." She smoothed his tie one more time, using the gesture to avoid his eyes.

"Do we really want to live on Bell?"

"The further out we go, the cheaper things are," she said. "And Bell isn't Pearl. It's even closer than Sanctuary."

A flash of determination crossed through his expression. "I'll call on my lunch break."

"I just want us to have our own space. I love your parents, but—" She shook her head, not sure how to explain her need to have their own space. They'd had it for so long, and living with someone else choked her.

"But you want to get the nest set up." He hugged her tightly. "I'll call at lunch and let you know."

The words *the nest* sent a familiar pang through her chest. She'd been tracking her cycle religiously, taking vitamins, doing everything the fertility websites suggested, but month after month brought the same disappointment. Maybe they should look for more of a starter home, instead of assuming they'd have a family anytime soon.

Mandie smiled at him. "Go." She gave him a gentle push toward the door. "You don't want to be late on your first day."

After Charlie left, Mandie threw herself into preparing for the day ahead. She reviewed her project binder for the fifteenth time, checking and rechecking timelines, supply orders, and contractor schedules. The familiar ritual of organization usually calmed her, but today it felt like trying to hold water in her hands.

She studied the architectural plans again, though she'd memorized every detail weeks ago. She'd color-coded her notes, created backup schedules for potential delays, and even researched weather patterns to anticipate how rain might affect their timeline.

Control the controllable, she told herself. It was a mantra that had gotten her through so much in her life, though she still found she worried about the things she couldn't control way too much.

Still, demolition and renovation felt like two things she could plan thoroughly enough, anticipate every possible problem, and then, maybe she could make this project run smoothly despite all the variables she couldn't manage.

Like finding a house. Like getting pregnant. Like whether Charlie would truly be happy working in Five Island Cove instead of pursuing opportunities in bigger cities.

The Black Sand Bungalow looked like a skeleton when she arrived, its bones exposed after two weeks of careful and thorough demolition. The exterior walls stood bare, stripped of their rotting shingles and decades of accumulated damage. Window openings gaped like empty eye sockets, and the roof had been reduced to its basic framework.

But the bones were good, just as Casper had said. The foundation stones sat solid and true, the main support beams showed no signs of structural damage, and the proportions promised a beautifully finished product.

"Morning," Suzie called from inside what had been the living room. She wore work clothes and safety glasses, her blonde hair pulled back in a practical ponytail. "I'm just finishing up final measurements."

She must've arrived a couple of hours before their nine a.m. start time for that, but Mandie wasn't shocked.

She joined her in the open room. "Any surprises?" Mandie pulled out her tablet to cross-reference Suzie's findings with their plans.

"Nothing major. The kitchen wall removal went exactly as planned, and the bathroom plumbing is in better shape than we expected."

Mandie nodded, making notes. "Oh, that's great news." She looked up quickly, flashing a smile.

Suzie let out a sigh. "Yeah, it's great."

Mandie watched her for a moment, detecting something in her friend. "The electrical contractor arrives tomorrow, and I want to make sure we're ready for him. Did you check the second-floor access? I want to confirm the new panel location before—"

"Mandie." Suzie's voice carried a note of exasperation. "I've checked everything twice. We're ready."

"I know, I just want to make sure we haven't missed anything."

"We won't." Alicia's voice came from the back of the house as she appeared in the doorway that would eventually connect the kitchen to a new mudroom. "Everything's been triple-checked." She held up a piece of paper, her smile rivaling the sun. "Look what I have."

Mandie practically lunged at her. "Is that the structural engineer's sign-off?" Giddiness pranced through her and Alicia let her rip the paper out of her hand. She scanned down to the bottom, where Ethan Briggs's name sat.

Beaming, she looked up. "Thank goodness." Now, she just needed to get this filed, and everyone would be happy. Her. The team. Candace. All the officials in Five Island Cove who had to deal with this project.

"You look a little tired," Alicia said, probably as kindly as she could.

"Charlie started at the hospital this morning," she said by

way of explanation. She threw a look over to Suzie. "How was the weekend with Daniel?"

Suzie's jaw jumped. "Fine." She took a few steps away, her tactic when she wanted to hide something. "I found something I want to show you guys."

She led the way into the kitchen, which had been reduced to the walls and subflooring. Sunlight streamed through the window openings, illuminating dust motes that danced in the air like tiny spirits.

Mandie could see it once it came to life again, filled with laughter and the scent of freshly baked bread or chocolate chip cookies. A family could gather here and take salads and sandwiches down the steps to the beach, where they'd make memories and have great experiences together.

Suzie crouched and removed a section of drywall that Mandie knew butted up against a small room behind it.

"What?" Mandie asked, because she'd had quite enough of secret compartments with the restoration of the yacht. And if not then, the Hampton House had revealed more secret passages than anyone needed to know about in their lifetime.

"False wall." Suzie ran her hands along the exposed wooden framework. "Look at this."

She'd uncovered a small built-in safe, its metal door hanging open on corroded hinges. The interior was mostly empty except for what looked like debris in the bottom.

"Anything valuable?" Mandie asked, her project manager instincts kicking in. They'd need to document any historical artifacts for the restoration records—and she wouldn't keep anything from Candace this time.

"Not exactly." Suzie carefully lifted out two items—a

tarnished silver button and a scrap of faded blue fabric. "But these were wrapped together in some tissue paper."

Mandie studied the objects in Suzie's palm. The button was ornate, with an intricate pattern that had been obscured by decades of tarnish. The fabric looked like it might have been silk once, though it was so faded and fragile it was hard to tell.

"Could be from a dress," Alicia said. "Or maybe a man's vest. That button looks formal."

"Hidden away like this?" Suzie turned the button over in her palm. "Along with that tile I found in the bedroom wall? Someone in this house had a secret."

A chill ran down Mandie's spine that had nothing to do with the ocean breeze flowing through the empty window frames. Every old house had stories, but something about these carefully hidden objects felt different. Deliberate. Important.

"We should research the Prescott family more thoroughly," she said, her mind already spinning with possibilities. "Find out who lived here, when they left, why the house was abandoned."

"I can handle that," Suzie said quickly. "I love genealogy research."

"Actually, I think I should—" Mandie began, then caught herself. There it was again, the need to control every aspect of the project, even tasks that played to her teammates' strengths.

Suzie raised an eyebrow. "You think you should what?"

"Nothing." Mandie forced herself to step back, literally and figuratively. "You're right. You're better at that kind of research than I am." She gave Suzie a smile and then looked at

Alicia. "I just hate that we can't control what we find when we start tearing into the walls."

Alicia smiled and then started to laugh, but Suzie gazed down at the button and fabric scrap in her hand.

"These might be the beginning of a much bigger story. Are you okay with me following where it leads, even if it takes us in unexpected directions?"

Mandie looked at the artifacts in her friend's hand, then at the faces of the two women who'd become like sisters to her. They were competent, capable, trustworthy. She didn't need to control every aspect of their work—she needed to let them do what they did best.

"Yes," she said, and meant it. "Follow the story. I'll try to focus on the things that actually need managing."

"Good." Suzie grinned. "Because I have a feeling this house is going to surprise us in ways we never expected."

"Are there any other walls we haven't looked into?" Mandie actually turned in a circle, scanning, because no, they hadn't torn open every piece of sheetrock.

"We're not tearing open every wall here," Alicia said.

Mandie glared at her. "We might need to."

"It's a button and a scrap of fabric." Alicia glanced over to Suzie. "Suze will look into things, but this doesn't stop the project."

"Right." Mandie took a deep breath. "I want to go over the timeline of deliveries. Our construction team will be here on Wednesday to get started, so we'll have a load of lumber delivered tomorrow. We have plumbing and electrical coming tomorrow to go over the scope of our project and to get on their schedule. Then—"

"Ladies," Flint said from behind her, and Mandie turned toward him. He lifted his camera in one hand and a drone in the other. He looked well-rested and cheerful, probably because he only had to show up for the good stuff.

"Hey, Flint," Mandie said, crossing to shake his elbow.

"Ready to make some magic?" He only had to show up for the good stuff, and then he'd be off to shoot another project. Flint did a ton of work in between appearances, and Mandie didn't even know what it took to turn raw footage into the beautiful films Flint made.

She suddenly felt lighter than she had in weeks. And lucky to be surrounded by so many good people, who had such talents that made her look smart and capable.

No, probably nothing about this project would go exactly as she had planned. Deliveries to the cove could be unpredictable, as Mandie had experienced plenty growing up here. People sometimes got sick or had other projects. Budgets had to be considered and met, and everyone in this room had a personal life that brought challenges, disappointments, and triumphs.

Oh, and it was summertime, which in and of itself made working a full day hard, what with friends, family, and the beach calling.

Yes, this project could get fouled up at any time, for any reason.

But Mandie said, "Ready," and for the first time in a long time, she meant it.

Chapter Six

S uzie stepped back from the newly framed kitchen wall, wiping sweat from her forehead with the back of her work glove. The early afternoon sun streamed through the window openings, casting long shadows across the construction site that had become her second home over the past three weeks.

Jake, the lead carpenter from the construction crew, approached. "Looks good, Suze."

She smiled at him, even though he had one of those bushy mountain man beards she disliked. "Hey, I'm going to take off now. I have some research to do."

He took her nail gun. "Yeah, sure. Thanks for all your help this week."

She nodded, surveying the transformation that had taken place in just five days. The Black Sand Bungalow had gone from a gutted shell to a structure with real promise. New floor joists stretched across the foundation like the ribs of some great beast coming back to life, and the freshly framed walls outlined rooms that would soon house a family's dreams.

The satisfaction that flowed through her felt bone-deep. This was what she lived for—taking something broken and forgotten and breathing new life into it. Every nail she'd driven, every board she'd measured and cut, every problem she'd solved with her hands and her mind had brought them closer to the vision Candace had laid out months ago.

With satisfaction humming through her, Suzie picked up her water jug and headed out to the front of the property. Mandie had erected a tent there, where she and Alicia did their tactical work until they had a place inside the cottage to do it.

"I'm going home," she said, poking her head into the tent. Both Alicia and Mandie looked up from the long table where they worked. A huge binder full of fabric samples sat between them. "I'm going to finish the research on the Prescotts, and then I'm picking up Daniel at seven-fifteen."

Mandie smiled at her. "Did you want to meet about the Prescotts?"

"Yeah." Suzie entered the shade of the tent. "Monday? What are we doing?"

"Construction," Alicia said dryly.

Suzie rolled her eyes. "It's going well in there." Alicia still wore ankle boots or sandals to the construction site, for crying out loud. Of course, her role wasn't the Bulldozer, the way Suzie's was, and Suzie actually wouldn't change her proper, sophisticated friend for anything.

"Let's meet to go over Suze's research at..." Mandie focused on her laptop and clicked a few times. "Ten-thirty?" She looked up.

"Sure," Suzie said. She never slept very late, and she made

it to Rocky Ridge on the first ferry here, which left Diamond Island at six-thirty. That put her on-site by seven-thirty, and the construction team arrived by eight.

After all, the morning hours were cooler and everyone wanted to get as much done before the sun baked them into this early June weather.

"Ten-thirty," Alicia said, clapping her hand over a pile of papers that started to flutter in the breeze. Probably invoices, budget projections, receipts, and quotes, as Alicia dealt with everything numbers. "We're actually running slightly ahead of schedule, which never happens."

"Don't jinx it," Mandie warned, but she wore a smile. Working in the cove had been an amazing experience so far. Mandie seemed much more relaxed, and Suzie could admit she loved leaving a little earlier in the day and finding a nice spot of sandy beach to soak in the sun.

Life felt slower here than in the city, and she could see why Mandie and Charlie had wanted to move back here.

Alicia's laptop chimed, and she focused on it. "Oh, this is about the windows."

If Suzie stayed, she felt sure she'd be embroiled in window drama, and she had her own family saga to deal with. She finished tucking her tools into her bag, and she waved to her friends. "I'll see you guys Monday."

"Have fun with Daniel," Mandie said with a smile.

Suzie nodded, but as she walked away her mind shifted to the research she'd been conducting in the evenings. The artifacts she'd found—the button, the fabric, the decorative tile —had been haunting her thoughts and sometimes following her into her dreams.

Suzie let herself decompress from the physical demands of the day on the ferry. Her muscles ached in the satisfying way that came from productive labor, and her hands bore the small nicks and calluses that marked her as someone who worked with her hands for a living.

She'd rented a small one-bedroom condo on the third floor of a converted beach house, with a view of the harbor and enough space for her laptop, research materials, and the growing collection of historical documents she'd been accumulating. It wasn't fancy, but it was a sanctuary where she could think and work without interruption.

After a quick shower and a strawberry yogurt with granola, Suzie settled at her small dining table with her laptop and the notebook where she'd been tracking her research. The Prescott family tree was starting to take shape, though significant gaps remained.

She opened the genealogy website she'd been using and pulled up the records she'd bookmarked. James Prescott had owned the Black Sand Bungalow from 1923 until 1968, when he'd abruptly left Five Island Cove with his wife Priscilla. They'd had three children: Robert, born in 1951; Denise, born in 1953; and Margaret, born in 1956.

Suzie made careful notes in her notebook, drawing lines to connect the family members and noting dates wherever she could find them. The 1960 census showed all five family members living at the Rocky Ridge address, but by 1970, James and Priscilla had moved to Florida, taking Margaret with them. Robert had joined the Army and was stationed in Germany.

But Denise was nowhere to be found in the 1970 census.

Suzie frowned, tapping her pen against the notebook. A seventeen-year-old girl during that time didn't just disappear from the records. She'd either moved with her parents and been missed by the census takers, or she'd stayed in Five Island Cove and was living with someone else.

"Or as someone else," she muttered.

She opened a new browser tab and searched for marriage records, typing in "Denise Prescott" and "Five Island Cove." The results loaded slowly, but there it was—a marriage certificate dated June 15, 1970.

Denise Prescott had married Connor Williams at the age of seventeen.

Suzie stared at the screen, her heart beginning to race. "Scandalous," she whispered. While yes, people used to get married at a younger age, most weren't hitched by seventeen unless they had to be.

Connor Williams. That was a name she hadn't seen yet, and she wrote it down next to Denise's and drew a line between them, adding the date and age of Denise.

She found a few more records—a birth certificate for Alice Williams in 1975, and another for Scott Williams in 1977, both before Denise had turned twenty-five-years-old.

Suzie had never felt so old, living a life so completely different than the one she currently researched.

The pieces of the puzzle were starting to come together, but Suzie couldn't shake the feeling that she was missing something important. Why had the Prescott family left so suddenly? Why had Denise gotten married so young? Where was she now?

She made more notes, sketching out a timeline of events. The house had been abandoned in 1968, when Denise was only fifteen.

"And where did they go?"

Suzie shuffled through some paperwork in the thin

manilla folder she kept. Candace had bought the property from... She shifted through a few pages until she found it.

"The Prescott Family Trust." Suzie's eyes zipped right and left, trying to find the executor of the trust, but sometimes that was the whole point of a trust—to keep names out of the spotlight.

She found a signature on the last page of the closing docs, and the name there made her breath catch. "Connor Williams."

Suzie looked up, her mind buzzing. Had Denise owned the house all these years?

Suzie dug some more, finally finding an old property record that had never been updated. She blinked, reading it once, then twice. "They put Denise's name on the trust when she was fifteen?"

That made no sense, not when there were older living relatives. At least she'd never seen it before.

She found death certificates for James and Priscilla Prescott—both had died in Florida in the 1980s. Margaret had married and moved to California. Robert had been killed in Vietnam in 1971.

But Denise's story remained frustratingly incomplete. She'd married Connor Williams in 1970, had two children, and then...nothing. No death certificate, no divorce records, no indication of what had happened to her.

And through all of it, the house had sat there, seemingly uninhabited since the family moved to Florida in the 1960s.

Suzie leaned back in her chair, rubbing her eyes while her mind continued to whir and whir and whir.

She couldn't help thinking about the parallels between Denise's life and hers. Of course, she hadn't been married and had two babies by the time she was twenty-five years old, but the last time she'd seen either of her parents was when she was fifteen years old.

A flash of love for her grandmother filled her, and Suzie let her soft feelings reign. A keen sense of missing flowed through her, and while Suzie had pushed such things away in the past, today she simply let herself feel it.

So much had changed in the past couple of years, as she would've never let herself be vulnerable like this, even alone in her own home, before the project in the Hamptons.

Tears pricked her eyes, and she startled when an alarm on her phone went off. Her eyes flew open, and she fumbled to silence the shrill noise. Her nerves buzzed at her as she left everything right where it sat on her dining room table and got to her feet.

A quick swipe of her phone and a bottle of water, and she headed out the door. The sunshine blinded her just as she realized she had no car here, and frustration built within her that she'd forgotten.

Luckily, the RideShare system operated far and wide, and it only took three minutes to get a car to take her to the airport.

"Will you wait until my fiancé comes out?"

"Yep," the driver said, meeting her eyes in the rearview mirror.

Suzie nodded, and she did enjoy being chauffeured around, and she determined to make the most of it this summer.

The driver pulled into the tiny park-and-wait lot just as Daniel texted. *Just landed. Can't wait to see you!*

Suzie's stomach fluttered with that awful mixture of excitement and anxiety. A fun beach weekend with the man she was going to marry should be like a vacation after a week of hard work.

But ever since his proposal at Alicia's wedding, she'd been wrestling with doubts and fears she couldn't quite articulate.

She loved Daniel—she was certain of that. But marriage felt like such a monumental step, one that required the kind of faith in the future she wasn't sure she possessed. What if she wasn't cut out for marriage? What if her independent nature, her need for solitude and space, made her unsuitable for the kind of partnership Daniel deserved?

Did Denise feel like this? Suzie wondered, the thoughts coming out of nowhere. She shook it away, because while her and Denise had a couple of things in common, that didn't mean she and Denise were actually anything alike.

As she watched her phone, she reminded herself that she often felt an emotional connection to the people she researched. She loved thinking about them as real human beings, and imagining what their lives were like, and making promises that their stories would be told—or at least learned by her.

She ran her hands through her still-damp hair, suddenly mortified. She'd showered, eaten, and plopped herself in front of the computer. She hadn't taken even five minutes to fix up her hair before heading to the airport, and her heartbeat thrashed for a new reason now.

She took a breath, the keen thought sliding through her mind now that Daniel didn't care about what her hair looked like. He'd probably just pull her ponytail out and carry her to bed the moment they stepped foot inside her condo anyway.

The blood in her veins thrummed at the thought, and then Daniel's name popped up on the screen. *1A.*

"He's outside," she told the driver. "Station 1A."

"You got it," the driver said, and he eased the car into drive and pulled out of the parking spot.

Suzie swallowed, then did it again, and then the driver rounded a curve, and her wonderful, gorgeous Daniel stood there with a messenger bag over his shoulder and a carryon suitcase standing at his side.

An instant smile burst onto her face, and she leaned forward. "He's right there. The one in the navy sweater vest."

Mm, yes, she loved his sweater vests.

He looked tired from the journey but happy, his face lighting up when he spotted her waving like a loon from the back seat. With the sweater vest, he wore the pale yellow button-down shirt covered in sailboats that she'd bought him for his birthday, and his dark hair was slightly mussed, as usual.

The car came to a stop at the curb, and all of her fears and doubts evaporated. Just, poof. Gone.

She slid over to the other door and got out. "Hey." She couldn't stop smiling, and she threw herself into his arms as he laughed and caught her. This was Daniel—her Daniel, who made her laugh, who listened to her theories about historical mysteries with genuine interest, who had somehow seen past her prickly exterior to the woman she was becoming.

"I've missed you," she said against his neck, breathing in the familiar scent of his tangy cologne.

"I've missed you too." He set her down but kept his arms around her, studying her face with those perceptive eyes that saw too much. "How was your week?"

"Amazing. Exhausting. Productive." She reached up to smooth his hair. "I have so much to tell you."

"And I want to hear all of it." He kissed her forehead,

then her nose, then her lips. She kissed him, and kissed him, and kissed him, not caring who saw them or how much it cost to have the RideShare driver sit there waiting.

She loved him, and he made her feel like she'd just come home to a warm, inviting place simply because they were there together.

He finally pulled away and hummed in the back of his throat. "It's twenty minutes to your place, sweetheart. Let's pick this up again when we get there." Then he reached for his bag and went around to the trunk of the car to stow it there.

Suzie couldn't wait to be alone with him, and she couldn't wait to run everything she'd learned about the Prescotts by him. Daniel had a history-research brain, and perhaps he'd see or think of something she hadn't.

Chapter Seven

A licia sliced through the watermelon with practiced precision, the sweet juice running over her fingers as she worked. The kitchen of their rented beach bungalow left a lot to be desired, especially space. Two people could barely be in the area together, but the morning light streaming through the salt-stained windows made everything feel bright and cheerful.

"Mom, can I have a piece?" Gray burst through the screen door, his swim shorts dripping seawater onto the weathered hardwood floors. Sand clung to his legs and feet, leaving a trail behind him.

"At lunchtime," she said, lifting another knife-full of watermelon chunks into the bowl. "You're getting sand everywhere. You're supposed to rinse off in the outdoor shower before you come inside." She waved the knife toward the door when he just froze. "Go on."

He groaned dramatically but headed back outside, the screen door slamming behind him with a satisfying bang that reminded Alicia of her own childhood summers.

"I think I'm done, Mama." Lily perched on the kitchen stool a few feet down, and she looked over to Alicia with her announcement. Alicia left her knife and picked up a towel to wipe her hands as she took two steps to look into the bowl.

She'd stirred together the mayonnaise and mustard, along with a bit of diced pickle, for the deviled eggs. Lily's eyes shone with hope, and Alicia grinned at her.

"You absolutely are, sweetheart." Alicia smiled at her daughter, marveling at how easily they'd all settled into this summer rhythm. Three weeks in Five Island Cove, only a month since the wedding, and it felt like they'd been here forever.

Ryan had agreed to let the kids spend the entire summer with her and Henry without a single argument or demand for makeup time. His new girlfriend, Jessica, was apparently planning a European backpacking trip, and Ryan had jumped at the chance to join her.

An uncomfortable pinch twisted in Alicia's stomach at the thought of Ryan gallivanting around Europe while she juggled work and parenting. Not jealousy exactly—she had Henry now, and their life together had become everything she'd hoped for. But something about how easily Ryan had signed away his summer with Gray and Lily stung in a way she couldn't quite name.

Oh, and Jessica was only twenty-six, a decade younger than Ryan. That didn't really help the pin in Alicia's side.

"Now we can start filling the eggs." She moved the tray of hard-boiled egg whites closer to Lily and handed her a small spoon. "Just a little bit in each one."

The screen door opened again, and Henry appeared with two large paper bags balanced on the cooler he pulled behind him. His hair had been the victim of the breeze here in the cove, and his t-shirt clung to his chest in a way that still made her heartbeat pulse.

He grinned at Alicia and Lily in the kitchen, heading their way. "Sandwiches from Lighthouse Bakery." He set the cooler on all four legs and picked up the bags. "And enough ice to keep the drinks cold." He glanced around. "Where's Gray?"

"You're amazing." Alicia stood on her tiptoes to kiss him, tasting salt and sunshine on his lips. "And Gray is outside. You didn't see him rinsing his feet in the outdoor shower?"

It was conveniently located at the end of the sidewalk, in plain view of the door Henry had just come through.

"No, he wasn't there."

"So he's probably back out on the beach." Alicia sighed and rolled her neck. "I'll go get him."

"I'll do it," Henry said. "It's his job to fill the cooler with soda pop." He turned and retraced his steps, leaning outside and whistling through his teeth for Gray to come back.

Alicia resumed cutting watermelon cubes as her son yelled from somewhere outside, and Henry returned to the end of the counter. "He's coming in."

She slid another several cubes into the bowl and smiled at him. "Gray's been talking about teaching Daniel how to paddle board all week." She raised her eyebrows.

"He's going to get up today." Henry twisted when the screen door opened again. "Did you wash up?"

Gray groaned and headed back out again, and this time, Henry followed him. They returned a few minutes later, and though Gray leaked water all over the floor, at least it wasn't sandy water.

"All the soda?" Gray asked, looking at the cases and cases Henry had stacked next to the fridge.

"All of it," Henry said. "And I don't want to hear any complaining. We're all working to get the picnic together today, and *then* we get to go paddle boarding, all right?"

"All right," Gray said, and he ripped into the first box of ginger ale.

Alicia finished with the watermelon and dumped all the rinds in the trashcan and helped Lily fill the last of the deviled eggs. "These go in the fridge," she said, and she opened the door and slid the tray of eggs inside. She moved a few things around to add the bowl of watermelon, and as she turned to help Gray with the last of the soda, someone knocked on the front door.

Her pulse bumped for a minute, because this was the first beach day here in the cove, and she wanted it to be perfect. She'd gone out with her friends before, and Alicia told herself she didn't have to be perfect today to keep them.

"We're coming in," Suzie said through the screen door before Alicia could tell her to do just that.

"Suzie!" Lily jumped down from the barstool and flew toward her. "Come see my sandcastle prints."

Alicia wiped her hands on the towel again, then moved to greet Daniel and Suzie too. "You found it."

"This place is incredible," Daniel said when she leaned in to hug him. "It's right on the water."

"Just a few steps down the sidewalk." Henry shook his hand as Lily towed Suzie over to the coffee table in the living room. She already wore her swimming suit, and she started showing Suzie all the drawings—her "blueprints"—she'd done for the sandcastles she wanted to build that day.

Daniel put down the beach bag he carried and glanced around. "Do you need any help?"

"I'd love to get some help putting up the umbrellas and

shade," Henry said, and he took both Daniel and Gray outside with him.

"Lily, Henry's going out to the beach," Alicia said.

"Okay," her daughter chirped, and Lily gave Suzie a quick neck-hug before running after them.

"This place is perfect," Suzie said, getting to her feet and wandering over to the wall of windows that faced the beach. "I can see why you love it here."

Alicia nodded, though she didn't get to enjoy the view as much as she'd like. "The sound of the waves is incredible at night, I'll say that."

Suzie glanced at her. "And Henry's getting some work done?"

"A little bit, yes." Alicia flashed a smile, her gratitude doubling that he had a forgiving job that had allowed him to work remotely for the summer. "He gets up early and stays up late, so he can spend most of the day with the kids."

She folded her arms and watched the water, something roiling in her stomach. She wished she could be the one getting up with the kids and slathering sunscreen on their skin while they spent the day at the beach. Balancing a career and motherhood often felt impossible, and she could sink deep into this hole if she let herself.

To stop the spiral, she drew in a deep breath and let it out slowly. "Daniel's here again."

Suzie nodded, her smile lifting only the corners of her mouth. "He's great."

"Suze," he yelled as he jogged in front of the windows. "Come see these paddle boards, sweetheart."

She gave half a groan that disappeared as she turned. "Coming." She threw Alicia one more look before going with her fiancé, and Alicia smiled at them as they walked by the windows again, this time with Daniel chattering excitedly about the paddle boards and Suzie nodding like she agreed.

Alicia giggled to herself, because while Suzie wasn't afraid of physical things, she wasn't exactly into water sports—at least that Alicia knew of.

"Hey, hey, hey."

Alicia turned as Mandie and Charlie entered the bungalow. "Hey, you two."

Mandie carried her own colorful beach bag and looked around the place. "This place is great. My old boss at the library lives in one of these." She grinned and moved right over to Alicia and hugged her. "You probably know her. Tessa Martin? She lives here with her husband, Dave. He owns a soda shop on Diamond where I worked one summer."

Alicia shook her head. "I haven't met them, but that's not surprising. I'm not here much, and when I am, I'm consumed with the kids." She glanced over to Charlie. "Hey, Charlie. How's the hospital?"

He'd started there two weeks ago now, and Mandie hadn't said much more about it. "Great," he said with a smile. "I finally feel like I'm settling in there."

"That's great," Alicia said. "Starting a new job can be the worst."

He nodded. "We brought one of our beach tables. Well, it's my mom's. We've used it a bunch on our beach days." He hooked his thumb toward the door. "Should I go set it up?"

"Yeah, that would be great," Alicia said with an appreciative smile. "Everyone else is out there already, getting things set up."

"Perfect." Charlie headed out, and Alicia turned back to the kitchen.

"I brought chocolate chip cookies," Mandie said.

Alicia studied her friend, noting the slight shadows under Mandie's eyes that makeup couldn't quite hide. "How are you feeling?"

"Good. Really good." Mandie's smile was genuine, but Alicia caught the slight hesitation. "It's been nice having the house to ourselves this week."

"I'll bet," Alicia said just as the screen door opened again. She was honestly tired of it, but the kids loved the beach so much that she'd said nothing about their constant back and forth from outside to in.

"Mama, Henry says we need a bag of stakes."

Alicia glanced around, finding the stakes for the shade beside the fridge. "Right there, baby doll. That blue bag."

Lily skipped over to them, picked them up, and headed back out.

Mandie watched her go, then turned back to Alicia with a more subdued expression. "She's gotten so big."

"Kids do that." Alicia smiled and then reached over to pat Mandie's hand. "No house yet?"

Mandie shook her head, and Alicia's heart went out to her. "No house, and you know what?" She looked up with a fiery blaze in her eyes. "It doesn't matter. Charlie and I can just get a condo like Suzie's, because I can't get pregnant."

Alicia blinked, surprise coursing through her. "At all?"

Mandie shook her head, her expression turning sad. "Charlie says it's not now or never, but I feel like it is."

Alicia didn't know what to say to make this okay. There weren't words for such a thing. She loved Mandie like a sister, and she put her arm around her. "Every body is different, every timeline is different."

"I know that. Logically, I know that." Mandie finally

looked up, and Alicia saw the vulnerability her friend usually kept hidden. "I guess I have to just swallow my pride and go to the doctor." Her lower lip trembled. "I just don't want to be told I can't have kids at all."

"You can't think like that," Alicia said, though she understood the fear. Sometimes it was better not to know than to be told the truth in such stark terms. "I'm really sorry, Mandie."

She nodded, some of the tension leaving her shoulders. "Thanks." She drew in a breath as voices neared. "What do you need help carrying outside?"

She brightened as Gray led the way inside, yelling, "Mom, everything is ready, and I'm *starving*."

Charlie followed him, chuckling. "Henry said he can't go paddle boarding until he eats lunch."

Alicia grinned at her son. "That sounds about right." She nodded to the two brown bags Henry had brought home. "We have sandwiches and salads in there, and I have a few things to take out from the fridge."

She moved to get the fruit and eggs, as well as a batch of cookies she and Lily had baked last night. With all of them, they easily got all the food outside with one trip, where Alicia lined it all up on the table. "Wow, you guys got everything done."

Someone had set up chairs too, and Alicia just wanted to sink into one of those, have someone bring her food, and listen to the ocean talk as it came ashore.

Henry and Daniel had positioned a large umbrella to provide shade, while Charlie currently set up a spikeball net in the sand while Suzie unwrapped the paper plates and set them on the end of the table.

The kids darted between the adults, their excitement infectious.

"This is perfect," Alicia said, a smile sinking way down into her soul. The ocean stretched endlessly before them, its surface sparkling under the midday sun. White clouds drifted lazily across the brilliant blue sky, and a gentle breeze carried the scent of salt and seaweed.

"It really is," Suzie agreed, settling into one of the beach chairs.

"We're eating first, right?" Mandie asked, picking up a plate.

"Yep." Alicia turned from the fantasy that was this Five Island Cove summer and called, "Gray; Lily; come get lunch."

Gray cheered, and everyone congregated at the table to pile sandwiches, salads, and watermelon onto their plates.

"The whole thing, Gray," Alicia said. "And I want to reapply sunscreen before you go out again."

"All right," he said, taking his food over to a blanket someone had spread out. He sank onto it and popped a cube of watermelon into his mouth.

Mandie helped Lily with her food, becoming the last to find a chair in the shade. Alicia smiled at her but said nothing. She listened to Daniel and Charlie talk about their jobs, and life in the cove, and she ate way too many deviled eggs before Gray got up and appeared in front of her.

"Can I go paddle boarding now?"

"Let me spray your shoulders again." Alicia bent to get the sunscreen out of her bag, and she made Gray stand there while she did his back, shoulders, ears, and chest. "Okay, go."

He moved over to Daniel and Charlie. "Do you guys wanna come paddle boarding with me?"

"Absolutely," Charlie said, and he handed Mandie his empty plate. Daniel went too, with Henry taking a couple of extra minutes to get Lily ready to go out into the sun and surf too.

She watched as Henry helped Lily onto a paddle board, his patient instructions evident in his expression. Gray sat on the other paddle board, and all three men stood waist-deep in the gentle waves, taking turns steadying the kids as they tried to find their balance.

"They're good with them," Suzie said, her voice carrying a note of something Alicia couldn't quite identify.

"The best," Alicia said. "Henry's been amazing with Gray and Lily this summer."

"Yeah, he's great."

Something in Suzie's tone made Alicia study her friend's face. "How are your wedding plans coming along?"

Suzie's expression immediately grew guarded. "We haven't really...I mean, we've talked about it, but nothing concrete yet."

"Have you set a date?" Mandie asked.

"Daniel wants to get married as soon as possible," Suzie said, twisting her engagement ring around her finger. Alicia wondered if she even knew she was doing it. "But I keep thinking we should wait until the project is finished, or until we figure out where we want to live, or..." She trailed off with a frustrated sigh.

Alicia exchanged a glance with Mandie. "Or until you're not scared?"

Suzie's head snapped up. "I'm not scared."

"Oh, come on." Mandie rolled her eyes. "You're terrified, and you know what? It's fine. Getting married is a little scary."

"Not helping," Suzie said, glaring at her. She breathed out, everything about her softening. She cleared her throat, and Alicia shook her head at Mandie, who'd just opened her mouth as if she'd say something.

"I've never had a real family," Suzie said after several long moments. "I mean, I had my grandmother, and she was wonderful, but that was different. My parents...I didn't have parents, really."

Alicia watched her, her heartbeat accelerating with every passing second. She had amazing parents to this day, and she didn't—couldn't—understand what Suzie meant.

"I don't know how to be part of a couple, how to make decisions together, how to..." She gestured helplessly to the surroundings. "Do married life."

"He fell in love with you exactly as you are," Alicia said, her throat so dry. "Your independence, your strength, your brilliant mind—that's what he wants."

"But what about the wedding itself?" Suzie asked, looking at her with pure desperation. "I don't know anything about planning weddings. I don't have a mother to help me pick out a dress, or order flowers, or any of that...stuff. I don't even know where to start."

Mandie's face brightened, and Alicia hoped Suzie was ready for her to say something. Sometimes they still butted heads, but usually only at work. "My mom would love to help you."

Suzie blinked and turned her head toward Mandie. "Your mom?"

"She's a wedding planner," Mandie said, practically bouncing in her chair. "She's been doing it for years, and she's *amazing* at it. She'd be thrilled to help you figure everything out, whether you want something big and elaborate or small and intimate."

Suzie frowned and looked out at the kids again. "I don't know."

"My mom would be all over it," Mandie said. "She says everyone needs a wedding planner, whether they have a big support system or not." She wore wide eyes as she nodded, though Suzie didn't even look at her.

Alicia hadn't heard Suzie talk about her parents or grandmother very much, and she hadn't known she didn't have parents. She wondered where they were, and if perhaps she'd lost them in a tragic accident. Perhaps that was why she loved doing the family history research about their projects, too.

Maybe it helps her feel like she belongs somewhere.

Alicia gave her a smile, which Mandie apparently took as encouragement. She pulled out her phone and started tapping.

"I'm giving you her number right now. Just call her and talk through some ideas. No pressure, no commitment, just someone who knows what she's doing and would love to help."

Alicia watched Suzie save the contact information, noting the mix of hope and anxiety on her friend's face. "You don't have to figure it all out at once," she said. "That's why you're engaged for a while. It gives you time to plan it, one step at a time."

Suzie nodded, though that little frown between her eyes didn't go anywhere.

A shout from the water drew their attention back to the group in the waves. Gray had successfully stood up on the paddle board and pumped his fists in triumph while the adults cheered.

Alicia jumped to her feet. "Look at him." She took out her own phone and snapped a couple of pictures, cheered for him, and retreated back into the shade. As she sank back into her seat, a happy sigh escaped her lips.

"One thing you can't wait for," Mandie said.

Alicia glanced over to her. "What?"

"My mom and her friends have all these things they do," she said with a smile. "Tell-Alls and stuff. I just want us to say one thing we can't wait for—and it has to be something new, something we haven't said before."

She looked at them with brightness in her blue eyes. "I'll go first. I can't *wait* to see that stained glass in the beach cottage."

Alicia's mood instantly lifted. The stained glass was supposed to arrive this past week, and it hadn't. That had caused a half-day of phone calls and emails to find it, and the last thing Alicia wanted was to have to account for the very expensive glass if they didn't even have it.

Even now, she swallowed down her nerves, because she'd have to deal with Candace sooner or later about the exorbitant expense of the glass. But Mandie was right—it would be phenomenal in the beach house, and Alicia also couldn't wait to see it.

"Oh, I see." Suzie cleared her throat and shook her blonde hair over her shoulders. "I can't wait to talk to Alice about the Prescotts." Her eyes gleamed with the same excitement Alicia had seen when they'd first started demolition, which was one of Suzie's favorite activities.

"You really think she'll know something?" Alicia asked.

"If anyone would, it's Alice," Mandie said. "She grew up here, and her parents have been on Rocky Ridge for generations."

"Her dad is Connor," Suzie said. "Do you think you can ask her to meet with us tomorrow?" She looked over to Mandie, who suddenly raised her thumbnail to her mouth and started to chew.

"I'll see how they are when they get back," she said. "They're traveling from three time zones away, so."

Suzie nodded, though her displeasure rode in the tightness of her mouth. She exchanged a glance with Alicia, but thankfully didn't press the issue. Finding out that her in-laws might be connected to the Black Sand Bungalow had been shocking for Mandie, to say the least.

"Your turn," Mandie said, and all eyes landed on Alicia.

Her heart skipped a beat, and her mind went blank. "Oh, um." She glanced out to the ocean again, her mind churning like the waves coming ashore. "I guess I can't wait for the next weekend we can all get together for a beach picnic."

She beamed at her friends, and while Mandie looked like she wanted to call Alicia on her "can't wait," she just pressed her lips into a line and nodded.

The truth was, Alicia couldn't wait for the stained glass to arrive either, and she couldn't wait to find out more about the Prescotts, and she couldn't wait to get back to the city.

Because then this project would be done, and they wouldn't be temporarily living in someone else's house anymore, and her life could get back to normal. But she couldn't say that to her friends right now, and she *did* want to do this weekend beach day again.

Now, they just needed to get the cove cottage done to Candace's satisfaction.

Chapter Eight

Mandie wiped her palms on her jeans for the third time in ten minutes, watching Suzie pack her research papers into a neat folder. The construction crew had left an hour ago, and the Black Sand Bungalow sat in the golden afternoon light like a patient waiting for surgery— half-transformed, full of promise, but still holding its secrets.

"You ready for this?" Suzie asked, shouldering her bag.

"As ready as I'll ever be." Mandie's stomach twisted with nerves. She'd interviewed dozens of property owners and historical society members over the years, but this felt different.

Alice wasn't just Charlie's mother; she was the woman Mandie had always secretly measured herself against.

Alice possessed the kind of effortless grace that made everyone feel welcome while simultaneously making Mandie feel like she was trying too hard. Even now, after years of marriage to Charlie, Mandie sometimes caught herself straightening her posture when Alice entered a room, smoothing her hair, checking her lipstick.

The sound of tires on the sandy lane made them both turn. A car appeared around the bend, Alice visible in the passenger seat. Mandie's pulse quickened, and she pulled her small makeup compact from her purse.

"You look fine," Suzie said, but she waited patiently while Mandie touched up her lipstick and checked her teeth for wayward poppy seeds from lunch.

The RideShare driver pulled over onto the shoulder, and Mandie's courage got a boost when Charlie opened the back door and stood. He didn't smile, though. "You guys ready?"

"Yep," Suzie said, marching in her steel-toed boots with such confidence.

Mandie glanced at Alice, who watched her with a cool expression. Her stomach rumbled, and Mandie told herself she could eat afterward. She forced a smile to her face. "Hey, baby."

She approached Charlie and swept a kiss across his lips. "Thanks for coming."

He didn't work on Thursdays, and they'd planned this meeting with his grandfather for this afternoon deliberately. Plus, Alice had been out of town for a week, and she'd needed a few days to get caught up with her clients.

Mandie slid into the car and scooted over into the middle, leaving the last seat for her husband. When Charlie closed the door behind him, he said, "It's the next house down."

The car eased onto the road, drove another few hundred yards, and this time, turned left into a driveway. Mandie had been here before, of course. This was Charlie's grandfather's house, and Mandie had always enjoyed coming here.

She pressed her eyes closed, remembering the way Della —the only grandmother he'd ever known—had welcomed her and Charlie, fed them the most delicious apple pie, and let them lounge on the back deck, the black sand beach, or their boat.

And now, she had to ask them questions that could dredge up a painful past.

Well, Suzie would, at least.

"Well, we can't sit here," Alice said, her voice touched with a hint of dryness. With that, she opened her door and rose like a phoenix from the ashes as she got out of the car.

"Thank you," Mandie said to the driver, and she followed Charlie out his door. She faced the house, watching Alice glide forward in her blue sundress that somehow managed to look both casual and elegant on this summer afternoon. Silver had started to streak her dark hair, the same as it had Mandie's mother's.

A familiar tightness wove through her, despite Charlie taking her hand and gently urging her forward. "Come on, sweetheart," he said. "They know why we're coming." He shot a look over to Suzie, and Mandie did too.

She wore her mouth in a battle line, and Mandie wanted to tell her to shelve the Bulldozer for an hour. At the same time, she hoped Suzie would bring out that bluntness that she so often exhibited. Then Mandie wouldn't have to be the one to ask the hard questions.

She didn't want to ask any questions at all. Talking to Alice, Arthur, and Charlie about the family history research and the artifacts they'd found in the house had been bad enough.

The late afternoon breeze carried the scent of beach roses and sunshine. The house sat nestled among mature pine trees, its shiny black shingles and white trim speaking of decades of careful maintenance. A wide porch wrapped around the front, dotted with hanging baskets of petunias and potted plants with wide, green-and-white leaves.

Alice reached the door first, and she called, "Dad," as she entered. Mandie and Charlie entered next, followed by Suzie. She flowed through the house to the back, where the kitchen sat just off the deck.

A genuine smile came to her face as she eased into Della. "Hello," she said, inhaling the powdery scent of her.

"We have bruschetta," she said, grinning from ear-to-ear as she moved to hug Charlie.

Mandie shook Connor's hand and glanced over to Suzie, who could absolutely be professional when she had to be. She radiated warmth and firm handshakes, introduced herself with ease, and smiled around at everyone like they'd gathered for afternoon tea. Mandie marveled at the different sides she could have and how she stayed so calm under pressure.

For it seemed that someone had encased her insides in gelatin, and she wobbled slightly as she moved out of the way for Suzie to finish greeting Connor. Once all the hellos finished, Mandie took a seat at the dining room table, where yes, Della had laden the surface with food.

"This is fire roasted tomato bruschetta," Della said. "And Connor did steak bites while he had the grill on." She continued to point out the different sauces she'd put together to go with the meat, and then Connor pulled out a tray of potato skins laden with cheddar cheese and bacon that made Mandie's mouth water.

He sat, and the atmosphere in the quaint beach cottage changed. Still, he wore a smile as he surveyed everyone, finally saying, "Alice tells us you've discovered some connection between our family and the house you're working on."

"We think so, yes." Mandie glanced at Suzie, who held up the folder.

She set it down and flipped it open. "We found some artifacts during demolition, and the purchase records have your signature on them, sir." She glanced up, then went back to shuffling paperwork for no reason. "On behalf of your late wife's trust."

She picked up the paper she'd shown Mandie and Alicia last week and placed it in the middle of the table, in neutral ground.

Mandie stared at it, though everyone at the table had seen it, except Della and Connor.

Della reached out and picked it up. "Yes, we decided it was time to see something done with the house." She smiled over to Connor and handed him the paper. "It was the last thing in the trust, which is simply a shell now."

Mandie swallowed and waited for someone else to say something. Alice, as a lawyer, had looked all of this up since Mandie and Suzie had spoken with her on Monday. She'd already texted them to say the trust didn't hold anything else, though she hadn't known about the trust until a few days ago.

Connor reached for his reading glasses, but he barely looked at the paper before handing it back to Suzie. "Yes, that house belonged to my wife's family. They hadn't used it for a long time, and I never found the gumption to do anything with it."

He glanced over to Alice, who covered his hand with hers, a tight smile on her face. "Della and I decided it was time to let it go."

"We found a few things, too," Suzie said. She laid out the button, the ceramic tile, and the faded fabric without saying where they'd been found. "I'm hoping you can tell us about the house, about your late wife's family, anything at all." She cut a glance over to Mandie, as they'd agreed to go into this with an open-ended format, without accusatory questions.

"We like to...how do I put it?"

"Feel the spirit of the house," Mandie said. "Suzie is an incredible historian, and she loves learning all she can about the *people* who lived in a place. We then try to curate items that speak to their heritage, to remembering them for who they were, to honor the past as we attempt to take the property into the future."

She could've been sucking on cotton, her mouth was so dry. She reached for a glass of pre-poured lemonade, hoping it didn't have an ounce of sugar in it.

Della, who still dyed her hair dark, leaned forward and then paused. "Can we touch them?"

"Yes, yes," Suzie said, moving the items closer. "We'll have them restored if they mean something. Otherwise, we'll probably just add them to our historical collection of items we've found on jobs."

Connor leaned forward too, his expression shifting from polite interest to something deeper. Recognition flickered in his eyes as he studied the objects.

He picked up the button, and the silence stretched as he turned it over, his weathered, fisherman's fingers tracing the intricate pattern. Mandie knew hands like his, because her father was a career fisherman, and no better people existed.

When he looked up, his eyes held a sadness that made Mandie's chest tighten. "This belonged to Denise," he said. "She had a beautiful green dress with buttons just like this one. She wore it to the last Christmas party we attended before she died."

Della reached over and squeezed his shoulder, her touch gentle and understanding. Mandie found herself holding her breath, waiting for more.

Suzie finished writing something. "Did you know her family before they left the cove?" Suzie asked, her inner historian shining through. "Can you tell us why they left, and why she didn't go with them?"

Connor frowned, his mouth drawing down with the movement. He'd obviously heard Suzie, but he didn't jump in to answer right away.

"Dad," Alice said. "It's not a trial. They're just trying to learn more about Mom and the house." She flashed Mandie and Suzie a smile and looked back at her father.

Connor nodded and looked across the table to Suzie. "Denise grew up in that house. Her parents, James and Priscilla, they owned it for decades. But they never really understood her." He set the button on the table with careful precision. "She was different from them—independent, spirited. She loved this place, loved the water, loved the freedom of island life."

He blew out his breath. "She loved me, but oh, her parents didn't." He smiled, but in a frowning sort of way. "We had a bad storm one spring, and it damaged the house pretty badly. They wanted to leave, and they made plans to move to Florida."

Mandie found herself leaning forward, almost desperate to know more.

"Denise refused to go with them."

"She was only seventeen," Suzie said.

"They established the trust for her and put the house in it." He glanced over to Alice, who wore a serious expression but said nothing.

"Who was the trustee?" Suzie's pen scratched, and she looked up expectantly.

Mandie wanted to also ask: *And they just left her behind in a defunct house? And moved to Florida? Really?*

She held her tongue and watched her grandfather-in-law. He shifted in his seat and glanced over to Della, then Charlie. No one said a word, and Mandie had the awful thought that whatever Connor said next would be false.

"My mother," he finally said, and Mandie couldn't tell if it was a lie or not.

"Your parents took her in?" Suzie asked.

"My *mother* did." Connor's frown softened though his eyes remained as steely as ever. "Mom always had a soft spot for strays—animals, people, didn't matter. She took one look at this defiant, scared girl and moved her right upstairs."

"While you were dating?" Alice asked.

"She didn't know about that," Connor said gruffly. "I mean, she found out when the Prescotts left the cove and Priscilla came by to say good-bye to Denise. Everything came out then."

He actually gave a low laugh. "My father was even more against the idea of Denise staying with us, and the two of us worked on the house enough for her to sleep there."

Della got up and brought over the coffee pot. "Coffee?" she asked, her cheerfulness almost out of place.

Mandie shook her head along with everyone else, her attention still riveted to Charlie's grandfather. No one had touched the food, but now, he reached out and picked up a steak bite, dipping the last piece on the short skewer into the bowl of spicy sauce.

"I loved her, and I wanted to prove it. But my father absolutely forbid me from marrying her, and we decided not to press our luck. Denise worked as a seamstress for one of the wealthy families here on the Ridge. She had enough to keep herself fed and clothed, and my mother made up the rest."

Suzie wrote out more notes.

"I slept there most nights," Connor continued, his gaze down now. "I'd never been more relieved than when she got pregnant."

Mandie pulled in a breath, and even Suzie stopped writing mid-sentence. The air turned heavy, and Mandie's heart struggled to beat through it.

"Because of that, we were finally allowed to get married." He shook his head sadly. "But she lost that baby. It was hard on both of us, but especially on her."

"I'm so sorry," Mandie whispered, a tether forming between her and Denise Prescott, though she'd never met the woman. Still, something about the story sang to her, made her feel seen and known, because she wanted a baby so badly too.

Connor nodded, his eyes distant with memory. "It took a few more years before she got pregnant with Alice. We'd almost given up hope." He blinked, and his expression cleared. He smiled and took the bite of steak.

"We had Alice and Scott pretty close together. My parents retired to Diamond Island, and we built our life right here in this house until…"

Alice reached for her father's hand. "Dad, I've told them the rest."

He looked at her, something challenging in his expression. "Have you? I don't even think I've told you the rest."

Alice leaned away from him as if he'd flicked something in her face. "You haven't?"

"Yes, you have," Della said. "About the storm and all of that?" She nodded decisively, though Mandie got the distinct impression there was more. "Yes, everyone knows the rest of that story, Connor. We don't need to hash it out again"

Suzie looked at Mandie, who nodded. She'd already told her of the storm that had claimed Alice's mother's life. How they'd called in rescue organizations far and wide, but they'd never found her or the boat.

She looked dissatisfied, but she didn't ask another question. Mandie almost wished she'd left Alice out of this, because she'd shut down the conversation just when it had started.

"So you two just kept the house all these years?" Mandie asked.

Connor nodded, still focused on the food. Charlie reached out and picked up a slice of bruschetta too, though they had dinner plans once this meeting concluded. Mandie's stomach swooped.

More than dinner plans. He'd gotten them a reservation at The Loft, an upscale restaurant right here on Rocky Ridge, with a room at the adjoining cliffside hotel. Just one night, but it felt like a luxurious escape.

"We saw no reason to get rid of it. It still needed a lot of work, and well..." He threw a look over to Alice. "Your mother still loved going there. It became a—a—a refuge of sorts for her."

"A refuge from what?" Suzie asked.

Mandie noticed Della's expression tighten slightly, a flicker of something crossing her features before she smoothed it away. Connor simply exuded sadness, and he shook his head again.

"Denise suffered from some mental illness," he said

quietly. "Depression. Anxiety. She held onto a lot of things, because she couldn't let them go."

"Did it help?" Alice asked. "Going to the house?"

Connor was quiet for a long moment. "Sometimes. She'd come home from those visits seemingly lighter somehow, like she'd found something she'd been looking for. But other times..." He shook his head. "Other times she'd be so sad I didn't know how to reach her."

"The night she died," Suzie said carefully, shooting a look to Mandie. But she had no idea what might come out of her mouth next. With Suzie, it was hard to tell sometimes. "Do you know why she went out on the boat during the storm?"

The question seemed to suck all the air from the room. Connor's face went pale, and Alice gripped his hand tighter.

"She'd been to the house that afternoon," he said finally.

"Dad, you never told me that."

"Connor, this probably isn't relevant," Della said.

Oh, whether it was or not, Mandie wanted to hear it.

Connor smiled softly at Alice and then threw Della a slightly more acidic look. Mandie wanted to get him alone too, because Della clearly didn't want all of this shared.

"It's just for us," she said. "We don't publish anything, though we have made monuments and whatnot with some of our projects."

"It just helps us feel the presence of the family more," Suzie said. "We definitely won't use the personal things, and we always check with the family first anyway."

"Right." Mandie nodded and reached for her lemonade again. It was slightly too sour, but she didn't mind at all.

Connor drew a deep breath. "When she came home that afternoon, she was agitated. Upset about something. I tried to talk to her, but she said she needed to be alone." His voice broke. "Later, she said she wanted to take the boat out. She'd done so before, after a particularly memorable visit to the house. But I should have stopped her. Should have known she wasn't thinking clearly. We both knew the storm was coming—it just came in faster than expected."

"Dad, it wasn't your fault," Alice said firmly.

"Wasn't it?" Connor looked at his daughter with eyes full of old pain. "She was my wife. I should have protected her."

Della reached across the table and gripped his fingers. "You can't blame yourself for choices other people make."

The words carried a weight that made Mandie study Della's face more carefully. There was something there—knowledge, perhaps, or understanding that went deeper than simple comfort.

"Do you think she meant to..." Suzie cleared her throat. "End her life on purpose?"

"I don't know." Connor's honesty sounded brutal in its simplicity. "She was an excellent sailor, and she knew these waters better than almost anyone. For her to go out in that storm." He shrugged helplessly. "It broke me, and I've spent the past thirty years trying to understand it."

Tears pricked Mandie's eyes as she watched this man wrestle with decades of guilt and unanswered questions. Beside her, Charlie was unusually quiet, his jaw tight with emotion.

"The Coast Guard searched for weeks," Alice added quietly. "Everyone did. The whole community turned out to help look for her."

Suzie made careful notes, her pen scratching against the paper in the otherwise silent room. "Is there anything else you can tell us about the house? About why it might have been important to her?"

Connor considered the question. "I don't know. I think it was a place of comfort for her." He nodded. "Yes, she loved going there more than anywhere else." He spoke with a subtle finality, and Suzie nodded.

She closed her notebook, placed it on top of the pages in the folder, and closed it all. "Thank you so much. I'm so sorry about your wife, Connor, but I really, really appreciate you talking to me."

"Me too," Mandie chimed in, shooting Suzie a look.

Suzie stood. "I'm afraid I have to get going. I have another appointment soon, and if I'm not on the four-forty ferry off Rocky Ridge, I won't make it."

Good-byes started, and Della wouldn't let them leave without containers of bruschetta and steak bites. Mandie couldn't wait to get out of the house; her skin itched with the need of it, and when she finally made her last wave, an intense wash of relief flowed over her.

"Thanks, Mom," Charlie said, hugging his mother in the driveway. "That was intense, right?"

Alice stepped back and looked south. "I didn't know my mother owned that house. I never knew she went there."

"You can come see the place," Mandie said. "Though we've torn most of it out."

Alice smiled and reached to slide her slender fingers down the side of Mandie's face. "No, it's okay. I knew my mother had some issues." She sighed out a breath while Suzie said she'd call a ride.

Charlie pulled out his phone to do the same. "Shoot, I left my backpack in the other car. Maybe I can get him to come." He took a few steps away to handle that.

"It's going to be an amazing house when we're finished,"

Mandie said. "And this will help us make sure it retains the spirit that your mother loved."

Alice nodded, and then she turned back to her father's house. "I'll be right back." She hurried inside, leaving Mandie to wonder what else she needed.

"That was incredible," Suzie said as she lowered her phone. "*So* much information to process."

"Definitely." Mandie simply watched Charlie talk on the phone, and when he turned back to her smiling, she knew he'd found his backpack with their overnight essentials. Not that they needed much. She'd been tracking her cycle, and she should be ovulating today. She just wanted to be alone with him—not in his parents' house—and make love to him.

"I'll type up my notes tonight and share them with you and Alicia tomorrow," Suzie said. "There are so many threads to follow up on."

"Sounds great," Mandie said.

"Two minutes," Charlie said as he came to her side. "Mom went back in?"

"Yes." Mandie reached for his hand.

He leaned down and pressed a kiss to her temple. "We can check-in as soon as we get there."

She nodded, knowing what that meant. Their car arrived, and she gave Suzie a quick hug. "See you tomorrow," she said.

"Yep, tomorrow." Suzie grinned at them, and Mandie followed Charlie to the car, giggling as she joined him.

"I love you," he whispered as the car backed out of the driveway and started north again. "Baby or no baby, I'm glad you're mine and I'm yours."

She leaned into his kiss, because she loved him the same way. But she did really want a baby too.

Chapter Nine

Candace adjusted the sleeves of her ivory silk blouse and surveyed the bullpen of her new Long Island office through the glass walls of her corner suite. The space buzzed with controlled energy—keyboards clicking, phones ringing, the soft hum of conversations about deadlines and client meetings.

Her gaze settled on Emma Chen, the newest addition to her team. The young woman hunched over her desk, furiously scribbling notes while juggling two people at her desk and a third on a phone call. Her dark hair fell across her face as she leaned forward, and her blazer hung slightly too large on her petite frame.

The sight triggered a memory of Mandie several years ago—eager, overwhelmed, desperate to prove herself worthy of a field assignment. Emma possessed that same hungry determination, that willingness to work twice as hard as anyone else just to earn a seat at the table.

Candace's chest tightened with an emotion she couldn't quite name. Pride, perhaps. Or loss.

She turned away from the window, pulled the blinds, and settled behind her mahogany desk, the familiar weight of her pearl earrings swaying as she moved. The morning light streamed through the floor-to-ceiling windows, casting geometric shadows across the stack of project files awaiting her attention.

She couldn't believe in the upgrade of her workspace since working in the also-being-renovated yacht club. She did miss that space for just a moment, as so much had happened in her life while she worked from the Captain's Quarters on the second floor of the club.

Still, she was glad to be back in the city, in a proper office space fit for the type of work she oversaw at PastForward.

Her phone buzzed with a text from Lana. *Can't wait to see you for lunch today - I have news!*

Candace smiled as she started to type a response. Lana's enthusiasm for their growing relationship still caught her off guard sometimes. Twenty-one years of separation couldn't be erased overnight, but they were building something real together. Something that felt like family.

Can't wait. Just come up and into the office. Tell Jerome I know you're coming, or he won't let you through.

She had told her assistant not to let anyone into her office, after all.

Her computer chimed with an email notification, and she forced herself to put aside her phone and focus on the work at hand. The autumn project lineup required her attention—two major restorations in Upstate New York and a historic brownstone renovation in Brooklyn. Each would need a capable team leader, someone who could handle the pressure and complexity of high-stakes restoration work.

Emma would need at least another year before she'd be

ready for that kind of responsibility. The other junior associates showed promise, but none possessed the intuitive understanding of historical architecture that made the difference between a competent renovation and a transformative one.

The kind of understanding Mandie had developed.

Candace's jaw tightened as she thought of her team in Five Island Cove. Mandie would finish the Black Sand Bungalow and then what? Stay in that quaint little island community, maybe open her own small restoration business? Waste all the training and mentorship Candace had invested in her?

She scoffed at the idea, though she knew it could very well come to fruition. A slip of irritation drove under her skin at the thought of it, because that was the exact reason Candace hadn't wanted to let her begin down the team lead path in the first place.

Young women like her...

Candace stalled the thought there, because she'd started wondering if young women like Mandie didn't know and understand more than she'd ever given them credit for.

At the very least, just because Mandie was married and wanted a family didn't mean she wasn't really good at her job too.

"People can't have everything," Candace muttered to herself. She'd often wondered what would've been different about her life had she kept Lana and raised her as her own, but she'd made a different choice.

She'd chosen her career over becoming a mother, over a family, and she was just now learning how to juggle and balance both.

Setting aside her worries about Mandie's potential two-week-notice coming at the worst possible time, Candace focused on the upcoming projects she needed to arrange into dossiers. Then, she could pass those out to her employees and start to weed through them in brutal weekly meetings.

Brutal for them, at least.

She worked on the files for the upcoming projects, so many possibilities ahead for PastForward. She loved this company, and she loved taking some of the most run-down properties in the world and making them new again.

She'd been around long enough to know that even if Mandie quit, someone would rise to take her place. Candace looked up from the folder where she'd just placed a full-color photo of the brownstone in Brooklyn, wondering if she should start to do some discreet mentoring.

Perhaps Emma, or even Jolie.

Her phone chimed again, but this time the sound told her the message would be from Bradley, and a sour taste filled her mouth. He'd left town again, and while she couldn't really blame him, she also didn't have to support his globe-trotting lifestyle.

Once again, people couldn't have everything.

He couldn't have the same relationship with their daughter as Candace did if he was never there—and no, an online relationship was not the same as a live, in-person, face-to-face one.

Candace knew, as she'd tried both with various people over the years, and she needed to see people, talk to them, judge their body language, all of it to truly have a friendship or working relationship with them.

That was one reason she had set the idea of a satellite office on the backburner. Already, she felt like she needed to get back to Five Island Cove and check on her team there, though she rarely stopped by active worksites, even if they were only a block away. No, she relied on reports, invoices, receipts, and emails to tell the story of how a project was progressing.

Something she needed to do with the Black Sand Bungalow, actually. Perhaps that was why she felt the need to book a plane ticket to the cove. Instead of doing that, she clicked around on her computer until she reached the cloud file for the project on the beach.

Alicia would have every slip of paper scanned, coded, labeled, and uploaded on time, as meticulous as she was.

Sure enough, Candace double-clicked to open the Black Sand Bungalow project and found neat folders for the weekly reports, unpaid invoices, paid receipts, the timeline, and all correspondence.

She clicked through the weekly reports, her practiced eye scanning budget projections and timeline updates. Everything looked solid—construction costs within parameters, no major delays, quality control measures in place.

Then she reached an unpaid materials invoice.

Candace blinked, certain she'd misread the number. She scrolled back up to double-check the line item, her pulse accelerating with each digit she confirmed.

Stained glass windows. Custom-designed, hand-crafted, imported from a specialty artisan in Vermont. Twenty-eight thousand dollars.

"What in the world?"

She grabbed her phone and scrolled to Alicia's contact, her fingers moving with sharp, precise motions. The call went straight to voicemail.

"You have got to be kidding me."

Alicia always had her phone with her. Always. If she wasn't answering, she'd *chosen* not to answer.

"Alicia, it's Candace." She spoke crisply after the sound of the beep. "I need you to call me immediately about the stained glass order. This is completely outside the discussed parameters."

She ended the call and immediately dialed Mandie's number. How in the world were they going to make the budget work with such an extravagant purchase?

Voicemail again.

Frustration bubbled up from her chest, hot and acidic. These women were supposed to be professionals. They carried company phones for a reason. The fact that both calls had gone unanswered felt deliberately dismissive.

A knock on her office door interrupted her spiraling thoughts. "Come in."

Jerome appeared in the doorway, his expression uncertain. "Miss Ewing? I have the Henderson contract ready for your review, and Mister Patterson from the possible Brooklyn project called about the timeline for possible purchase."

"Not now." Candace's voice came out sharper than she'd intended. "Come back after lunch."

Jerome's face flushed pink. "Of course. Sorry to interrupt."

The door closed with a soft click, and Candace immediately felt the familiar stab of guilt. Jerome was a good assistant, but he had caught her at a bad time. A very bad time.

Mandie's voicemail beeped. "Mandie, I'm assuming you and Alicia aren't on speaking terms, which radically concerns me. Otherwise, I'm certain you wouldn't have authorized a *twenty-eight-thousand-dollar* stained glass window order that is going to take at least fifteen percent of your overall budget."

She drew in a breath, her chest so tight. "Call me back immediately."

She hung up and pulled up the stained glass invoice again, studying the detailed specifications. The design was admittedly beautiful—a coastal motif that would perfectly complement the renovated bungalow's aesthetic. The craftsmanship would be exceptional, the kind of artistic detail that elevated a good restoration to an extraordinary one.

But twenty-eight thousand dollars represented nearly fifteen percent of their total materials budget. For windows.

Her phone buzzed with another text, and she made the mistake of looking down at her screen. Bradley: *Flying to Seattle. Back next week. Give my love to Lana.*

Candace stared at the message, her irritation shifting targets. His casual cancellations reminded Candace too much of her own past behavior—putting work first, assuming personal relationships would simply wait.

She typed back: *I am not your messenger, and I'm not telling her. You need to text her yourself.*

He didn't respond, and Candace still hated herself that she'd passed on his cancellation message the first time. Well, no more.

She set the phone aside and pulled up the site to book a plane ticket. If her team in Five Island Cove couldn't be bothered to answer their phones, she'd handle this conversation in person.

The Friday afternoon flights to the regional airport were nearly full, as it was summertime now and tourists flocked to the cove on the weekends. She managed to find a seat on the three-forty departure—expensive and last-minute, as well as not in her preferred class, but necessary.

She fired off a group text to Mandie, Alicia, and Suzie: *I'll be arriving Friday evening to review the project status. Please clear your schedules for a comprehensive walk-through either around 6:30 that night or early the next morning.*

She didn't care if it was a weekend or not. Perhaps they should answer their phones when she called. She stared at her phone, expecting one of them to answer, which would only prove they'd purposely ignored her.

Another knock interrupted her thoughts. This time, she didn't bother looking up from her computer screen. "I said after lunch."

"Candace?"

Candace's head snapped up at the sound of the familiar voice. Lana stood in the doorway, her face glowing with excitement. She wore a sundress the color of the pure summer sky, her blonde hair falling in loose waves around her shoulders.

"Lana." Candace's frustration melted away, replaced by the warm rush of affection that still surprised her with its intensity. "You're early." She got to her feet and rounded the desk.

"I couldn't wait." Lana practically bounced as she entered the office, her gaze sweeping across the space with obvious admiration. "I still can't get over how incredible your office is. The view, the furniture, everything. It's *so* amazing."

"Thank you." Candace watched her daughter's face. The excitement radiating from Lana was almost tangible, electric in its intensity. "You mentioned you have news?"

"I do." Lana held up her left hand, where a modest but

elegant diamond ring caught the afternoon light. "Ted proposed last night." She giggled and bounced on her toes.

The words hit Candace like a physical blow. Joy and terror warred in her chest, creating a sensation she couldn't quite name. "Congratulations," she gushed, pulling Lana into a hug.

"Thank you." Lana's voice came out muffled against Candace's shoulder. "I said yes, obviously. We're thinking next summer, after I graduate."

Candace held her daughter tighter, breathing in the familiar scent of her vanilla perfume. Marriage. Another milestone she'd missed, another life event she'd have to navigate from the sidelines.

"Tell me about the proposal," she said as they separated.

Lana launched into the story. First, dinner at her favorite restaurant in Times Square, Ted's nervous fumbling with the ring box, her tears of happiness. Candace listened, nodding in all the right places, but part of her mind remained fixed on a single, selfish thought: she was losing Lana just as she'd found her.

Her daughter flopped into the chair opposite the desk and exhaled mightily. "I was hoping you might help me plan the wedding. I know it's a lot to ask, because you're so busy with work, but I got this appointment—"

"Yes." The word came out before Candace could second-guess herself. "Of course. I'd be honored." She moved behind her desk and retook her seat. "You aren't going to ask your mother?"

"Yes, she's helping too," Lana said, like having both of them in the same room would go swimmingly well. Sure, if the definition of *well* was a bottomless pit in Candace's stomach.

Lana's smile could have powered the entire building. "I was thinking we could start with dress shopping. There's this *amazing* boutique in SoHo that specializes in vintage-inspired gowns, and I thought maybe we could make a day of it? Lunch, shopping, maybe get our nails done?"

The domestic normalcy of it—mother and daughter planning a wedding together—felt both foreign and wonderful. But Lana would be there with two women, only one of which was her mother. "That sounds perfect."

"I was thinking in a couple of months, once we get through the summer bustle and things settle down with the start of yet another semester." Lana pulled out her phone, already scrolling through her calendar. "Maybe October?"

"October works." Candace made a mental note to block out the entire day, no matter what work crises might arise.

"Great." Lana bounced to her feet again. "I can see what they have at lunch." She scanned Candace behind the desk. "Are you ready?"

"Yes." Candace cleared her throat and opened her bottom desk drawer to collect her purse. She stood and smiled at Lana, beyond grateful that she'd been invited to help with the wedding. "I'm ready."

They left the office together, and Candace noticed how everyone immediately stopped their conversations and bent their heads over their work. Such a thing used to give her a rush, make her feel powerful, remind her of everything she'd worked for and built.

Now, almost a slithering guilt moved through her. Was this really how she wanted her employees to treat her? To feel at work?

"Jerome," she said, stopping at his desk. "You had paperwork for me?"

"Yes, ma'am." He practically fell out of his chair to get it for her.

She gave him a smile. "Thank you. I'll get it done over lunch and get it back to you."

"Oh-okay."

Candace nodded at him and turned to face the rest of the office. Out of everyone, Emma Chen looked at her and met her eye. Candace took the first steps toward her, keeping her smile on her face.

"Miss Chen," she said. "Will you please meet with Jerome and schedule a meeting with me for early next week? He'll know my schedule."

"For what?" Emma asked.

"A new mentoring program." She nodded at her, finally feeling her smile reach across her whole face.

Emma's face lit up with the same eager hope Candace remembered from her own early career. "Absolutely. Thank you."

As Candace watched Emma's reaction, something shifted inside her chest. The recognition that she had the power to *nurture* talent instead of simply demanding results. The understanding that mentorship was a gift she could give.

She looked over to Lana, who waited a few feet away. The stained glass invoice still demanded an explanation, and her Five Island Cove team's failure to respond still rankled. But for now, she had somewhere more important to be.

"Let's go, dear," she said.

As they left the office, Candace caught several employees watching her with obvious curiosity. Tomorrow, she'd share some of what she'd learned about balancing ambition with humanity, about the importance of building relationships alongside projects and resumes.

Today, she'd focus on the relationship that mattered most —the one with the daughter she'd thought she'd lost forever, who was now planning a wedding and asking for her help.

The stained glass windows could wait until Friday. Some things, Candace was finally learning, were more important than work.

Chapter Ten

A licia smoothed one hand down the front of her navy blouse for the third time in ten minutes, her tablet clutched in the other. The late afternoon breeze carried the scent of sawdust and fresh pine, mixing with the fresh air that perpetually clung to Rocky Ridge.

Candace would be here any minute, and Alicia had everything ready. Every invoice scanned and categorized, every receipt coded and uploaded, every timeline adjustment documented with meticulous precision.

Henry's digital rendering of the stained glass windows sat waiting on her tablet, the afternoon light captured in brilliant blues and greens that would soon flood the back wall of the restored cottage.

Her phone buzzed against her hip, and Alicia dipped her hand into her pocket to retrieve it. Henry's name flashed across the screen, and she swiped it to voicemail without hesitation. The walk-through, report, and conversation about twenty-eight thousand dollars in custom stained glass required her full attention.

The phone buzzed again almost immediately

Alicia stared at the screen, her pulse quickening. Henry never called twice in rapid succession unless something was wrong with the kids. She started to answer, then caught sight of a black sedan turning onto the sandy lane.

"Mandie," she called over her shoulder. "She's here."

The car pulled to a stop beside their small construction camp, and Alicia tucked her phone into her back pocket as Candace emerged from the back seat. But instead of the usual navy blazer and designer heels, Candace wore navy-and-white striped cotton pants and a plain navy blue tank top that looked like it was made with the finest fabric in the world. Her blonde hair had been pulled back into a casual ponytail, and she'd traded her signature pearls for simple silver hoops.

Relief flooded through Alicia's chest. This version of Candace felt approachable, almost vacation-ready rather than battle-prepared.

"How was your flight?" Alicia asked as she approached, extending her hand.

"Surprisingly pleasant." Candace's smile reached her eyes as she shook Alicia's hand. "Though I'm still getting used to these small regional airports."

"I hear that." Alicia gestured toward the house, where Mandie and Suzie waited on the newly constructed front porch. "How are things at the office? How's Lana?"

Something softened in Candace's expression at the mention of her daughter. "She's engaged. Wedding planning has officially begun, and she's asked me to help her and her mother."

"Wow, engaged." A genuine smile tugged at her lips even as another slip of shock moved through her. She had no idea how to navigate an adoption relationship, and surely Candace didn't either. But she'd likely handle it with dignity and grace, the way she did everything.

"That's wonderful. You must be so excited." She gestured for Candace to go in front of her and toward the house.

"Terrified and thrilled in equal measure." Candace's laugh held a note of vulnerability that Alicia had rarely heard before. She stepped past her, her gaze going up into the trees they'd pruned but left untouched. "She wants me to help plan everything. Dress shopping, venue tours, the whole experience."

"Wow," Alicia said.

They reached the porch, where Mandie stepped forward with her usual project-manager efficiency. "Ready for the grand tour?"

"More than ready." Candace surveyed the transformed exterior with obvious approval. "The progress is remarkable. This looks nothing like the photos from six weeks ago."

"Wait until you see the inside." Mandie led the way through the front door, immediately launching into her detailed explanation of structural improvements, timeline adjustments, and quality control measures.

Alicia followed, her tablet ready to insert her voice with budget breakdowns and vendor contracts when necessary. They'd met the moment all of them had finally seen Candace's text, and they'd split their responsibilities down team lines.

Mandie, as the team lead, would take Candace through the house. Alicia would add budgetary and analytical details as they went, and Suzie would pipe in with all structural and historical details about the construction work and the family.

The interior of the bungalow had been completely transformed, and Alicia still took a quick breath as she entered. New subflooring stretched across the main living area, and fresh drywall created clean lines where rotting plaster had once peeled from the walls. The thick wall that had once separated the back of the house from the front had been mostly removed, with a strong beam now in place to support the weight of the second floor.

The kitchen framework on the left outlined a space that would soon house gorgeous cabinetry, and the bathroom rough-in promised a luxurious master suite just on the other side of the remaining wall in the footprint of the main floor.

"The electrical and plumbing contractors start Monday," Mandie explained as they moved through the space. "We're on schedule for flooring installation the following week, then cabinetry and fixtures in the coming weeks."

Candace nodded, making notes on her own tablet. "The budget tracking?"

"Exactly where we projected." Alicia pulled up the financial dashboard on her screen. "Even with the stained glass investment, we're within the established parameters." She tilted the tablet toward Candace. "We've saved a lot on a few things by sourcing them here in the cove, including the white pine we're using upstairs, and the upcycled cabinets that are standard instead of custom."

Candace held her gaze for a moment before switching it to the screen. "Standard, not custom," she muttered.

True, they usually did everything custom in their renovations at PastForward, but Alicia didn't think anyone would notice in this cliffside cottage, because it would be absolutely stunning.

"We're going to paint them and one of Mandie's friends is trying to get into custom cabinetry carving. He's going to do a design on knobs that will make them seem custom without the price of custom."

She looked over to Suzie. "We found a ceramic tile here in the house," she said without missing a beat. "It had a few symbols on it, and we've come to learn that one of them represents the Prescott family in a non-obtrusive way."

Candace lifted her head from studying the numbers, flipping back her reading glasses. "We don't put that kind of personal touch on our houses," she said. "We have to be able to resell this to someone who's never heard of the Prescotts."

"But someone who loves and appreciates the history here in the cove," Mandie said.

"It's a bird," Suzie said, practically blurting out the words. "It won't be intrusive. The only way anyone will know what it means is if we tell them." She shot a look to Alicia, who held her tongue.

"I want to see it before any carving is done." Candace refocused on the numbers, scrolling quickly through the line items with practiced efficiency.

"Let's continue," she said.

The fact that she didn't ask a question or demand to be shown something more unsettled Alicia slightly.

"You can see we have no windows in the house as of yet," Mandie said. "They're on the way, and should be here by the time we're doing the wallpaper and flooring."

"Including your spanning stained glass?" Candace came to a stop on the cusp of the living room and kitchen. "I see where they go. They're certainly impressive."

"You'll be able to see them from the front door," Alicia said. "They'll bathe the entire house in beautiful light that streams from west to east, north and south."

"There's one in the master suite in the corner here,"

Mandie said, having moved over to the doorway that framed in the bedroom. "So it's a continuous design we're sure the right buyer is going to appreciate greatly."

She met Alicia's eyes, and she startled when she realized it was her turn to show the rendering—and her phone had just started to buzz again.

"I have a rendering," she said. Alicia's fingers trembled slightly as she navigated to Henry's design file.

"A rendering?" Candace asked.

"Henry created it for us, and I'm so sorry, but he's called three times in the past twenty minutes, and I need to step out for two minutes."

She thrust the tablet into Suzie's hands and pulled her phone out of her back pocket. She'd seen the rendering—had gone over every moment of it with her husband—and she could imagine the way the image would fill the screen and show the back of the cottage transformed by three massive stained glass panels, each depicting coastal scenes in rich blues, greens, and golds. Late afternoon sunlight streamed through the virtual glass, casting rainbow patterns across the hardwood floors.

When she didn't get fired as she walked away, she pulled out her phone and returned Henry's third call.

"Hey, Mom," Gray said.

Alicia frowned. "Gray? What's going on?"

"I just wanted to know if I could go with Mrs. Lennox over to the splash pad."

Alicia turned back to her business meeting and found all three of the women in the kitchen still watching the rendering. "Where's Henry?"

"He's helping Lily with her braiding."

"Gray," Alicia said, her patience razor thin for this type of interruption. "Go ask Henry. He's in charge of you. I'm working."

"Okay, but—"

"Gray, does he know you called me?"

Silence.

"Take him the phone right now and tell him what's going on. Then tell him that I said, no, you *can't* go to the splash pad with Mrs. Lennox."

"But, Mom—"

"You should've asked Henry. I'll be home later, Gray." With that, she ended the call, trying to soothe the lightning-hot irritation with her son. She took a few angry steps toward the group, which drew the attention of everyone in the kitchen.

"Is everything okay?" Mandie asked, genuine concern on her face.

Candace handed her the tablet. "If you need to go, Alicia, go ahead."

Alicia blinked, that response from Candace—caring, concerned, almost maternal—not quite lining up in her head. She shook it, trying to find the right train of thought to be on. "I'm okay," she said. "Henry's handling it, just like he did for this rendering."

"I can't believe Henry made this." Candace nodded to the tablet. "Maybe I need to recruit him over to PastForward." She wore a small smile that spoke volumes of mischief. Alicia had never seen anything like it.

"He has experience with architectural visualization from his museum work." Alicia's voice steadied as she spoke about Henry's talents. "He captured how the light will move through the space at different times of day."

She glanced over to Suzie. "Did you show her that? Morning versus afternoon versus evening?"

"We watched it all, yes," Suzie said with a smile. She too wore concern in her face, and Alicia almost wished she wouldn't. She knew Daniel had come in on the same flight as Candace and would be waiting for Suzie in her condo. Mandie had a husband waiting at home too.

And yet, the three of them were there, standing in this half-rebuilt cottage for a job they each loved.

"It's extraordinary." Candace smiled at Alicia. "The craftsmanship will be exceptional?"

She nodded crisply, finding her professionalism for long enough to put Gray on a shelf in her mind to deal with when she got home. "The artisan in Vermont has a waiting list of six months for new commissions. We were fortunate to secure a cancellation slot."

Candace nodded slowly. "This is exactly the kind of detail that elevates a good restoration to an unforgettable one."

The knot in Alicia's chest loosened. No lecture about budget overruns, no demands for explanations or justifications. Just professional recognition of artistic value. Of Alicia's research and judgment.

They continued upstairs, along a new staircase that would remain open, Mandie detailing the progress. "We'll have three bedrooms and two full bathrooms up here, plus a reading nook that takes advantage of the ocean view."

Alicia provided financial context for every decision, including the one where they'd install double-panel clear windows in the upstairs nook instead of more stained glass.

"I want that to be truly special for the ground floor."

Candace nodded, and as they went back downstairs,

Suzie chimed in with historical insights about the original construction, her enthusiasm for the Prescott family research evident in every comment.

Alicia brought up the rear, and she'd barely reached the main floor when Candace asked, "What's that?" She pointed across the room, to the southwest corner that rarely saw any light.

Alicia followed her gaze, squinting into the distance. "I don't see anything."

"There." Candace moved closer, crouching down. She moved to the left. "Something's sticking up." She looked over her shoulder. "I can see it catching the light."

With that, the sun shifted down even more, and as Alicia took another step closer, she saw the flash of evening summer sunlight catch something and illuminate it into a bright white.

Alicia knelt beside her, finally spotting the edge of what looked like paper or fabric wedged between the boards. "Suzie, can you get this board up?"

"Seriously?" Suzie's voice carried her trademark exasperation. "We're ready for electrical and plumbing, and now I'm doing demo again?"

But she pulled a hammer from her belt, working the prying head under the floorboard with practiced efficiency. The board came up with a protesting creak, revealing a gap in the subfloor beneath.

Suzie gasped, her hand flying to her mouth.

Alicia leaned forward, her heart racing as she peered into the opening. Nestled in the space between floor joists sat an old-fashioned hatbox, its faded floral pattern barely visible in the shadows.

"What is it?" Mandie asked, crowding closer.

Alicia reached into the opening with reverent care, her fingers closing around the box's edges. It was heavier than expected, and something shifted inside as she lifted it out. The cardboard felt fragile with age, and the ribbon that had once secured the lid hung in what once was white.

Part of it had crept up through the boards and caught the light.

As Mandie knelt beside her, crowding in close, Alicia set the box on the floor and carefully lifted the lid, her breath catching at what lay inside.

"Letters," she breathed out. Dozens of them, tied with faded ribbons and stacked in neat piles. The envelopes were yellowed with age, and the ink had faded to a soft brown, but the handwriting was still legible.

Alicia lifted the top envelope, a loose one not banded together with any others, her fingers trembling.

"Denise" sat proudly across the front, written in a masculine hand, the letters flowing with the careful penmanship of another era.

She looked up at her friends, her voice barely above a whisper. "I think they're love letters."

Chapter Eleven

S uzie kicked off her work boots, having unlaced them on the ferry, and let them fall beside the door of her condo with satisfying thuds. She groaned at the relief of not having the heavy steel-toed things attached to her body anymore.

The blessed air conditioning blew hard, and Daniel sat at her small dining table, his laptop open and papers scattered around him. His eyes tracked her movement as she padded across the hardwood floor in her socks.

"How did it go?" He closed the laptop and pushed his chair back, opening his arms.

She sank into his lap, breathing in the familiar scent of his cologne mixed with the faint smell of coffee. "Better than expected." She pressed her face against his neck, letting the tension of the day melt away. "She loved the stained glass rendering Henry made."

"That's great, sweetheart." His hand found the small of her back, fingers tracing gentle circles through her work shirt. "I'm sure you charmed her with your knowledge of all things horned lark." He grinned at her.

"She wants to see it first, of course." Suzie sighed. "We didn't talk about it all that much, but I think I can win her over in the end."

Daniel's laugh rumbled through his chest. "I'm positive of that."

She traced the edge of his collar with her finger. "We found something else today. More letters, hidden under the floorboards in a hatbox. Love letters addressed to Denise."

His eyebrows rose. "From her husband?"

"That's what we need to figure out. We're meeting for brunch tomorrow to go through them." She shifted in his lap, suddenly restless. "I'm sorry. Candace promised it would be two hours."

"Baby, I can entertain myself for two hours."

"I just—you come all this way every weekend." She peered up at him through her eyelashes. "I want to pick a date tonight."

"For the wedding?" His hands stilled on her back as his eyes widened.

"Yes." The word came out more forcefully than she'd intended. "For the wedding."

Daniel studied her face with those perceptive eyes that saw too much. "What's changed?"

Suzie stood and moved to the window, wrapping her arms around herself as she stared out at the harbor. Boats bobbed at their moorings, their masts swaying gently in the evening breeze. "Seeing Candace today, hearing about Lana's engagement. Everyone's moving forward with their lives, making commitments, building futures." She turned back to him. "I don't want to be the woman who's too scared to take the next step."

"You're scared?" Daniel rose and crossed to her, his hands finding her shoulders.

She'd told him this. Maybe not in those exact words, but close enough. She leaned into his touch despite the knot forming in her stomach. "I think it would be nice to get married in the spring. The city in the spring." She turned into him, wrapping her arms around him and looking up into his handsome face. "Maybe May?"

"May sounds perfect." His smile was warm, uncomplicated.

"It'll be a small ceremony, just family and close friends." She pulled out her phone, scrolling to find the contact Mandie had given her weeks ago. "Because you know, I don't even have any family to invite."

"Suze."

She stepped back, fighting the familiar bitterness that had been staining her tongue since she'd gotten engaged. Funny how she didn't mind being alone in the world until she had something amazing to celebrate. Then she just felt so... isolated. And foolish, like it was her fault she had no one to invite to her own wedding.

She pulled out her phone. "I should call Mandie's mother now, before I lose my nerve."

Daniel settled back at the table while she dialed, his presence steady and reassuring as the phone rang.

"This is Robin," a friendly voice chirped.

"Hey, Robin, uh." Suzie started to pace, the color in the room draining from her vision. "This is Suzette Paxman. Mandie's friend? She gave me your number for wedding planning?"

"Suzie, of course." Robin's voice brightened immediately. "Mandie's told me so much about you. Congratulations on your engagement."

"Thank you," Suzie said, her feet finally stopping and growing roots next to where Daniel sat at the table.

He reached for her free hand and tugged her into his lap again. He nuzzled the side of her neck and whispered, "Put her on speaker, love."

Suzie pulled the phone away from her ear and did as he'd asked. "You're on with me and Daniel," she said, finally able to meet his eyes. "We're thinking New York City in the springtime."

"Oh, the city?" Pages flipped on Robin's end of the line while Suzie's stomach tumbled to the floor.

"Do you only do weddings here in the cove?" she asked.

"No, of course not," Robin said. "I can do May. It's still a bit chilly, with unpredictable weather, here in the cove. I'm free the whole month."

The whole month. Suzie's mind fractured.

"Nothing elaborate," she heard herself say. "Maybe thirty or forty people."

"Maybe up to eighty," Daniel said. "I have a lot of cousins that might creep out of the woodwork, and Suze has all her work friends she's forgetting about."

"That's not a terribly large number," Robin mused. "Are you thinking indoor? Outdoor? Wedding? Reception? Dinner? All in the same place?"

Suzie blinked and stared at Daniel, who chuckled.

"I think right now, we're thinking we'd like to set a date. Suzie—well, she just wants to do one thing at a time."

"Well, you tell me. If you have a specific place you want to be married in, that might influence the date."

Suzie looked at him, and he gazed back at her. Her mind

churned, like she had a gear out of place. "Maybe that Greek restaurant where we had our first date?"

"You want to get married in a restaurant?" Robin asked.

"I don't know." Frustration built within Suzie. "Where do people get married in New York City?"

Silence came through the line, and then Robin giggled. "Anywhere, Suzie. Literally, anywhere. Here's what I think: You and Daniel make a list of places that mean something to you, and I'll do some research on what it would take to get married there and host up to eighty guests in the process. Okay?"

"Okay," Suzie said.

"And then, you can pick one, and I'll call them and find out what their May calendars look like. And we'll pick a date that way."

She nodded, noting Daniel's wide smile. "Sounds good, Robin," he said. "Thank you so much."

"I'll text you a list," Suzie said. "Really soon." Because while she'd made the call, she didn't actually have a date on the calendar yet.

The call ended, and she slid her phone onto the table and curled into Daniel's chest.

"Hey," he said gently, and Suzie looked up at him. "May, next year. We're getting married." His eyes shone with so much love, and he closed the distance between them and kissed her.

His hands moved into her hair, and he growled, "I love you, Suze," just before he gently nudged her off his lap and led her down the hall and into her bedroom.

LATER, AS THEY LAY TANGLED IN HER SHEETS WITH the windows open and the sound of waves lapping against the harbor, Suzie traced patterns on Daniel's chest in the darkness.

"Before she finally left, my mother would disappear for days at a time, leaving me home alone."

Daniel said nothing, but the gentle swirling of his fingers tracing a pattern up and down her arm didn't stop either.

"If it started to be five or six days, the neighbors would notice, and they'd come get me to stay with them."

"I'm sorry," he murmured, his voice sounding drowsy, but his muscles tight with attention.

"She was gone for sixteen days once, and then she came back for less than forty-eight hours. She spent most of that packing up everything we owned."

Suzie could see the apartment where she'd lived for a couple of years as a young pre-teen. Feel the fear as it struck through her with the force of a venomous snake. Hear the way the neighbors would knock and call for her to come out, that she was safe and they'd care for her.

"I was twelve," she said. "And she dropped me off at school that second morning she was home. My teacher got a call about a half-hour after we'd come back from lunch. He took me out in the hall, and he was crying."

Suzie shook her head slightly, trying to get the memory to go away. It wouldn't, cemented as it was in her mind. "I thought he was going to tell me my mom had died, and honestly, as I waited for him to say something, I had this horrible sense of relief. Like, maybe then, I'd be able to go into the foster care system and have someone who actually wanted me."

Tears burned her eyes, and Daniel held her closer. "He

said my mom had called, and that I needed to find my way to my grandmother's after school got out. He said he and the principal would go with me, that I'd be living with her from now on."

She let her tears slither out of the corners of her eyes and down her cheeks. They crawled, carving a path of fire that soon cooled to the point that she shivered. "Grams didn't live anywhere near the school, and I had to transfer somewhere else. I didn't see my mother again for over a year."

But she also never got left home alone again. Grams had dinner on the table every night, and she made Suzie do her homework. She bought her shoes and clothes and she took care of her.

"I'm afraid I'm going to be just like her," Suzie whispered into the dark, her eyes open and seeing only a future where she inflicted the same kind of pain on someone else that her mother had done to her.

"That's not true," Daniel whispered back, his voice fierce and strong. He shifted and sat up, but Suzie simply rolled away, turning her back to him. She couldn't face him right now.

He curled into her from behind, his arms encircling her and holding on. "I know it's not true, sweetheart, because I've seen you and I know you. You would never, ever, ever abandon people who mean something to you." He pressed a kiss just behind her ear. "Can you imagine ever just turning your back on Alicia and Mandie and walking away in the middle of a project?"

He scoffed softly. "No, it would never happen. That's not who you are."

She wept softly, because she couldn't ever see herself

doing that either. "I never imagined I'd get married. I won't be a good wife."

"I don't think that's something you get to judge," he said. "And I think you'll be an amazing wife and partner. We've been together for over a year, Suzie. I told you ages ago that if you needed space to just tell me, and you've never told me that. Not one single time."

She nodded and clasped her hands and arms around his. "I'm sorry," she whispered. "I will try."

"You don't need to try," he said. "You just have to be you."

Suzie turned again and pressed her face against his shoulder, breathing in the familiar scent of his skin. Maybe he was right. Maybe she'd already broken the cycle that had defined her mother's choices.

"I love you too," she whispered. "I'm terrified about it, but I do want to marry you."

He touched his lips to her forehead and swept his hands through her hair. "And that's how I know you're nothing like your mother."

Suzie let his words sink into her ears and move deeper. They penetrated her heart too, and glided down into her stomach and then into her soul. Perhaps she wasn't like her mother, and she wouldn't let fear or inadequacy drive her.

She could do things that scared her, and she could do things she'd never done before—including getting married.

THE NEXT MORNING DAWNED CLEAR AND BRIGHT, with the kind of crystalline light that made Five Island Cove look like a postcard. Suzie dressed carefully in khaki shorts, a pale green sleeveless blouse, and sandals, her hair loose around her shoulders. The Glass Dolphin sat perched on a bluff overlooking Diamond Island's western coast, its floor-to-ceiling windows offering panoramic views of the water.

Once she'd entered, frilly music danced down from hidden speakers, and she barely knew what to do in a place like this. She met a well-dressed hostess at a podium and said, "I'm meeting a group? Candace Ewing?"

"Yes, I just seated Miss Ewing. This way." The woman smiled and led Suzie through the pristine restaurant to a booth big enough for six and curved around so that one would have to stand right in the exact spot to see what was happening inside.

Candace and Mandie had already arrived, and they both held menus as Suzie said, "Thank you."

Candace had traded yesterday's casual attire for another set, this one in purple and black, and her expression remained more relaxed than Suzie had seen in months. Mandie wore a floral dress that brought out the blue in her eyes, and as Suzie bounced around the seat to get closer to them, Alicia arrived.

She looked polished in navy and white stripes and a pair of capris that fit her like a glove. Suzie really needed to up her game in the fashion department—or did she?

You are who you are, she told herself as she picked up a menu.

"Morning everyone," Suzie said as she finally settled into place on the springy bench seat beside Mandie.

"How was your evening with Daniel?" Alicia asked, taking the spot next to Candace and placing her enormous purse on the bench beside her. Suzie had a thread wallet, for crying out loud. What did Alicia have in that thing?

Despite the obvious difference in purse size, Suzie

couldn't suppress her smile. "I called your mom, Mandie." She steadfastly kept her gaze on her menu, as if she needed all her concentration to read a few English words.

Mandie pulled in a breath. "You did not."

"Did you set a date?" Alicia asked, her tone just as tinged with disbelief as Mandie's.

Suzie lowered her menu and grinned at them. "No, unfortunately. That was my goal, but your mom asks hard questions."

Mandie tilted her head. "She does? Like what?"

"She wanted to know *where* we wanted to get married," Suzie said. "She said that would probably influence the *when*."

"Oh, sure," Mandie said.

"So where are you getting married?" Alicia asked.

"I have no idea." Suzie sighed like she was trying to blow up a balloon with one breath. "I've never thought about it."

Even Candace blinked a few extra times. "You've never thought about where you want to get married?"

"She never saw herself getting married," Alicia said, almost out of the corner of her mouth, as if Suzie wouldn't be able to hear it that way.

"We narrowed it to New York City."

Candace scoffed. "Suzie, the city is huge."

"You know where you should do it?" Mandie suddenly brightened, her blue eyes firing joy at Suzie.

"Mandie, hello." An older woman with beautiful blonde hair stood at the end of the table, and all eyes went to her. She wore an elegant yet understated dress in black, and her blue eyes beamed fondness toward Mandie. "I heard we had a VIP group here this morning, and it seems I've found them."

Mandie scoffed and then laughed. "Hardly," she said.

"Though this is my boss and my team from the city." She grinned around at everyone. "Maddie is a good friend of my parents'," she added. "And me. She's amazing, and she manages this place."

"It's wonderful," Candace said, her old schmoozy voice emerging as she lifted her mimosa flute.

"You haven't ordered," Maddie said. "I'll get Luca over here." She nodded, her smile stuck in place. She seemed a tiny bit stuffy, almost like Candace, but the beach-version of her. "I'll make sure you have privacy for your meeting. Just wave if you need anything."

After she left, Suzie returned to her menu, relieved the topic of her wedding didn't resurface. They chit-chatted about the menu, and then Luca arrived to take their orders.

Once he'd gone, Alicia twisted and opened the hat box. "I got up early this morning, unable to sleep."

She pulled out a manila folder and set it carefully on the table. "I wore gloves, of course, and I opened them all. I kept the envelope with the letter, and I put them in acid-free sheets."

She flipped open the front of the binder, and Suzie practically started salivating. She loved old things. Adored them. Wanted to simply pet the letters as she memorized every word, every sentence.

"There are forty-three letters in total, spanning about two years."

"What years?" Candace asked.

Suzie watched as Alicia slowly flipped the pages, the aged envelopes they'd discovered the day before carefully preserved. Even in the bright morning light, the paper looked fragile, the ink faded to sepia tones.

"The two years before Denise's boat accident." Her

words seemed to drip across the table, taking their sweet time to enter Suzie's ears and make sense in her head.

"Wow," Mandie said.

"Not all of them are dated," Alicia said, snapping open the metal rings that held the sheet protectors in place. She unhooked one and handed it across the table to Suzie. "That's the first one with a date, and it's March, 1988."

Suzie leaned forward to study the letter, the envelope on the back side of the paper. The handwriting held a confident, masculine stroke, filled with passion even decades later.

"My dearest D," Suzie read aloud. "I can't stop thinking about yesterday afternoon. The way the light caught your hair as you stood by the window, the sound of your laugh when I told you about the sailing mishap. You make me feel alive in ways I'd forgotten were possible."

Mandie's eyebrows rose. "That doesn't sound like something a husband would write to his wife."

Suzie scanned ahead, her historian's instincts tingling. She drew a breath and kept going. "I know this is complicated, that we're both walking a dangerous line. But when I'm with you in our little sanctuary, nothing else matters. The world falls away, and it's just us, just this perfect bubble of time we've carved out for ourselves."

She swallowed, her blood vibrating as she looked up. "This is definitely...not from her husband."

Mandie and Alicia shook their heads, but Candace simply watched Suzie with a thoughtful expression on her face.

Suzie glanced down again. "I can't wait to see you again. Leave a note in our usual place. Yours always, M."

M.

Not a C for Connor. Not a W for Williams.

She lowered the sheet and looked around the table.

Candace reached for the binder, and Alicia let her pull it in front of her. "July eighth." She read silently for a moment, then looked up. "She's written this one, 'To my dearest M,' and it says—Let's meet at our place by the water, taking care to wait until the morning fishermen have gone out. Then no one will see us, and we can walk and talk until we reach the stairs."

Suzie's mind raced, trying to connect dots and build timelines. "So she was using the cottage as a meeting place. That's why she went there so often, why it was her refuge."

"But who was she meeting?" Mandie asked, peering over Candace's forearm at the letter in the binder.

Alicia shuffled through more letters, scanning signatures and salutations. "He signs them 'Forever yours, M,' and she's always saying, 'My dearest M.'" She reached for her water and took a sip.

"M." Suzie looked down at the letter in her hand again. "Could be a first name or last name."

"There's another pattern," Candace said, studying several letters. "He mentions his work taking him away from the cove for weeks at a time. Something about contracts and negotiations."

"Business travel," Alicia said. "That would explain the sporadic timing of the letters."

Mandie took a sheet out of the binder and started reading it. "Listen to this." She drew in another breath and turned the sheet over. "No date. And not 'my dearest M' either."

Suzie waited, her heartbeat throbbing in the vein in her neck now. She'd felt such a connection to Denise before, and she couldn't wait to read more of her words and try to piece together who she was.

But this changed the picture she had in her head, and Suzie didn't like the fuzziness of the woman now.

"I can't stand these separations anymore," Mandie read. "Every day away from you feels like a lifetime. I've been thinking about what we discussed, about the possibility of a different future. Are you serious about leaving with me?'"

The table fell silent. Suzie could hear the gentle clink of silverware from other tables, the murmur of conversation, everything feeling distant and far away.

"She was planning to leave Connor," Mandie said quietly.

"It looks that way." Alicia sorted through more letters, her expression growing more troubled. "But she never did. She died in that storm instead."

"Or did she?" Suzie found herself asking. The question hung in the air like smoke.

Candace leaned back in the booth, her coffee forgotten. "You think she faked her death?"

"I don't know what I think yet." Suzie handed her letter back to Mandie, and the binder got passed back to Alicia. She ringed everything back together the way she'd had it, the final snap of the metal teeth coming together making Suzie jump.

"We need to create a proper timeline with them," Suzie said. "There's a story here, and we're only seeing pieces of it."

"That's a lot of work," Mandie said.

"What about Connor?" Alicia asked. "Do we tell him what we found?"

Mandie's face paled, and she wore a fierce look of protection. "He's my husband's grandfather. This could be bad for everyone."

"Or it could give him answers he's been wondering about for thirty years," Suzie said. "Either way, we need to know the whole truth before we decide what to do with it."

She looked around the table at her colleagues, her friends, these women who'd become her chosen family, and found them all staring back at her.

"What?" she asked.

Alicia grinned at her and slid the binder toward her. "You said it. You need to create a proper timeline."

Suzie gaped at the bulging binder, the forty-three letters. "Me?"

"It's what you do," Mandie said simply. "You give past people a voice. You tell their stories."

Suzie nodded and pulled the binder closer, her eyes glued to the front though it was blank. Denise Prescott Williams had been a real person, with real feelings. She wasn't just a tragic footnote in history, even if her family had left her in the cove, and her life had been filled with ups and downs.

It was precisely those Suzie wanted to know about.

"All right," she said. "I'll take the letters, organize them, create a complete timeline." She looked up and into the eyes of each woman at the table. "But eventually, we're going to have to talk to Connor again."

Alicia nodded, and Candace said, "I agree. At some point."

Suzie looked at Mandie and found her jaw clenched and her entire demeanor tight. But even she nodded.

Then Suzie swiped the binder off the table and onto the bench seat beside her, thinking maybe she'd ask Alicia if she could borrow her purse to get it home once they finished eating brunch.

Chapter Twelve

Mandie adjusted the brim of her wide sun hat as she watched Charlie emerge from the waves with water streaming from his shoulders. The familiar stretch of Diamond Island's southwest beach buzzed with the controlled chaos of a summer Sunday—children's laughter mixing with the crash of waves, the sizzle of grilled burgers competing with the cries of seagulls overhead.

She sighed, trying to relax. After all, this was her favorite place in the world, surrounded by the people who'd shaped her life. A restless energy crawled beneath her skin, making her shift constantly in the beach chair that had felt comfortable an hour ago.

"You're fidgeting again," her mother said from the chair beside her, not looking up from the romance novel balanced on her knees.

And that was why she couldn't relax, though she loved her parents and all the women she'd grown up with. She'd loved their beach days as a teen, and she loved them now.

But she had a secret she didn't want to tell anyone; she

hadn't even told Charlie about the love letters from his grandmother to an unknown man who wasn't his grandfather.

"I'm fine." Mandie forced herself to still, gripping the arms of her chair. The lie tasted bitter on her tongue, but she simply leaned her head back and closed her eyes. Mom moved and looked at her, the weight of her gaze something Mandie had always been able to feel, even across miles and miles of ocean.

"You look pale. Are you drinking enough water?"

"Mom." Mandie reached for her water bottle, taking a deliberately long sip to avoid further questions. The liquid cooled her dry throat, but did nothing to settle the churning in her stomach. "I just put on a pound of sunscreen." She flashed Mom a smile. "It's probably not rubbed in all the way."

Yes, she sat in the shade. That didn't matter, not to her pale skin, which only seemed to freckle in the sun.

Alice approached from the direction of the coolers, her elegant swimsuit cover-up flowing around her like silken water. She wore her hair up into a topknot, and she looked every bit the wealthy aristocrat having a "down day at the beach."

"We're out of raspberry lemonade. Should I send Arthur to get more?"

"We put two cases in our cooler," Robin said, closing her book and getting to her feet. "Are we really out?"

They moved over to the bank of coolers, which sat in the shade made by the tables carrying various toppings, buns, and condiments. Dad and Parker—a twenty-five-year-old home for a summer visit—manned the grill, cooking up hamburgers, bratwurst, and chicken.

Mandie loved eating charred food on the sand, but today, her stomach shrank at the very idea.

Parker's mother, Kelli, was one of Mom's good friends from her childhood, and Mandie watched her glide across the sand as she went after her ten-year-old, Daphne. The sight triggered an unwelcome image of another woman walking a similar beach decades ago—Denise, meeting her mysterious lover in secret, planning an escape that never came.

The images faded, leaving Mandie with the present reality. She loved people-watching, and with so many different people right here in her close circle, she could easily see how life could be unique.

Her parents had been married for over thirty years, for example. But Kelli had been divorced and had Parker from that marriage. She'd gotten remarried and had a daughter in her late forties, and now she ran a yoga and health-forward studio while her husband did sailing tours around the cove.

Life morphed and changed, and a small smile filtered from her soul to her face. Kelli and AJ, another of Mom's friends, had had babies really late in life, probably after they'd thought they could.

She was twenty-seven. She and Charlie had time.

"You hungry, baby?" Charlie reached for the towel in the chair next to her, dripping salty ocean water on her right arm and leg.

She shook her head, pressing her mouth into a tight line. "I had a bowl of crab salad earlier." And it felt like it might come back up if she had to keep talking.

He nodded and looked over to the grill. "I'm gonna go get something. Robin? Mom? Are you eating?"

"No, thank you, dear." Alice swept one hand along her

son's shoulders, and then sat on the other side of Mom, who didn't pick up her book again.

Not good.

Thankfully, her phone buzzed against the metal frame of her beach chair, and she pulled it from her bag, hoping for a satisfactory distraction.

Suzie: *Organized the first ten letters chronologically. The timeline is even more interesting than we thought. Can we meet tomorrow?*

Mandie stared at the message, her pulse accelerating. So not distracting, at least not in a good way. She shielded her phone slightly, turning it more to the right so Mom couldn't see it.

We have deliveries all day tomorrow.

Maybe we can find a pocket of time over lunch, Alicia said.

"How are things going at the cove cottage?" Mom asked, and Mandie almost threw her phone in the sand.

She tapped to silence it all the way and tucked it back into her bag. She let out a sigh. "It's a high-stress project, that's how it's going."

"Your boss came in on Friday, right?" Alice asked.

Mandie nodded, trying to find a way through the maze of information in her head. "We appeased her about the stained glass windows. The project is on-target. It's just a lot of moving pieces and we're moving into the detail-phase, which is like managing shards of glass."

"You're talking about work?" Charlie sank into the chair beside her. "It's the weekend."

Mandie smiled at him and reached over to run her hand through his still-damp, salty hair. "You're right." She flashed her mom and Alice a look. "I don't want to talk about the cove cottage."

"You work on the weekend," Alice pointed out.

"Some of us have to," Charlie said. He lifted his burger to his mouth and took a huge bite. After he swallowed it, he added, "But you don't hear me talking about pharmacy stuff all the time."

"That's because your job is boring," his mom teased.

"Ha ha." Charlie took another bite of his hamburger, his eyes latching onto Mandie's. He wanted to move out of his parents' house as much as she did.

"Have you checked with Ginny today?" Mandie asked, moving the conversation somewhere that would be more comfortable for Charlie. Not for her, but it didn't matter. She was determined to be nothing but overjoyed for her best friend and sister-in-law.

"Nothing yet," Alice said. "They're inducing her tomorrow no matter what, so we'll have a baby soon." She smiled widely, and Mandie wished she could *feel* the smile the way Alice obviously did.

"I'm going to text her and remind her I want five million pictures." Mandie pulled her phone out to do that.

Wish you were here, she sent instead. *It's the perfect beach day, but it's not the same without you and Bob.*

Me too! Ginny said back. *We're planning to bring the baby in September, so if you can't come before then, you'll get to meet her.*

Mandie smiled softly, because of course she wanted to meet Ginny and Bob's daughter. And she'd be here in September; the cove cottage wouldn't be done until near the end of the month, and then Mandie needed to decide what to do about her job.

Another sigh filled her lungs, but she controlled the air as it left her mouth. No need to alert her mother of anything more than she already was.

Oh, and totally random, but do you remember Marcus DeLeis? I went out with him a couple of times in high school. Anyway, his wife is from Boston, and we've gotten together with them a few times. They live in the cove right now, but they're moving back here, because her parents live here and they're having their second baby in December.

Mandie frowned as the message cut off there, and she had to tap "more" to keep reading. Did she really want to? Another person her age, married with almost two kids.

She tapped.

They're selling their house on Diamond Island. It's not up for sale yet, and I told him to send it to me, that you and Charlie might want to look at it.

Mandie's pulse picked up again, and she sat up. "Charlie, look."

A picture had come through—a one-story, clapboard white beach cottage with postage-stamp sized patches of pure green lawn out front, a driveway to a garage, and a bright red door.

She handed her phone to her husband. "Do you remember Marcus DeLeis?"

Charlie frowned at the message, his expression lightening until he was grinning by the end. "Look at that, Mandie. It's not bad."

She took the phone back. "It's small," she said.

"I remember Marcus," Charlie said. "I might have his number." He mumbled the last few words, already on his own device.

This is great, Mandie sent to Ginny. *Charlie's looking for his number.*

I'll send it to him, Ginny said.

"She's going to send it to you," Mandie said.

"Maybe we can go look at it today."

Mandie shook her head. "It's Sunday, baby. They want to relax like we are." Or at least, how she was trying to.

"You're swamped this week," he said, glancing over to her with a challenge in his eyes. She couldn't deny it, so she said nothing. "And I don't have time off until Thursday. If we can go today...I'm just going to ask."

His fingers flew across the screen, and Mandie decided to let him handle it. She had too many other things on her mind, and she couldn't hide the sigh that came out of her mouth as she sank back into her chair again.

Three days ago, she would have told him everything— about the letters, the mystery, her growing anxiety about what they might mean for his family. Now the words stuck in her throat like concrete.

"Mandie, come settle an argument," Eloise called from a cluster of beach chairs twenty feet away. Her dark hair was pulled back in a ponytail, and she wore a patient expression that suggested she'd been moderating disputes all afternoon.

"What kind of argument?" Mandie called back.

"Kelli thinks we should have brought the volleyball net. AJ insists nobody wants to play volleyball in this heat."

"I vote for no volleyball," she said. "It's too hot to move that much."

"See?" AJ gestured triumphantly from her position under a large umbrella. "Mandie agrees with me."

Kelli laughed, having collected Daphne, James, Emily, Heidi and Asher—the younger generation of kids from their group—and was playing a game with them on a huge blanket.

Mandie missed her own generation in that moment. Ginny and Bob. Her younger sister, Jamie, who'd gone to school in Colorado and currently lived in the Rocky Mountains studying trees.

Parker, though he was here visiting.

Billie and Grace, Aaron and Eloise's girls. Billie currently lived in Maryland, where she was pursuing a Master's degree in computational security, and Grace, who'd gone to the city to become an artist.

"You sure you're okay?" Mom's voice carried genuine concern now. "You've been moody and sighing all morning."

"Just tired." She managed another smile, this one feeling more natural. "Yesterday was a long day, and I didn't sleep well last night."

It wasn't entirely untrue. She'd lain awake for hours, staring at the ceiling while her mind raced through possibilities. Who was M? What had happened to Denise Williams? And why did the discovery of those letters feel like opening a door she couldn't close again?

"Maybe you should head home early," Alice said. "Get out of this heat."

"He says we can come anytime." Charlie shoved his phone at Mandie and stood up. "I'm going to get packed up."

"What's going on?" Mom asked.

Mandie stared at his phone. *Sure, man! Come anytime! We're just home today, getting things packed up and ready. We're moving in a couple of weeks, and while it's not a palace, we've loved living here.*

An address sat there, with a road name of Beachwalk Avenue.

Having grown up in the cove, Mandie knew exactly where Beachwalk Avenue was.

Just off the coastal highway on the southeast side of the island.

"Right here on Diamond," she whispered.

"And it's in our price range," Charlie said, grinning. He took his phone and dropped it in his pocket. "We're going to look at a house."

"Good luck," his mother said fondly, and Mandie jumped to her feet too.

Hope fluttered in Mandie's chest, competing with the anxiety that had been her constant companion. Beachwalk Avenue was only about a mile south of the lighthouse, a place Mandie had loved growing up. It sat on the rockier side of the island, where it was windier—but also had less tourists.

She let Charlie get her chair while she shouldered her bag. Saying good-bye could take an astronomical amount of time, so Mandie hurried to sweep a kiss along her mom's cheek with, "I'll call you later."

She followed Charlie, taking only a moment to hug her father with the words, "We're going to look at a house."

"Oh, okay," Dad said. "I hope it's amazing."

"Me too." Mandie forced a smile to her face, because she'd looked at a dozen not-amazing houses in the past several weeks.

"Two bedrooms," Charlie said when she caught up to him. "Two baths. It's a cedar cottage with brand new painted and sealed white trim."

"Wow," Mandie said.

"It's small, like you said."

She stumbled in the loose sand, everything in her world swooping. Her vision turned white, and she wondered if she should've eaten something or had more to drink, as her mother had said.

"Hey, you okay?" Charlie paused to steady her with his hand. He watched her intently, and Mandie fought the tears threatening to spill down her cheeks.

"There's so much going on at work," she said in a tinny voice. "I'm so tired."

Fierce determination entered his eyes. "So we'll spend a half-hour at this house, and then I'm taking you home for a nap."

Home.

The word twinged through her bloodstream. She nodded, because she didn't really have a home. But she did have a bed, and if she was lucky, Charlie would lay beside her until she fell asleep.

They made it to the sidewalk, where a car waited. Charlie put everything in the back while Mandie got in. When he joined her, he gave the driver the address, and off they went.

It only took fifteen minutes to arrive, and the white house Ginny had sent her came into full existence right before Mandie's eyes.

Even from the sidewalk, her restoration-trained eye automatically started cataloging potential improvements. The lot was generous, with room for expansion if they decided to add on later. "The lawn looks nice," she said, wishing there were bigger trees.

But trees could be planted.

Charlie dumped their beach bags and chairs on the lawn. "Let's go, baby." He took her hand, and they approached the house together.

The door opened, and a dark-haired man came outside. He wore the kind of bright smile that suggested he really didn't mind an old acquaintance stopping by on a Sunday afternoon.

"Hey, man." He chuckled as he shook Charlie's hand. "Mandie. It's good to see you guys again. You've moved back?"

"Yeah," Charlie said. "Just a few weeks ago."

Seven weeks ago, but Mandie said nothing.

"Come in," Marcus said. "It's a bit messy, but you can see the space."

The late afternoon sun cast everything in golden tones, making even the cottage's weathered exterior look charming rather than tired. A small garden struggled against the sandy soil, and beach roses climbed a trellis beside the front door.

"Built in 1962," Marcus said. "This is my wife, Hannah."

"Hey," she said, rising from where she taped a box in the middle of the living room floor.

The hardwood floor. Big windows that looked over the lawn. The living room flowed into a galley kitchen, and a short hallway led to the two bedrooms and bathrooms.

"It's cozy," Charlie said diplomatically as they stood shoulder-to-shoulder in the doorway of the second bedroom, which was probably only big enough to hold a desk and a twin bed.

But it could hold a crib and a changing table.

Mandie walked through the space slowly, her mind already working. Remove the wall between the kitchen and dining area to create more flow. Update the appliances and add an island for storage. The master bedroom was barely large enough for a queen bed, but did they need more than that?

No. No, they did not.

"The lot is almost half an acre," Marcus said. "Plenty of room to expand if you wanted to add on."

Mandie followed him and Charlie out onto the back deck, looking out the window toward the lighthouse in the distance. The view wasn't spectacular, but it was peaceful. She could imagine waking up here every morning, drinking coffee on the front porch, building a life that belonged to them instead of borrowing space in someone else's home.

She could see precisely where to push out the back of the house to add more room to the master suite. Where the staircase could go at the end of the hall to lead to a second floor that they could fill with bookcases, a loft, and more bedrooms.

She blinked, her renovation mind finally shutting down. She put a smile on her face and turned to Marcus. "Thank you so much for letting us come. We'll get out of your hair."

"We'd love to sell it without an agent," Hannah said. "It saves on fees, so...I guess let us know."

"Have you shown it to many people?" Charlie asked. "I'm sure my mom could help us with the paperwork and contract." He looked at Mandie, his eyebrows raised.

"You're the first," Marcus said, hooking his arm around Hannah. "We just decided to move this week." And he didn't seem stressed about it at all. Mandie had planned their move to the cove for six months before they'd left the city.

"Thank you." Charlie moved over to them both and hugged them. Mandie shook their hands, her smile finally feeling real and settled on her face. Then she went with Charlie around the house, noting the back lawn looked crispier than the front. That made sense, as it bore the brunt of the western sun all afternoon and into the evening.

"What do you think?" Charlie asked once they stood alone beside their beach gear, waiting for another RideShare.

"It's not perfect," she said honestly.

"But?"

Mandie turned to face him, seeing her own cautious hope reflected in his eyes. "But it could be ours."

Charlie's smile started slow and built to something radiant. "You want to make an offer?"

"I want to make an offer." The words felt solid, real, like stepping onto firm ground after weeks of uncertainty. "It's not our forever house, but it could be our right-now house."

"Our starter house," Charlie said. "With room to grow."

As the car arrived and Charlie loaded up their stuff, her phone buzzed with another text from Suzie, but for the first time all day, Mandie didn't feel the familiar spike of anxiety.

Whatever secrets Denise Williams had kept, whatever truth the letters revealed, it belonged to the past. This moment—this possibility of a future with Charlie, of building something together—belonged to her, to them, right now.

She got in the car with him and squeezed his hand, already imagining the day when they'd drive this same road and turn into their own driveway, coming home to a place that was truly theirs.

Chapter Thirteen

Alicia balanced the clipboard against her hip as she scanned the chaos that had descended upon the Black Sand Bungalow's construction site. Thirty-seven boxes of materials sat stacked in precarious towers across the front of the property, each one labeled with cryptic codes that meant something to the company who'd sent them, but not to her.

Every box had to be opened, every item inspected. These had come a long way, after all, and anything that wasn't pristine would need to be repackaged, returned, and reordered.

Her back ached from the past three days of inventory management exactly like this, but at least this array of hastily unloaded boxes represented their last delivery for a few weeks.

To her left, on a tarp barely big enough to hold them, the white pine planks waited to be installed. Beside them stood about five thousand dollars worth of flooring. They had painting supplies, but no paint yet. Some fixtures, but mostly things like light switch plates and samples for the finishes in the kitchen and bathroom.

All of the kitchen cabinets stood waiting, and they had

molding for days, along with several rolls of premium wallpaper—which Alicia had actually fought Mandie for.

"No one hangs wallpaper anymore," Mandie had said.

"This won't even look like wallpaper," Alicia assured her. "It's going to be amazing, and it'll speak to the history of the house." It wasn't like she was pasting up some random colored covering with nautical symbols on it.

No, she'd ordered a gorgeously designed paper that they'd only put on one wall in the main living room, and it boasted texture, a faint rose pattern in a slightly darker color than the taupe paper, and gold threads throughout the petals, which would catch all the light from the stained glass and reflect it back into the house.

She couldn't wait to see it. But right now, Alicia's eyes burned from squinting at tiny print on shipping labels, trying to find corresponding materials on her clipboard, and check them off.

"This is everything that should have arrived this morning," she said, handing the clipboard to Mandie. "The kitchen pieces are probably in boxes twelve through sixteen, with the samples scattered between boxes twenty-one and twenty-eight, which should have all the outdoor deck accessories too, and the custom millwork pieces should be in the ones marked with red tape."

Mandie accepted the clipboard with the resigned expression of someone who'd been expecting this moment. "We've got this. You need a break."

Like Mandie didn't. Her hair currently stuck to her forehead in wisps, because of the heat. She and Suzie had been setting up the security tent now that they had so many supplies on-site, and that wasn't easy or non-sweaty work.

But they could zip it all closed, lock the zippers, and Flint would be by in a couple of hours to set up security cameras. The project had progressed to the point where Alicia would like to have supplies ready and waiting for them rather than the other way around.

"I feel terrible leaving you with this mess." Alicia gestured toward the boxes, where Suzie crouched beside an open container, pulling out what looked like cabinet hinges and sorting them into smaller piles. "The electrical contractor is coming at two, and if we can't find the outlet covers—"

"Alicia." Suzie's voice carried the firm tone she used when bulldozing through obstacles. "Go. Home."

Alicia looked toward the road, where a car waited to take her to the ferry station. She was going to go home, but she wasn't going to climb into bed and take a nap. No, Suzie had been texting them what she learned about the letters, and she'd finally found two initials in a single letter last night.

M.A.

It's in exactly one letter—one of the later ones in the series, she'd told them.

Alicia wanted to see what she could find in harbor logs, property deeds, anything else searchable online from the late 1980s. If they could find a name for the writer of the letters, it would help them construct a more complete picture of Denise—and solve the mystery of who she was seeing before she disappeared.

Alicia didn't want to think there might be foul play surrounding her death, but the truth was, there might be.

Everything moved forward with the relentless momentum of a project humming along, and the weight of managing every detail pressed against Alicia's shoulders like a physical burden.

Today was a great day to cut out a little early, though. She had plans with her bikini, laptop, and Henry and the kids. She could access the internet from the beach, and she'd just nodded when Mandie shrieked.

She startled. "What in the world?"

"Ginny sent pictures of the baby," Mandie said, the clipboard now discarded on the ground as she stared, eyes glowing, at her phone. She looked up, pure joy filling her face. "They named her Caroline. Isn't that so cute and so classic?"

Alicia smiled and took the phone, where yes, the most perfect newborn slept peacefully. "She's beautiful."

"Let me see," Suzie said, appearing in their three-way huddle. She too grinned at the little bundle all wrapped in pink. A soft fringe of blonde hair caught the light, and Alicia could practically smell the powdery scent of the baby.

"She's lovely," Suzie said.

"Oh, I can't wait to meet her," Mandie said, taking back her phone and diving into it. Alicia met Suzie's eyes, and a special type of understanding passed between them.

"Go," Suzie said. "She can look at a baby for an hour, and we'll be fine."

"All right." Alicia hugged Suzie quickly, and Mandie put down the phone for a fast hug too, and then she headed for the car.

She'd just boarded the ferry when her phone buzzed with a text from Henry. *The kids want to know if you're going to be home in time for lunch. Gray caught a hermit crab and Lily built a sandcastle with a moat.*

What does that have to do with lunch? Tell me we're not eating the hermit crab. She grinned at her own text as it blipped across the water to Henry.

Still, the message sent a familiar pang through her chest.

While she'd been drowning in shipping manifests and inventory lists, her children had been experiencing the magic of summer on Five Island Cove. Henry had been handling everything—meals, sunscreen applications, entertainment—with the patient grace that made her love him more every day.

But it also made her feel like she was failing at the one job that mattered most.

I'm on the ferry right now, so I should be home in about twenty minutes. Alicia had been using the ferry ride from Rocky Ridge to Sanctuary as pure detox-time. She never allowed herself to work on the way to the site or the way back.

She just wanted to feel the fresh air on her face, and feel it slide down into her lungs. She let her thoughts roam where they may, and today, she thought about the historical records she could access.

Alicia too loved history, though her job didn't lend herself to doing as much of it as Suzie or Mandie did. Not only that, but Mandie had put her in touch with Tessa Martin, a librarian here in the cove, and she'd learned that their historical records were extensive, thanks to the community's pride in preserving its maritime heritage. Property deeds, harbor logs, newspaper archives—all digitized and accessible through the library's online portal.

When she got in the RideShare to get from the station on Sanctuary to the bungalow, she pulled out her phone and scrolled to Tessa's name. *Hi Tessa*, she typed. *Working on a historical research project about Five Island Cove in the early 1990s. Any chance you could point me toward the best digital archives for that time period? Looking for property records, harbor logs, anything like that.*

The response came back before the car pulled up to the row of bungalows, which was only a five-minute drive. *Try the Harbor Master's database first - it goes back to 1975. Also check the Five Island Gazette archives. They're fully searchable. All of the property records in Five Island Cove are online as well, and they require legal names. You got your login credentials okay?*

Yes, Alicia said. *I logged in last night no problem. Thanks so much!*

The beach bungalow sat exactly how she'd left it that morning—windows open to catch the ocean breeze, Henry's coffee cup still sitting on the kitchen counter, evidence of a peaceful morning spent somewhere outside.

Alicia ducked inside, changed her clothes, and filled a water bottle. She then picked up her laptop and a notebook and tucked them both into her beach bag, where she had a towel and a can of sunscreen always ready to go.

She took a deep breath as she moved outside, settling her sunglasses into place before heading down the sidewalk to the beach. A few people had spread out there, including Henry, who'd staked out a place in the shade.

Two chairs, with a blanket in front of them, various toys scattered nearby, and a small cooler. She'd barely stepped onto the sand before Lily spotted her.

"Mama!" Lily's voice carried from the direction of the water. "Come see what I built!"

Henry turned toward her and rose to his feet, looking incredibly hot in a pair of blue and orange swim trunks, his sunglasses perched just-so on his face, and his dark hair windswept.

He grinned as he neared, and he stepped into her and

kissed her. "Hey." He took her bag and together, they faced the water. "You're wearing the red bikini."

As if it wasn't already hot enough outside. "Yep," she said, because she knew it was his favorite. "I might even get it wet. It's hot today."

"Go swim for a second," he said. "Say hi to the kids. I'll get you set up in the right place for the WiFi." He grinned at her, and Alicia moved to do just what he'd suggested.

Gray stood waist-deep in the gentle surf, a plastic bucket in his hands, while Lily crouched beside an elaborate sand-castle that sprawled across several square feet of beach.

"That's incredible, sweetheart," Alicia said as she arrived. The castle featured multiple towers, though one looked a bit crumbly, and what appeared to be a functioning moat system. "You've been busy."

"Gray's helping with the moat," Lily said. "Come on, Gray. Mom's here."

Her son came running in from the waves, which caused a lot of splashing, of course. And water and sand didn't exactly mix in the way Lily would like.

"Gray, stop it," she complained, though she'd literally just called him in. "You're ruining the princess tower." She crouched to start to fix it.

Gray dropped the bucket, clearly unconcerned about pouring the water carefully in the moat, and wrapped his arms around her waist. "You're back."

"Did you get up on the paddle board again?" Alicia asked, smiling at him as she hugged him back.

"No, but I can do a handstand."

"In the ocean?"

"If I stay in the calm part." He started to run back out into the water, and Alicia cupped her hand over her eyes to watch him. Her nerves rioted at her, because it didn't feel safe to go upside down in a body of water with a current. The ocean wasn't a swimming pool, after all.

But Gray only went out to about mid-thigh, and then he dove straight down. Alicia cringed slightly at the white-water splash-fest that ensued, but after several long moments where it looked like Gray was wrestling with a shadow version of himself, his legs finally straightened and stuck up above the surface while he found his balance.

Alicia clapped enthusiastically when he surfaced, water streaming from his hair. "Very impressive. Just be careful not to go too deep."

"I'm being careful," he called back, already preparing for another attempt.

Alicia smoothed back Lily's hair and went to sit in the shade with Henry. She sighed as she sank into the chair and pulled out her sunscreen. She didn't burn very easily, but she didn't want to experience even a hint of discomfort.

After several long moments of just breathing, Alicia retrieved her laptop and settled back into the beach chair, the computer balanced on her knees. The wireless internet connection held strong, and within only a minute she'd accessed the Five Island Cove Library's digital archives.

The Harbor Master's database loaded, decades of records organized by year and vessel type. She started with 1990—the year Denise Williams had died—and worked backward, scanning through lists of registered boats, passenger manifests, and docking fees.

She'd just spotted the name of a boat she'd already seen when Lily yelled, "Mama!"

She flinched and looked up, but Lily wasn't kneeling in the sand anymore.

No, now she'd moved out into the shallow water with Gray, and the two of them sat on a boogie board as Gray paddled them around.

"Wow," she called with as much enthusiasm as she could muster. "Looks fun, baby." Alicia looked up long enough to wave and cheer, then returned to her screen, the name of the boat forgotten.

The 1990 records showed the usual mix of fishing boats, pleasure craft, and small commercial vessels that served the island community.

She scrolled through months of entries, her eyes scanning for any mention of the initials M.A. or variations thereof. The work required patience and attention to detail—exactly the kind of methodical research that played to her strengths.

"There," she whispered, her pulse quickening as a name caught her eye. "Sea Sprite."

She reached for her notebook to write down the name of the boat. She went down that rabbit hole, and before long, she had a whole page of notes.

Sea Sprite
Small passenger boat
Licensed for trips between the islands in Five Island Cove, as well as between the cove and Nantucket
Can hold up to eighteen passengers
Seasonal trips, usually operates between May and October
Does day tours in the western waters of the cove
Not authorized for the eastern shore

At that point, Alicia had learned that hardly any boats were authorized to be sailing around the eastern shore of the cove in the 90s.. And even if there were vessels that could, it required the captain to complete special training and hold a valid permit to do so.

The ocean was one of the most dangerous things on the planet, after all. It never slept. It always rocked. It went wherever it could to survive, and it existed at the mercy of gravity, earth tremors, wind and storms.

Alicia looked at her notes and added: *Captain of the Sea Sprite?*

She couldn't find a name outside of who owned the company that operated the Sprite. That honor belonged to Atlantic Ventures.

Alicia turned the page and wrote that at the top of the second one. She kept searching, and Atlantic Ventures operated out of Massachusetts and was a private company held by an M. Adams.

Her heartbeat spiked, and she didn't even look at the paper as she scrawled out his name.

Well, part of it at least, but it gave her another rabbit to chase down another hole.

Alicia's fingers flew across the keyboard as she searched for more references to an M. Adams. The Harbor Master's logs showed regular entries throughout the spring and summer of 1985—passenger trips to Nantucket, supply runs between the islands, occasional private charters for fishing or sightseeing.

Again in 1986 and 1987, but the name on the manifests never said anything more than M. Adams.

1988, 1988, 1990.

Then, the entries stopped.

The last mention of the Sea Sprite appeared in late October 1990, with a notation that the vessel had been "permanently decommissioned due to owner departure from service area."

Alicia stared at the screen, her heart racing. Denise

Williams had died in the summer of 1990. M. Adams had stopped operating his boat service just a few months later.

Why?

"Mom!" Gray's voice carried a note of urgency that made her look up immediately. He stood in the shallows, pointing toward something in the water. "There's a really big fish out here."

Henry stood, already moving toward the water's edge. "Where?"

"Right there." Gray pointed again, his finger following the movement of a fish in the water, his excitement palpable. "It's huge!"

Alicia closed the laptop, following Henry down to the water. "Come in," she told the kids just as Henry reached the water's edge.

Thankfully, they obeyed her, and the four of them lined up where the water nipped at their toes to watch the fish.

"I think it's a bluefish," Henry said. "Remember we looked up how they have silver sides that flash?"

"Yeah," Gray said, utterly transfixed by the sighting.

The fish wiggled out into deeper water and disappeared beyond the surf line, and Alicia breathed out.

"That was cool," she said, smiling at the kids.

"So cool." Gray pumped his fist and the moment embedded itself in Alicia's memory—this amazing summer day with a family on a beach, marveling at the simple wonder of marine life.

As she returned to her chair, Alicia's stomach growled. She'd not eaten lunch, and she pressed a kiss to Henry's forehead and bent to get her bag. "I'm going to go get us something to eat."

"We made sandwiches before we came out."

"Okay." She went into the bungalow and opened the fridge. She didn't want to eat her sandwich with a side of sand, so she unwrapped hers and perched on a barstool with her laptop open once again.

She searched for the Sea Sprite and M. Adams together, and a newspaper article appeared second in the search results.

The September 12, 1990 edition of the Cove Chronicles loaded slowly, its pages preserved as digital images of the original print layout.

She scanned the headlines—local election coverage, fishing and weather reports, a feature about the island's lighthouse restoration—until a small item in the social section caught her eye.

Local Captain Announces Retirement from Passenger Service

The brief article mentioned Mark Adams, age 42, who had operated the *Sea Sprite* passenger service for five years. He cited "personal reasons" for his decision to end the service and relocate off-island. The piece included a quote from Adams thanking the community for their support and expressing regret at leaving "this beautiful place and the people who have become like family."

Alicia could only stare.

Mark Adams.

She returned to the Harbor Master's database, this time searching for any references to Mark Adams. The records showed he'd first registered the Sea Sprite in April 1985, listing his address as a small office in Diamond Island's harbor district.

Property records for that address revealed he'd rented the space from a local family, but had never owned property on the islands. No marriage license, no business partnerships, no other official documents that might provide more details about his life or background.

But when she put in Mark's name with Denise's, she found seven trips where Denise was listed on the passenger manifest of the Sea Sprite.

A day trip around the cove.

A half-day fishing expedition.

A trip to Nantucket on a Tuesday, with return passage that Saturday.

Alicia's mind raced, and she started taking screenshots to send to Mandie and Suzie. Names, documents, manifests.

She couldn't believe her interest had been so completely invested in two people she'd never met. A boat captain and a married woman, conducting a secret affair that had lasted at least two years. Clandestine trips to Nantucket, hidden letters, plans for a future that never came to pass.

But what had happened to Mark Adams after Denise died? Had he really left the island, or had he simply disappeared into the same mystery that surrounded her death?

Chapter Fourteen

Suzie hummed as she flipped the last blueberry pancake, the sweet aroma of vanilla and cinnamon filling her small kitchen. Her phone buzzed against the counter, and she glanced down to see Robin's name on the screen.

All set! May 17th at the Maritime History Museum. They have a beautiful ceremony space overlooking the harbor, and the reception hall can accommodate up to 100 guests. You two are going to LOVE IT. Congratulations again!

Suzie forgot everything in that moment.

Somehow, her hand still knew how to reach out and pick up her phone. Her eyes knew how to read as she scanned the message again. Her mouth remembered how to smile as she realized what a monumental thing had just happened.

Oh, and her nose still worked, as the blueberry pancake in the pan told her it was getting a little bit too brown.

She hurried to slide the spatula underneath it and flip it onto the stack beside the stove. Then she leaned against the counter and re-read Robin's text again.

May 17th. A real date, a real place, a real wedding.

Her doorbell rang, accompanied by a couple of hands knocking, and Suzie jerked her head up. "Come in."

The door opened, and Mandie and Alicia appeared at the same time, both balancing coffee cups, obviously coordinating their arrival.

"Morning," Alicia said as she entered the condo. "Something smells incredible in there."

"Come in, come in." Suzie wiped her hands on the dish towel she'd thrown on the counter. "I went a little overboard with breakfast."

Mandie straightened her neat ponytail and entered wearing her usual work clothes—in this case, a pair of jeans and a blouse in bright blue that brought out her eyes. "Your place is so cozy. I love those curtains you put up."

Alicia wore a pair of slacks and a polo the color of the blueberries in the pancakes, her dark hair loose around her shoulders. She glanced around the small living space with obvious appreciation. "It feels like a real home."

"And it smells like Daniel's cologne underneath all the pancake goodness," Mandie added with a teasing smile.

Heat crept up Suzie's neck, but she laughed anyway, because everyone knew Daniel came every weekend and stayed with her.

She gestured toward the small dining table, which she'd set with real dishes instead of paper plates. The morning light streamed through the windows, casting everything in a warm golden glow that promised a lot of heat later.

"This is nice," Alicia said, settling into one of the chairs. "You didn't have to go to all this trouble."

"Look, bacon *and* pancakes," Mandie said, picking up a strip of bacon.

"I wanted to." Suzie carried the plate of pancakes to the

table, followed by a bowl of fresh berries and a pitcher of maple syrup. "Besides, I want to do the can't-wait thing."

Mandie's eyebrows rose as she reached for the syrup. "The can't-wait thing?" She looked over to Alicia. "We have a thing?"

"It's your thing," Suzie said. "I thought I could invoke it, though."

"You can." Mandie waved at her to invoke away.

"Okay, great." Suzie couldn't contain her smile as she took her seat. "Mine is...May seventeenth, at the Maritime History Museum in New York City." She picked up her fork and stabbed a couple of pancakes onto her plate, deliberately not looking at anyone.

Mandie shrieked, and Alicia said, "Suzie, congratulations."

Suzie giggled and leaned over to hug Mandie. "It was your mom, really."

"The Maritime History Museum is *perfect* for you and Daniel," Alicia said as she tipped some bacon onto her plate.

"Right?" Suzie started slathering butter over her pancakes. "Daniel suggested it. He said it would be perfect because it combines history with the water, and it's beautiful without being too fancy."

She beamed at her friends. "Your mom worked her magic and got us the harbor-view ceremony space."

"I bet she's so excited. She loves weddings, but she especially loves helping people who don't have a lot of family support." Mandie's expression softened. "She's going to treat you like one of her own daughters."

Something warm and unfamiliar settled in Suzie's chest at those words. The idea of being claimed by someone's mother, of belonging to a family that chose her, felt both terrifying and wonderful.

"Okay," she said, clearing her throat and reaching for the syrup. "Your turn. Can't-wait."

"I can't wait to have keys to my own house." Mandie looked like the one who'd eaten a whole jar of cookies before coming for breakfast now.

Alicia nearly choked on her coffee, and Suzie froze with the pitcher of syrup in her hand. "What?"

"Charlie and I put in an offer on a house earlier this week, and the offer was accepted yesterday." Mandie's smile could have powered the entire island. "Alice is handling all the paperwork and legal stuff. We should close in three weeks."

Alicia blinked and looked over to Suzie. "They put an offer in on a house earlier this week, and we're just now hearing about it."

"Yeah, I heard that part." Suzie looked back at Mandie. "Maybe she was just really busy with the baby news, and the inventory, and—"

"And keeping all kinds of secrets from my husband and my mother-in-law." Mandie gave Suzie a pointed look and stabbed her fork into the air toward Alicia. "This week has been *so* hard, on so many levels."

Boy, Suzie could feel that, though she wasn't trying for a baby. Nor did she have a best friend and sister-in-law who'd just had a baby. Nor was she keeping secrets—family secrets —from Daniel.

"Mandie, I'm so happy for you." Suzie reached across the table to squeeze her friend's hand. "I can't believe you're going to have your own place." She passed the syrup to Alicia and cut into her pancake. "I've never bought a house before."

"But you have your grandmother's place," Alicia said.

"True." She grinned, and Suzie turned to Alicia. "Your turn."

Alicia's expression grew more contemplative as she set down her fork. "Honestly? I can't wait for this project to be finished, so we can get back to our normal life."

The words hung in the air, and a small pang of disappointment cut through her. She'd been hoping Alicia would say something about the research, or the mystery, or even just spending time together. Something with the kids, or Henry, or something.

"The summer has been amazing," Alicia continued quickly, her eyes darting to Suzie and Mandie and back as the mood shifted. "The kids love it here, and Henry's been incredible. But I'm ready to get back to our routine in the city. The kids need to start school, Henry needs to get back to his regular work, and I need to not be managing a project from two hours away."

"You're moving to Yonkers, right?" Mandie asked, her voice a touch cooler than before.

"Into Henry's house, yes. It's a big change for all of us; the kids will have to move schools, that kind of stuff." Alicia picked up a berry and popped it into her mouth. "I love the cove. I don't love the...wildness of summer, and it feels even more out of control because we're not in our normal place."

"I get it," Mandie said, but so much still hung in the air.

After all, Mandie had just bought a house here in the cove. She wouldn't be moving back to the city when the cove cottage project ended. That fact settled like raw dough in Suzie's stomach, and she looked over to the woman who had become one of her most treasured friends.

"We probably won't work together on another project, will we?" She switched her gaze to Alicia, who suddenly wore anxiety in her expression.

"We don't know the future," Mandie said firmly. "And it doesn't matter if we work together or not." She reached over and covered Suzie's hand with one of hers, and Alicia's with the other. "We are friends for life, and Suze, I will be at your wedding in the front row, and Lish, if you need me to babysit, I'm there. If you have another baby, I'm there. I'll be there for both of you, even if you don't want me there."

She grinned. "We're not going to be sad about this. We have phones, and it's a quick trip to the city. Charlie and I love it there too, and it's an amazing weekend trip." She nodded like that was that, and Suzie did the same.

"All right. "Alicia blew out her breath. "You're right." She cut into her pancakes too, and the conversation turned to lighter things. Work things, and once they finished eating, Suzie got up and started to clear the table.

Her condo didn't have a lot of space, and she needed the dining room table to lay out everything she'd put together for her letter presentation.

She then moved into the living room and picked up the moving box she'd put all of her research in. "I can't wait to show you what I've figured out about Denise and Mark." The words came out with more confidence than she expected. "I think I've cracked the timeline."

She pulled out the letters, which she'd organized chronologically in acid-free sleeves, each one labeled with dates and cross-referenced with her timeline. She'd printed out harbor logs, weather reports, and ferry schedules, all color-coded and annotated with her careful handwriting.

"This is incredible," Alicia said, leaning over one of the reports. "You've been busy."

"Look at this timeline." Suzie unrolled a large sheet of paper across the table, revealing a detailed chart that spanned two years. "I've mapped every letter against the harbor logs and weather reports."

And now that she knew the names of things, thanks to Alicia's research, the picture had started to become clearer.

"The timeline shows a clear pattern. Mark Adams operated the *Sea Sprite* on a regular schedule during tourist season, traditionally from May to October, but there were specific days when he'd made unscheduled trips to Rocky Ridge. Those same days corresponded to letters from Denise mentioning meeting at 'our place.'"

She looked up to make sure Mandie and Alicia were still with her, which of course, they were.

"See here." Suzie pointed to a cluster of entries in July 1989. "Mark made three unscheduled trips to Rocky Ridge this week. Look at the letter from July fifteenth."

She pushed the corresponding letter toward Alicia. She picked it up and read, "My dearest M, yesterday was perfect. Walking along our beach, talking about the house we'll have someday, the life we'll build together. I can almost taste the freedom."

Mandie leaned forward, studying the timeline. "She's talking about a future with him."

"It gets better." Suzie pointed to another section and picked up the letter. "September 1989. The boat is ready, and I've made the arrangements we discussed. All we need now is the right weather window."

"Arrangements for what?" Alicia asked.

"I think she was planning to fake her death." The words

came out matter-of-factly, but the weight of them settled heavily on Suzie's shoulders. "Look at this one from October."

She handed the letter to Mandie, who wore apprehension in her gaze before she swallowed and looked at it. "I've been practicing holding my breath underwater, and I've gotten much better at swimming in rough conditions. You were right, my love, and the current patterns are predictable if you know what to look for. Because of you, I know what to look for. It's more of a feel, though, isn't it?"

She looked up, and her next breath sounded like a gasp. The room fell silent except for the gentle hum of the air conditioning and the distant sound of waves against the harbor.

"You think Mark helped her stage the boat accident," Mandie whispered.

"I think they planned it together." Suzie plucked a weather report out from underneath the timeline, which she'd made by taping together the ends of a few sheets of regular office paper.

"Mark knew these waters better than anyone. He'd been operating passenger services for five years. He knew weather patterns, and he would've studied them to know when he could schedule tours and fishing expeditions."

"He was a swim instructor," Alicia said, her voice a ghost of its usual tone.

"He what?" Suzie blinked at her. "You didn't say that."

"I found another article last night," Alicia said. "It was out of Nantucket, not here in the cove. He taught scuba diving and open water swimming for the Polar Bears. Stuff like that."

Suzie leaned back in her chair. "He would have known

exactly how to make a boat disappear without leaving recoverable evidence, and he knew how to survive in open water."

Alicia picked up one of the weather reports and looked at it. "The storm that night was perfect cover. High winds, rough seas, limited visibility for search and rescue operations."

"And look at this." Suzie pointed to the final item in her timeline. "Mark Adams officially ended his passenger service and left the island only four months after Denise's supposed death. That's not a coincidence."

"Where do you think they went?" Mandie asked.

"I have no idea." Suzie sat back, feeling the satisfaction of a puzzle coming together. She'd spent countless hours cross-referencing documents, following paper trails, building a case that felt increasingly solid. This was what she was good at—seeing patterns others missed, connecting dots across decades of scattered information.

"The question is," she asked, focusing particularly on Mandie. "What do we do with this information?"

No one spoke, because so many other questions accompanied that one.

The weight of the decision to tell others settled over them. Connor Williams had spent thirty years believing his wife had died in a tragic accident. He'd remarried, built a new life, found happiness with Della.

Alice had lost her mother, and Suzie couldn't even imagine finding out thirty-five years later that someone she thought was dead actually wasn't. And then that brought up even more pain and heartache. Alice would want to know why her mother had left her—*abandoned her*, Suzie thought —when she was only fifteen years old.

The ripple effect of this theory didn't just affect one

person or one project. Something that had happened decades ago still had the power to bring people to their knees, and Suzie didn't want to do that to anyone.

"What good would it do at this point?" Mandie asked. "He's happy with Della. Alice and Scott have made peace with losing their mother. Why destroy that?"

"Because it's the truth." Suzie gathered the letters back into the box, always a proponent of truth. "And because maybe Denise is still alive somewhere. Maybe she wants to reconnect with her children."

"Or maybe she chose to disappear for good reasons we don't understand," Alicia said. "Maybe telling Connor would hurt more people than it helps."

Suzie looked between her friends, feeling the weight of responsibility while grappling with her own personal phantoms. In her mind, she fancied the idea that her own mother wanted to reconnect with her and simply didn't know how.

She'd uncovered this story, followed the threads until they led to an uncomfortable truth, and somehow twisted them to fit her own narrative. But maybe...

"We need more information before we decide anything," she finally said. "Maybe there are other documents we're missing."

"And then?" Mandie asked.

"Then we decide whether Connor Williams deserves to know that his wife might still be alive." Suzie looked at her timeline before rolling it up, at the careful documentation of a love affair that had led to deception and disappearance. She'd built a compelling case, and for the first time in her life, she was the one with answers. She was the one people looked to for guidance. The realization should have terrified her, but instead, it felt like coming home to herself.

She wasn't the kind of person who walked away from difficult truths. She was the kind of person who saw things through to the end, no matter how complicated or painful the journey became.

Now she just had to decide if telling others about her discoveries was the right thing to do.

Chapter Fifteen

Mandie pulled the covers up and over her face, groaning as Charlie switched on his lamp and rolled out of bed. "I get to sleep in today," she griped at him.

"Sorry, babe." The lamp snapped off again, and Charlie left the bedroom in favor of the shower. Mandie managed to doze back to sleep, even staying in bed after Charlie had gotten dressed and gone downstairs.

Her stomach rumbled, really roiling and boiling, and she curled further into a ball, sighing. She reached for her phone to check the time, and she'd gotten an extra hour of rest this morning.

The sunlight now filtered through their borrowed bedroom windows, casting everything in soft gold that should have felt peaceful. Instead, she simply couldn't wait to close on the house she and Charlie had bought.

"Next Thursday," she whispered to herself as her stomach started to play nice. She'd been feeling shaky and tired for a couple of days now, and she'd skipped breakfast too, thinking her stomach might not like it.

Today seemed like it would be another one of those days.

Mandie finally sat up, then stood and stretched her arms above her head. She loved wearing nightgowns to bed, despite Charlie teasing her about being eighty years old, and she looked down at the pale pink one she currently wore.

Her stomach lurched, and Mandie froze. She was going to throw up, and she spun toward the door and ran for the bathroom. She didn't make it to the toilet, and she retched into the bathroom sink, her whole body unhappy.

She panted there for a moment as everything settled, and then she flipped on the water. It ran cold up here, and she liked the coolness as the air flowed up and met her face.

Pressing her eyes closed, she muttered, "I should've known I couldn't have a real day off."

And she wasn't truly taking today off anyway. She was going with Suzie to the woodworker, to see the designs for the horned larks Suze wanted to carve into the knobs for the kitchen cabinetry.

The cove cottage had been progressing beautifully over the past several days. The white pine flooring upstairs gleamed under the construction lights, and the roofers had started installing the cedar shingles that would weather to the perfect silvery-gray within a year. Everything moved forward according to schedule, despite the stained glass windows remaining mysteriously delayed in Vermont.

To preserve her sanity, Mandie had thrown herself into managing every detail, coordinating with contractors, approving samples, and maintaining the timeline that would make Candace proud. In fact, the project might finish early at this pace.

Anything to obtain the blessed distraction from the weight of secrets she carried about Charlie's grandmother.

But this morning, even thinking about Denise made her stomach lurch violently. She dropped to her knees, everything clenching again as she tried to throw up something she didn't have in her stomach. The tile bit against her knees as she gripped the porcelain rim, her body shaking with the force of it.

The nausea passed, and she leaned her head against the coolness of the porcelain, her mind whirring. She'd been sick for a few days now.

She lifted her head. "For three days in a row."

The realization hit her like a ruthless wave. She'd been attributing the nausea to stress, to the sleepless nights spent wrestling with what they'd discovered about Denise Williams. To the exhaustion that had been dragging at her for the past week—all of it suddenly took on new meaning.

She looked toward the door, wishing she had her miniature notebook in front of her. Was her period late? Shouldn't she have started yesterday? Mandie tracked her cycle religiously, and the notebook would confirm it.

But she knew.

"Charlie," she called, her voice sounding hoarse to her own ears. She hoped with everything she had that he hadn't left for the hospital yet.

Her hands trembled as she reached for the edge of the bathtub to pull herself up. The room spun slightly, and she gripped the counter until the dizziness passed. In the mirror, her reflection stared back with wide eyes and pale cheeks.

"Charlie," she called again, louder this time. She had a pregnancy test here somewhere, and she dropped to the ground again, pulling open the doors on the vanity to check under the sink. "Charlie!"

Still nothing. The man could focus on his morning routine with laser precision.

Mandie found the pregnancy test and sank onto the edge of the bathtub, pressing her palms against her face. Could she really be pregnant? After months of trying, of tracking ovulation and timing everything perfectly, of disappointment month after month?

The possibility felt too fragile to examine closely, like a soap bubble that might burst if she breathed on it wrong.

And what if you're not? she asked herself. The crushing blow that would be... Mandie got up and walked back into the bedroom to get her notebook. It sat right there in her nightstand drawer, and she didn't even have to flip a page to get the information she wanted.

She was actually two days late starting her period.

"Charlie!"

"What?" he bellowed up the steps.

"I need you up here."

His footsteps thundered up the stairs, taking them two at a time. "I have to leave soon. What's going on?"

He appeared in the bedroom doorway, his hair perfectly combed and his tie on straight and neat. Concern creased his features as he took in her position next to the nightstand, a pregnancy test in one hand and her notebook in the other.

"I think..." She swallowed hard, her throat raw from being sick. "I think I might be pregnant." She held up the unused test.

Charlie's face went through a series of expressions—surprise, hope, fear, and back to hope again. "What?" He crossed to her in a few strides and looked at her as if he could tell that way. "Are you sure? I mean, what makes you think...?"

He trailed off, studying her face. "You haven't been feeling well."

"Only in the morning," she whispered. She nodded to the test in her hand. "I bought these months ago, just in case." She started to weep. "My period is two days late, Charlie."

Charlie drew her into his arms. "Let's take the test, okay? Is it too soon?"

"I don't know," she said, because Mandie didn't know anything right now.

"Come on." He led her back into the bathroom, and his hands shook as he opened the package. He pulled out the instructions and handed her the stick. "This says it'll detect the hormone as early as four days before the first day of your missed cycle."

He stared at her with wide eyes. "I'll be right outside," he said softly, pressing a kiss to her temple before stepping out and bringing the door almost all the way closed.

Mandie took a deep breath and followed the test instructions with the precision she brought to construction timelines, then set the plastic stick on the counter and forced herself to breathe.

She opened the door, met her husband's eyes, and started crying again. "I don't dare—" she said, feeling foolish.

"It's fine," Charlie said. "Whatever it is, it'll be fine." He helped her back to bed, pulling the covers up around her shoulders and smoothing her hair away from her face. His touch felt gentle and steady, anchoring her to the moment when everything else seemed to be spinning.

"How long do we wait?" he asked, kneeling down beside her side of the bed.

"Three minutes."

They waited in silence, Charlie's hand warm against hers. Outside their window, the morning sounds of Five Island Cove drifted up—seagulls calling, a boat engine starting up in the harbor, the distant sound of construction beginning at another job site.

Normal sounds of a normal day that might be anything but normal.

"Whatever it says," Charlie began, his voice quiet and serious.

"Don't." Mandie squeezed his hand. "Don't say it'll be fine again, because I don't know if I'll be fine."

He nodded, understanding filling his eyes. They'd learned not to make promises about being okay either way, because the disappointment had been real every month. The hope followed by crushing letdown had become a familiar cycle they'd both grown tired of navigating.

"Go check it, please," Mandie whispered.

Charlie stood and walked to the bathroom with the measured steps of someone approaching either the best or worst news of his life. Mandie held her breath, listening to the silence that stretched between them.

Then Charlie bellowed from the bathroom—a sound of pure, unfiltered joy that made Mandie's heart leap into her throat.

He came rushing back into the bedroom, the pregnancy test held high above his head like a trophy. "You're pregnant!" His voice cracked on the words. "Mandie, you're pregnant!"

He danced closer and held out the stick for her to take. The test showed two clear pink lines, undeniable and beautiful and real.

Mandie burst into tears—happy tears that had been

building behind her eyes for months. Charlie launched himself onto the bed, gathering her into his arms and rolling them both sideways until they were tangled in sheets and limbs and laughter.

"We're having a baby." She sobbed against his shoulder, the words feeling magical on her tongue.

"We're having a baby," he repeated, his own voice thick with emotion. He pulled back to look at her face, his eyes bright with unshed tears. "I can't believe it. I just can't believe it."

He kissed her through her tears, salty and sweet and desperate with relief. All the months of careful planning and disappointment dissolved into this perfect moment of pure happiness. Mandie felt like she could float away on the joy bubbling up from her chest.

Charlie peppered her face with kisses, touching her forehead, her cheeks, her nose, her lips. "I love you so much. I love you both so much."

The word *both* sent another wave of emotion through her. Not just her and Charlie anymore, but the three of them.

"I have to call in sick," Charlie said suddenly, sitting up and patting his pockets for his phone. "I can't go to work today."

"Charlie, you can't call in sick because your wife is pregnant." But Mandie laughed as she said it, because she didn't want him to leave either. She wanted to stay in this bubble of happiness for as long as possible.

"Are you going to go to work?"

Mandie wiped her face and couldn't stop smiling. "Yeah, of course."

He scoffed. "What are you doing today? The wood-working?"

"Yes," she said. "It's right here on Diamond, and Suze and I weren't even planning to go to the cottage today. They're just doing the cedar shingles and the roof. There's nothing to do there."

"Call her and tell her you need another half-hour." Charlie started tapping on his phone. "I'm going to tell Sarah the same thing."

"Why?" Mandie gazed at him and reached up to smooth his hair back. "What are we going to do?"

"Just be together." He twisted and put his phone on her nightstand, and then he rolled into her again and drew her into his arms. Mandie loved being held by him, and she cuddled into his chest and listened to his heart beating.

What would she tell Candace?

She pushed the thought away, because she knew what she was going to do. She and Charlie had bought a house here; they weren't going back to the city. She wouldn't continue with PastForward after the completion of the cove cottage.

Her thoughts moved to something else, and the little white house on Beachwalk Avenue came forward. It would become a home filled with laughter and bedtime stories and all the beautiful chaos that came with raising a family.

As the initial rush of excitement settled into something deeper and more sustainable, the weight of her secret pressed against her chest, making breathing hard.

Her stomach clenched again, but for an entirely different reason now. "Charlie," she said softly, her fingers tracing the collar of his shirt.

"Mm?" He pressed another kiss to the top of her head.

"There's something I need to tell you about the cove cottage. About what we found in the house."

His hand stilled on her back. "What kind of something?"

Mandie took a deep breath, gathering courage from the pregnancy test still sitting on her nightstand. If she could create life, she could certainly find the strength to tell her husband the truth about his family's history.

"We found forty-three love letters from Denise." She lifted her head to meet his eyes, seeing her own reflection in their blue depths. "But they're not to your grandfather."

Chapter Sixteen

C andace adjusted the angle of her laptop screen, ensuring the afternoon light streaming through her apartment's floor-to-ceiling windows wouldn't create a glare. Her home office occupied the corner of her Upper East Side penthouse, its walls lined with architectural photography from her most successful projects—visual reminders of what she'd built, what she'd accomplished.

The mahogany desk had belonged to her father, one of the few pieces she'd kept after his death. Today it held her laptop, a crystal tumbler of sparkling water with lime, and a leather portfolio containing notes about upcoming projects. The familiar weight of responsibility settled across her shoulders as she opened the video call application.

Her team in Five Island Cove appeared on screen moments later, crowded around a single laptop in what looked like the construction tent. Behind them, blue sky stretched endlessly, and the popping sound of a nail gun drifted faintly through their microphone.

Candace smiled at the sight of them—windblown hair,

sun-kissed faces, the easy camaraderie of people who'd been working together under pressure. And they looked happy about it. Happy together, and that made her happy.

When had she started caring about their happiness?

"Good afternoon," she said, settling back in her ergonomic chair. She let that slip of maternal fondness move through her. She couldn't be much older than Suzie, but she could've been Mandie's mother if she'd had a late teenage pregnancy.

After all, Mandie was only a handful of years older than Lana, and Candace had never made that connection until now.

"Hey," Mandie said cheerfully. She looked a bit pale, but that could've been the lighting. No matter what, she definitely bore the battle scars of working on a restoration project with high stakes. Candace knew this feeling well, as she'd lived it herself for years.

"Are you guys taking enough time away from the site?" Candace asked. "I expected you to perhaps be at a café or someone's house."

The three of them exchanged quick glances with one another. "My house is packed up," Mandie said. "Charlie and I are moving next week."

"The kids attach themselves to me the moment I walk in," Alicia said, and they both looked at Suzie.

She swallowed, and Candace catalogued it from across the ocean. "I had to be here today," she said simply. "So we figured this was just fine."

"I'm surprised you have service," Candace said.

"We're borrowing from my grandfather-in-law." Mandie leaned closer to the screen. "We're in his gazebo." She picked up the computer and turned it so Candace could see.

So they weren't at the job-site, and Candace wasn't sure why she cared. She did want them to be happy, because they'd had a lot of field assignments lately, and she didn't want them to burn out.

"Okay," she said. "You said there's something you needed to discuss with me?"

"Are you at home?" Suzie asked, ever the blunt one. "I don't think I've ever seen your home office."

"Me either," Alicia said. "It's nice, Candace." She offered a kind smile, and Candace returned it.

"Yes, I just needed to get out of the bullpen today." She gave a sigh. "I do have another call in a few minutes."

"Yes, of course," Mandie said, clearing her throat and glancing at Suzie.

Suzie leaned forward slightly now, and Mandie moved the computer so the camera focused more on her. "We need your guidance on something we've discovered. It's about the house's history, and we're not sure how to proceed."

Candace reached for her sparkling water while fighting the adrenaline as it lurched through her veins. "What kind of discovery?"

"Love letters," Alicia said, her voice carrying the precise tone she used for budget reports. "Forty-three of them, hidden in the house. They span about two years, ending just before Denise Williams died."

"Or *disappeared*," Suzie interjected, earning sharp looks from both Mandie and Alicia.

Candace leaned forward, her business instincts sharpening. "Explain."

For the next twenty minutes, her team laid out their findings with the thoroughness of a legal brief. The letters, the timeline, the harbor records, the mysterious Mark Adams who'd vanished from Five Island Cove just months after Denise's "supposed death."

Suzie's research had been meticulous, building a compelling case for an elaborate deception, and Candace was reminded of why she'd hired the woman in the first place. Yes, she wasn't afraid to go into any space, and she knew a great deal about construction and building mechanics.

But she adored history too, especially when connected to people, and she never missed a detail.

"So you believe she faked her death to run off with this boat captain," Candace said when they finished.

"The evidence strongly suggests it," Suzie said. "Mark Adams had the knowledge and resources to stage a convincing accident. The timing of his departure from the island can't be coincidental."

Candace studied their faces through the screen, noting the tension between them. Mandie's jaw sat tight with obvious stress, while Alicia maintained her professional composure. Only Suzie radiated excitement about the discovery.

"What's the question you need me to answer?" Candace asked, though she suspected she already knew.

"What's our obligation as historian-renovators?" Mandie's voice carried a note of desperation. "Do we have to tell any involved parties everything we discover?"

The question hung in the digital space between them, weighted with implications Candace had never considered. In all her years of restoration work, she'd uncovered family secrets before—hidden rooms, forgotten heirlooms, evidence of past scandals. But usually, those discoveries only added to the allure of the renovation. They highlighted them in cases and glowing shadowboxes so everyone would know how special the property was.

She'd never encountered something quite like this before.

"What do the three of you think?" she asked.

"Truth matters," Suzie said, glaring at Mandie. "What? It does." She shook her head, her blonde ponytail brushing her shoulders. "Part of what we do is uncover the truth. Connor Williams has spent more than thirty years believing his wife died in a tragic accident. Alice and Scott lost their mother and never got closure, because her body and the boat were never found. If there's even a chance Denise is still alive, don't they deserve to know?"

"What if she doesn't *want* to be found?" Mandie's voice cracked slightly. "What if she *chose* to disappear for reasons we can't understand? For reasons not stated in a few letters? For reasons that would only hurt Connor and Della and Alice and everyone else?"

Including her husband, Candace thought.

"We'd be destroying multiple families based on speculation and *half*-truths." Mandie could give as good as she got, and the thing was, Candace didn't disagree with her.

Candace watched Mandie's face, recognizing the particular strain of someone carrying a burden too heavy for their shoulders. Oh, how she'd done that in her life too.

"Have you told Charlie?"

"A couple of days ago." Mandie's admission came out barely above a whisper. "I couldn't keep it from him anymore. He's processing it, but he agrees we shouldn't say anything to his grandfather."

Alicia shifted in her chair, the movement drawing Candace's attention, as she folded her arms and leaned away from the camera. "I see both sides. The historian in me wants to follow every lead, uncover every truth. But the practical side knows that sometimes knowledge causes more harm than good in a situation like this."

"And your conclusion?" Candace asked.

"I think we should focus on completing the renovation." Alicia threw a glance down to Suzie, who frowned. "This mystery doesn't affect the structural integrity of the house or our ability to deliver a beautiful renovation on time and within budget." Alicia's words carried the weight of someone who'd made difficult decisions in her life, who'd weathered them, who'd survived.

"If Suzie wants to continue investigating, she should do it on her own time." She added a soft smile. "Sorry, Suze."

"It's fine." She waved her hand in a half-flap, which meant she didn't agree and didn't think anything was fine.

Candace absorbed their arguments, her mind automatically sorting through implications and consequences. The weight of decision-making had always energized her, but this felt different. More personal, somehow.

"I need time to consider this," she said finally. "It's not a decision to make lightly."

Relief flickered across Mandie's face, while disappointment shadowed Suzie's. Alicia simply nodded, accepting the delay with her usual professionalism.

"Let's continue with the renovation work," Candace said. "It's even looking like you'll be done a week or two early, and I'll be in touch soon." Candace's tone carried the finality that ended meetings, and after brief goodbyes, the screen went dark.

She closed the laptop and pushed back from the desk, suddenly restless. The apartment felt too quiet, too controlled, after the vibrant energy of her team's outdoor workspace. She walked to the windows, her heels clicking against the hardwood floors.

Manhattan stretched before her, thirty floors below. Traffic moved in predictable patterns, people hurried along sidewalks with purpose, and the city hummed with the constant energy of eight million lives intersecting. From this height, everything looked manageable, orderly, under control.

But control was an illusion, wasn't it? She'd learned that lesson with Lana, with Bradley, with the gradual recognition that her carefully constructed walls had kept out love along with pain.

The weight of secrets pressed against her chest. She understood the burden her team carried, the responsibility of holding information that could shatter lives or heal old wounds. How many times had she made decisions that affected others without considering the human cost?

The afternoon light shifted, casting longer shadows across her office. She had another call scheduled, one that represented the changes she'd been trying to make in her professional life. Emma Chen, bright and eager, reminded Candace of herself at twenty-three—hungry for opportunities, willing to work twice as hard as anyone else just to prove her worth.

She returned to her desk, pulling up Emma's file on her computer. The young woman had impressed her with detailed project analyses and innovative solutions to restoration challenges. More importantly, she'd shown the kind of passion that couldn't be taught, only nurtured.

The video call connected precisely on time, Emma's face appearing on screen with the backdrop of the PastForward office. Their new space had private pods for video calls, and Emma had sequestered herself in one of those.

Her dark hair was pulled back in a neat bun, and she wore a navy blazer that looked expensive but not quite designer.

"Good afternoon, Miss Ewing. Thank you for making time for this."

"Emma." Candace smiled, noting how the younger woman's posture straightened at the use of her first name. "I've been reviewing your analysis of the Brooklyn brownstone project. Your recommendations for the façade restoration are excellent."

Pink colored Emma's cheeks. "Thank you. I spent considerable time researching the original construction techniques, and it was so much fun."

Candace grinned at her, because who wanted to study historical construction techniques in Brooklyn?

Only the kind of people Candace wanted at PastForward. Those with a hunger to know the past and bring it back to life in the future.

"That level of attention to historical research and detail is exactly what separates good restoration from exceptional work." Candace leaned back in her chair, studying Emma's face. "Tell me what you hope to accomplish in the next year."

She'd been clear that Emma wouldn't be assigned any field assignments in the first year of her employment at the company. No one got those, because Candace needed her top people out in the field, with the hundreds of details that needed managing, and the ability to solve and handle countless problems that could happen.

But she wanted to help employees she thought had potential to do more than schedule mold removal or research properties for sale. They discussed Emma's career goals, her strengths and areas for development to help her learn the things she needed to know to be that team leader, and the types of projects that excited her most.

Candace found herself genuinely engaged, remembering her own hunger for mentorship that had never materialized. Not only that, but perhaps the Black Sand Bungalow could use an outsider's perspective...

"I have a special research project," Candace said as their conversation wound down. "It's not directly related to any current renovation, but it requires the kind of thorough investigation skills you've been developing."

Emma's eyes brightened. "Sure. What is it?"

"I need you to research two people who disappeared from Five Island Cove in 1990. Denise Williams and Mark Adams. I want to know if they're still alive, if they assumed new identities, any trace of what happened to them after they left the island."

"Missing persons research." Emma nodded, already taking notes. "What's the time frame for this?"

"Take your time. Be thorough. And Emma?" Candace waited until she had the younger woman's full attention. "This is confidential. Not to be discussed with anyone else in the office."

"Of course."

After the call ended, Candace remained at her desk, staring at her reflection in the dark laptop screen. The decision to involve someone else felt right, a way to mentor while also addressing the mystery that had captured her team's attention—and divided it.

But deeper questions remained. What *was* her obligation to the truth? To the families involved? To the woman who might still be alive somewhere, living under an assumed name, believing her secrets were safely buried in the past?

The apartment's silence pressed around her, broken only by the distant hum of traffic and the whisper of air conditioning. She'd built this life deliberately—controlled, predictable, insulated from the messy complications of human emotion. But isolation had its own costs, as she'd learned through her relationship with Lana.

Her phone chimed out Lana's tone, and Candace returned to her desk to pick up her phone. *I had lunch with Ted's parents today. They're so excited about the wedding! I can't wait for you to meet them, especially his mom. I think she's going to come wedding dress shopping with us in the fall.*

Of course she would, because Lana seemed to have a golden, magnetic personality that drew everyone to her.

Candace smiled, warmth spreading through her chest. Her daughter's happiness had become one of the few things that mattered more than business success or professional recognition. The realization felt like coming home to a part of herself she'd forgotten existed.

I'm looking forward to it. How are the dress preferences going?

I'm still trying to narrow down the style I like. Maybe we could look at some magazines together this weekend?

Candace's throat tightened with emotion. The simple request for shared time, for mother-daughter bonding over wedding planning, represented everything she'd missed during Lana's childhood. Everything she was determined not to miss now.

I'd love that, she replied. *Saturday morning? I'll order breakfast.*

Ted and I will be there.

She turned in her office chair and looked out the windows again. The past had a way of surfacing, especially when people like Suzie refused to let sleeping mysteries lie. The question was whether truth would bring healing or simply create new wounds.

The weight of decision settled across Candace's shoulders like a familiar coat. Tomorrow would bring new challenges, new choices, new opportunities to balance control with... compassion. Candace didn't have much experience operating from a place of caring, but she figured the house in Five Island Cove was giving her an opportunity to do exactly that.

Almost if the house knew she needed a mentor in this area.

Chapter Seventeen

S uzie stood at the back of the ferry, its wake catching the
early light and scattering it around like diamonds.

The air hummed with quiet anticipation, and the only
way Suzie knew how to relieve the nerves running through
her body was to work. When she accomplished things with
her hands, it somehow allowed her mind to work through
the problems she harbored there.

Five days had passed since their video call with Candace,
and still no word about what to do with the letters. The
silence gnawed at her like a splinter she couldn't dig out.

So she watched the water, enjoying the way it moved left
and right, trying to throw the ferry off-course. She loved the
way the boat fought back and kept its course, and she loved
the predictability of the sun as it continued to rise and paint
the day with beautiful, bright light.

She exhaled, trying to let go of the driving need to know
what had truly happened to Denise. *She probably really did
pass in the storm*, she told herself, hoping she'd believe it this
time.

Even if it's not true, does it matter?

Oh, the circle her thoughts could travel in.

Once she reached the job site, she unlocked the security tent and pulled out her tablet, scrolling through the day's checklist while the ocean breeze kicked up over the cliffs and around the cottage.

She turned toward it, marveling at the miraculous transformation. The new cedar shingles had been painted white on Friday, and fresh white trim outlined every window and door, crisp lines that spoke of craftsmanship and attention to detail. The front porch gleamed with new decking, and the railing Jake had installed yesterday curved gracefully around the corner, following the natural flow of the structure.

Suzie needed to talk to Mandie about the landscaping, as that sometimes took some time to design and coordinate. They'd have to get the tent cleared up soon, because the entire property needed to be transformed.

The construction crew had moved out of the house and had started construction on the back deck, and then the long set of steps that led down to the black sand beach. They'd demo and repair anything that needed it, and then install a new set of steps that should weather the storms and last the test of time.

They'd be painting inside this week, and Suzie should get the knobs for the cabinetry throughout the house by Friday. They'd move on to fixtures and finishes, which always took longer than anticipated.

She glanced down at her tablet. "And the stained glass windows."

Those still hadn't arrived from Vermont, and every call Alicia made ended with reassurances that they'd be there "soon." If they didn't come, they'd sure have some great big holes in the back wall.

The rumble of an engine announced the arrival of the construction crew, and Jake, the construction lead, drove a truck full of men down the sandy lane. Dust kicked up behind the vehicle, catching the coral morning light for just a moment before it resettled on the ground.

"Morning," Jake called as he climbed out of his truck, his thermos of coffee already in hand. His beard looked freshly trimmed, and he wore the satisfied expression of a man who knew his work was nearly complete. Others followed him, faces that had become familiar over the past several weeks but that Suzie probably wouldn't see once this project finished.

Just like Mandie. The thought flowed through her mind, unbidden, and Suzie really wished it would go. She couldn't stand the thought of going back to the city without the woman who'd become such a good friend.

"You'll have to," she muttered, because Mandie and Charlie had just bought a house here. Charlie had a good job here. Though Mandie hadn't said anything to anyone about her plans for her job, her actions spoke of a permanent move to Five Island Cove.

"Hey." She gestured toward the truck. "Did you get the millwork?"

"Sure did." He grinned and took a long sip of coffee. "Those pieces came out better than I expected. Your friend's carving work is incredible."

Suzie's chest warmed at the mention of the custom cabinet knobs. Each one featured a delicate lark in flight, carved with such precision that the tiny birds seemed ready to take wing. The design honored the ceramic tile she'd found in the bedroom wall, the one that had started her down the rabbit hole of Denise Williams's story.

The rest of the crew moved into the supply tent with the easy efficiency of people who'd worked together long enough to anticipate each other's needs. They exchanged morning greetings and finally, everyone gathered around Jake for the daily briefing.

"Kitchen cabinets go in first," Jake said, consulting the tablet Suzie handed him. "Then we'll install the crown molding in the living room and master bedroom. Suzie's handling detail work in the kitchen today, and we'll have a couple of you out back."

He nodded to Alex and Otto. "That's you guys."

"You got it, boss." Alex finished buckling on his tool belt, and then he headed around the cottage to the back.

Suzie let everyone else go inside, and then she stowed the tablet back in the tent. Alicia and Mandie weren't expected on-site today, as they'd set up a meeting to start to plan the grand reveal—the party and unveiling of the project. They'd need to get a date set, get invites sent out to the Mayor and other important figures in the cove, schedule Flint to do the final recording for the video, all of it.

In that moment, Suzie loved her role on this team and that it wasn't arranging all the fussy party details that Past-Forward had become known for.

She loved the precision required for finish work, the way every measurement had to be perfect, every joint seamless. It was the opposite of demolition, and as she used the table saw to cut a piece of molding to someone's specifications, she realized she preferred building to tearing down.

Maybe her nickname of the Bulldozer didn't fit anymore.

She frowned as she took the cut molding into the

cottage, her footsteps echoing against the gleaming hardwood floors. The interior smelled of new wood, with undertones of the ocean breeze that flowed through those huge gaping holes in the back wall.

In the back of the cottage, the kitchen cabinets waited in neat stacks, each piece labeled and organized according to Alicia's meticulous system. Suzie ran her hand along the smooth surface of one door, admiring the way the paint had dried to a perfect satin finish. They'd chosen a soft sage green that would complement the coastal palette without overwhelming the space.

She got out of the way as Trevor hefted the first cabinet into position and someone else called out another measurement for the next piece of molding. Since she stood there, Suzie helped guide the cabinet into place, her movements precise and confident. The cabinet slid into position with satisfying precision, and Jake immediately secured it to the wall studs.

They worked in companionable silence, the rhythm of installation as familiar as a dance. Suzie found herself thinking about Denise Williams as she worked, wondering if the woman had ever stood in this same space, planning her own kitchen, dreaming of meals she'd prepare for her family.

But those dreams had been interrupted by love letters and secret meetings, by plans for escape that had ended in disappearance. Suzie's hands stilled on the cabinet that would go up next, her mind drifting to the timeline in her bag.

"You okay?" Jake asked, his voice cutting through her reverie. "We're ready for that one."

She blinked to refocus on the task at hand and stepped back. "Yeah, just thinking about the history of this place."

He picked up the cabinet and passed it to Trevor, then moved into position to nail it in place.

"That's what makes restoration work interesting," he said, turning back to her. "You're not just fixing a building; you're preserving someone's story."

"Yeah." She turned away from the conversation, because she didn't want Jake to see the irritation on her face. When would Candace make her decision?

She stepped outside of the cottage, the back deck coming along nicely. A call came for more lumber for the steps, and Suzie said, "I got it."

She went around the house to the table saw, but stopped on the north side in the shade for just a moment. Just to check her phone really quick.

No text from Candace.

But she did have a message from Daniel she hadn't heard come in. *Thinking about you this morning. I hate coming back here on Sunday night. How's the cottage coming along?*

She smiled despite her frustration with Candace's silence. Daniel's steady presence in her life anchored her, something she could count on even when everything else felt uncertain, and reminded her that the house was just a house.

Amazing progress today, she typed back. *Installing the kitchen cabinets, working on the deck and the molding.*

Send pictures, he said. *I want to see everything before the big reveal.*

While technically, Suzie wasn't supposed to share any pictures with anyone outside of the project, she had sent some to Daniel over the weeks. She could snap a few of the cabinets and the molding and update the team—and Daniel —on the progress.

With a sigh, she tucked away her phone and returned to

work, but Candace's silence affected her more than she wanted to admit. It felt like judgment, like Candace had weighed her request for guidance and found it wanting. Suzie had always prided herself on being someone who finished what she started, but this mystery felt more important than any puzzle she'd tackled before.

The morning heat began to build as they worked, and by noon, sweat dampened her shirt as the breeze had sort of lilted to almost nothing. The millwork installation required precision and patience, each piece cut to exact measurements and fitted with care. Suzie lost herself in the work, finding peace in the repetitive motions and the satisfaction of watching the cottage start to take on a personality.

Jake called for lunch break just as they finished installing the crown molding in the living room. The crew scattered to find shade and food, but Suzie remained inside, drawn to the window where the stained glass would eventually be installed. She could almost see the way the colored light would dance across the walls and light the gold thread in the wallpaper, transforming the space into something magical.

She retreated to the supply tent, where she'd put her lunchbox. Finally alone, she pulled the timeline from her bag, along with her PB&J, and spread it across the table, her eyes scanning the careful notations she'd made. Forty-three letters, two years of secret meetings, and a love affair that had ended in disappearance. The evidence pointed to an elaborate deception, but doubt had been creeping in over the past few days.

Her phone rang, Daniel's name appearing on the screen. She answered immediately, grateful for the distraction.

"Hey, sweetheart," he said, his voice warm and familiar. "How's the most beautiful woman in Five Island Cove?"

"Frustrated," she said, leaning back in the chair and keeping her voice down. "And sweaty, and covered in sawdust."

"Mm, my favorite combination of things." He wore a sexy smile in his voice. "Except the frustration."

"Candace has said nothing," she said, blowing out her breath.

"I can see how that would frustrate you." A slightly frosty tone came through the line, and Suzie tilted her head.

"And?" she asked when he didn't go on.

"And nothing."

Further ire flashed through her. "There's something," she said.

"Suze—"

"I don't want you to keep things from me," she said, her bluntness making an appearance. Maybe she was more bull-dozer than she wanted to be, perhaps only in certain moments. "Because if you can't say what you think to me, what is this?"

"I know what this is," Daniel said quietly. "And so do you."

Suzie stared at the timeline, seeing the careful documen-tation of a love affair that had challenged everything she thought she knew about commitment and loyalty. "I used to think truth was always the answer."

"And now?"

"Now, I don't know." She closed her eyes and rolled her head, stretching her neck. "You agree with Mandie."

"I think sometimes it's okay to let the past live in the past, yes," Daniel said. "Even though I love history—adore it, right? I want to know everything about the past, but that doesn't mean everyone does."

Suzie wanted to know too, and as she took in a long breath, she heard the truth in his words.

"I think telling them might destroy everything they've tried to rebuild in the past thirty-five years," Daniel continued. "And that's not the kind of bulldozer you want to be. It's not the kind of bulldozer you are."

She traced one of the letter dates with her finger, thinking about what he'd said. "I'm not sure I know how to build." As she spoke, she looked up and out the door of the tent.

The cottage stood there in the noon-day shade of the trees, its careful restoration a stark opposite of what she'd just said.

"That's not true," Daniel said. "I've seen what you guys did at the house in the Hamptons, and on that yacht, and I'm pretty sure that the construction timeline would be complete chaos without you."

"Daniel—"

"You absolutely know how to find the beauty in lost, forgotten things—and people."

Tears pricked her eyes, and she worked hard not to sniffle so he wouldn't know of her emotion.

"You know how to strip them down, repair them, and build them back up again," he said. "You do it with buildings, sure. But you've done with the people around you, and with yourself."

The words settled into her chest like a key finding its lock. She had become that person, hadn't she? The woman who'd been too scared to set a wedding date had transformed into someone who could plan a future, who could trust in love enough to promise forever.

She couldn't help the sniffle that came out, and she

decided she didn't care. If she couldn't cry in front of Daniel, then what was this?

She could, because they had a relationship built on trust and loyalty and true love.

"I love you," she said, the words carrying more weight than usual.

"I love you too."

"Maybe being the kind of person that builds people up is more important than uncovering every secret."

"Oh, you'll *uncover* them," he said, a thread of happiness coming back into his voice. "But that doesn't mean you have to *expose* them."

Suzie folded the timeline and tucked it back into her bag. The cottage hummed with activity as the crew returned from lunch, their voices mixing with the sound of power tools and the undeniable beating of her heart.

She actually felt like she had a heart for one of the first times of her life.

"I'm getting a flight out in the morning," Daniel said.

Suzie blinked and straightened. "What? You don't need to do that."

"I want to," he said. "If I can't come see my fiancée whenever I want, what is this?"

She grinned, a giggle coming out of her throat. "Okay, but you'll have to get your own ride to the cove cottage. I have work to do."

"Okay," he said. "I'm sure I can manage."

She was sure he could too, and she picked up the sandwich she'd only taken one bite out of. "I have to go. I'll see you tomorrow, I guess."

"Love you, Suzie-sweetheart." He ended the call before

she could process the new nickname, and then warmth filled her as she stared at the screen on her phone as it turned black.

Suzie took her time with lunch, and she wanted to stretch out every aspect of this project. After all, this would be her last project with Mandie and Alicia, the end of a chapter that had defined the past few years of her life. The realization brought both sadness and gratitude—sadness for the ending, but gratitude for the friendship that she'd been able to find, cultivate, and...build.

The mystery of Denise Williams, just like the one surrounding her own mother, might never be solved, and perhaps that was as it should be.

Chapter Eighteen

Mandie stood in the doorway of her new kitchen, watching Charlie wrestle a box marked *DISHES* through the narrow hallway. The cardboard scraped against the freshly painted walls, and she winced at the sound.

Everything about this moment felt surreal—the keys in her pocket, the faint smell of fresh paint, the way the morning light streamed through windows that belonged to her.

To them.

"I think these dishes are made of lead." Charlie maneuvered the box around the corner and dropped it on the counter with an awful thud. Sweat beaded on his forehead, and his t-shirt already bore evidence of their morning packing up the storage unit. "That's the last of the kitchen stuff from the truck."

The kitchen looked impossibly small with boxes stacked on every available surface, but Mandie could see past the chaos to the potential underneath. Their dishes would fill those cabinets, their coffee maker would sit on that counter, their life would unfold in this space they'd chosen together.

A wave of nausea rolled through her stomach, and she gripped the doorframe until it passed. Six weeks pregnant, and the morning sickness hit at the most inconvenient times. She'd managed to hide it from everyone so far, claiming stress or lack of sleep when anyone noticed anything.

"Things okay in here?" Charlie appeared beside her, his hand warm against her lower back.

"I'm a little overwhelmed." She leaned into his touch, breathing in the familiar scent of his aftershave. "I can't believe this is ours."

"Our first house." His voice carried wonder that matched her own. "Remember when we used to talk about having a place that didn't share a wall with ten other people?" He grinned at her, and she smiled back.

"We still don't have room for a pool table," she said.

"Not inside, at least." He pressed a kiss to her temple. "But right now, I'll settle for a coffee table that doesn't belong to my parents."

She tipped her head back and laughed, because that was so true.

The front door banged open, followed by her father's voice calling, "Which bedroom is the master?"

Charlie stepped away from her. "It's the one at the end of the hall. I'll help you guys with the heavy stuff."

Mandie watched him disappear down the hallway, then turned back to survey the kitchen boxes. Each one represented a decision she and Charlie had made together—which dishes to keep when they'd gotten married, which small appliances they actually needed, which coffee mugs had enough sentimental value to justify the move across the water.

Alice came in the back door carrying a garbage can with a sticker still on it. She flashed a smile and looked effortlessly cool in a pair of khaki pants and a pale blue blouse. "This is going to be beautiful once you get settled."

She reached up and tightened her ponytail, and she carried herself with the same grace she brought to everything else.

"I hope so." Mandie gestured at the chaos surrounding them. "Because this just looks like a storage unit exploded."

Alice laughed, a sound that helped Mandie relax. She smiled, truly sinking into just being herself. She was never going to be Alice, never going to understand fashion the way she did, never be able to pull off anything but being herself.

And that was exactly who she needed to be.

"I brought you something." Alice lifted a wrapped package from behind a box. "A housewarming gift."

Mandie accepted the package with careful hands, noting the expensive wrapping paper and perfect bow. Inside, nestled in tissue paper, sat a set of linen kitchen towels in soft sage green, embroidered with delicate white flowers.

"They're gorgeous." Mandie held one up to the light, admiring the intricate stitching. "Thank you."

"I thought they'd complement the color scheme you described." Alice smiled warmly and stepped over to hug Mandie. She sank into the embrace as Alice said, "And you love a good hand towel."

Mandie giggle. "I do." She stepped back and grinned. "Thank you, Alice."

Charlie called something from outside, and Mandie's mother's voice drifted from the living room, where she was directing the placement of boxes with the efficiency of a seasoned wedding planner.

Alice gestured toward the kitchen boxes. "Let's get some of this unpacked."

"That would be amazing."

Alice opened a box by picking at the tape and then pulling it off. "This one has knives in it." The unpacking went faster after that, with Alice unwrapping dishes and unboxing utensils while Mandie put them in drawers and cupboards. The repetitive motions soothed her nerves, but her stomach lurched all over again when she thought about Alice's mother.

"Alice," Mandie said, setting a stack of plates on a shelf. "There's something I need to tell you about the cove cottage project."

Alice looked up as she pulled out Charlie's favorite coffee mug. "Oh?"

Mandie took a deep breath, gathering courage from the baby growing inside her. "We found some things during the renovation. Some letters that belonged to your mother."

"Letters?" Alice's voice carried the careful neutrality she undoubtedly used in legal situations.

Mandie met her eyes directly. "Forty-three love letters, hidden in the house."

The question that always came to her mind at this point in the story resurfaced: Why were Denise's letters in the house too? Wouldn't she have given them to Mark, and he'd have stored them somewhere else?

Her blood seemed to move through her body like lightning. "They were between your mom and...someone who wasn't your father."

Shutters dropped over Alice's eyes. "I know my mother had an affair before she died."

"You do? She did?"

The kitchen fell silent except for the distant sounds of moving day chaos. Alice gripped the edge of the counter, her knuckles white against the pale wood. Then she released her hands and her breath.

"Yes," she said. "When Joel died, and we all came back to the cove to help Kristen clean out her house, we found something to indicate as much."

Relief filled Mandie from top to bottom. "Oh, good." She immediately realized what she'd said. "I mean, it's not good that you found out your mom was having an affair. I'm just glad I'm not the one telling you about Mark."

Alice blinked. "Mark?"

Mandie blinked. Her mind whirred. Dots connected. "It wasn't Mark." She hung her head, wishing she hadn't brought this up at all. She hadn't wanted to tell Alice or Connor about the letters at all, but they gnawed at her. Chewed and chewed and chewed, and Candace still hadn't given her instructions for what to do about the letters.

"I'm sorry," Mandie said. "Forget I said anything."

"It's okay." Alice walked to the window that overlooked the backyard, her arms wrapped around herself. "It's okay." She turned, and she wore a smile now. "Really." She gave a light laugh, but Mandie had frozen to the spot.

"I'm sorry," she said. "It's just—I'm not good at keeping secrets."

"It's fine, dear, really." She swept into Mandie and hugged her. "I've made peace with the version of my mother that I remember," she whispered. "I don't need to know anything else."

She stepped back and nodded, her smile still radiant. "My dad found happiness with Della. Scott has his own family. I have Arthur and you and Charlie, and Ginny and Bob, and now Caroline. It's all fine, and you don't have anything to feel bad about."

Tears filled Mandie's eyes. "Okay." She nodded, understanding settling over her like a blanket. "I agree."

Alice looked around and exhaled. "Okay, let's finish this up so we can go see where they put all your furniture."

LATER THAT AFTERNOON, MANDIE STOOD ON THE front porch, a wave of exhaustion moving through her as she lifted her hand in a goodbye gesture to her parents. Finally.

She turned back to the house when Charlie did, and she entered behind him, a sigh pulling through her whole body. "I'm so tired," she said.

But her couch stood in the perfect spot in the living room, with a bookcase beside it and a storage cabinet with a TV across from it. They'd lived in the city for so long, and they both knew how to make the most of a small space.

Charlie sank onto the couch. "Me too," he said, grinning at her. "But guess what? We live here by ourselves, and we don't share a wall with anyone."

Mandie squealed and danced over to him, snuggling into his side on the couch. "Isn't it great?"

"So great."

She exhaled happily, and she closed her eyes and let the amazingness of this day flow over her. She could barely believe this had happened, though she and Charlie had worked and saved and seized opportunities whenever they came their way to get to this point.

"I need to call Candace," she said with a sigh.

Charlie sighed too. "Yeah? What are you thinking?"

Mandie sat up and looked at him, appreciating the way he deferred to her, asked her what she wanted, and listened to her. "I think—I've known for a while that this project will be my last one at PastForward."

Charlie blinked, a hint of surprise crossing his expression. "You love this job."

Mandie nodded and glanced down at her hands. "Yeah, but I love the cove, and we live here now." She met his gaze again. "We moved here, knowing that there's no office here. There aren't going to be a plethora of projects here."

She moved her palm to her belly. "And with the baby coming, that's all I want. I want to be your wife and our baby's mom, and..." She trailed off and shrugged one shoulder. "You have a great job, and we have money from the first two projects. When this third one sells, that's another decent chunk of money."

He nodded. "It's not about the money."

"You think I won't be happy?" If Mandie were being honest with herself, she'd had the thought too.

"If you're not, then we'll do something different." He sat up and laced his fingers through hers over her belly. "Okay?"

She nodded. "I'm going to text Candace and set up a meeting, so I can tell her."

"Yep." He got up with a groan and re-took her hand. "But first, we're going to take a nap in our bed, in our house." He grinned at her, and Mandie giggled as she got to her feet and followed her husband down the hall to the bedroom in their new house.

She could text Candace later, maybe when she sent pictures of moving day to the whole team.

Chapter Nineteen

A licia stood in the ferry terminal, her fingers clenched around the strap of her oversized purse, watching Henry guide Gray and Lily through the boarding process. Her son's backpack bounced against his shoulders as he practically vibrated with excitement about going back to the city, while Lily clutched the stuffed dolphin they'd bought at a fun shop in the downtown area of Diamond Island.

The morning air carried the salt tang of low tide mixed with diesel fumes from the ferry's engines. Other passengers moved around them with the bustle of traveling, and Alicia's kids moved right along with them.

Just before he needed to go with the kids, Henry turned back toward the terminal building, his eyes finding hers through the glass. He raised his hand in a wave, his smile so warm and amazing, and she matched the gesture from her side, the barrier between them feeling symbolic of something she couldn't quite name.

Gray appeared beside his stepfather, waving enthusiastically at her while Lily bounced on her toes, blowing kisses and grinning. The sight sent a sharp pang through Alicia's chest, and she forced herself to smile and wave back with enthusiasm she didn't entirely feel.

The ferry's horn blasted twice, signaling final boarding. Henry shepherded the kids toward the gangway, and they all simply disappeared onto the ferry which would take them back to the city, to Henry's house, to the registration table at their new school.

Though she couldn't see them anymore, Alicia watched until the ferry pulled away. She wanted to be the one going with them to the open registration day at the children's new school.

She wanted to be the one going through their rooms and making a list of the things they needed. She wanted to be the one packing up her life in the two-bedroom apartment where she'd lived with the kids since her divorce and help move it into the house in Yonkers where she and Henry would raise their family.

As it was, she couldn't take a week away from the cove cottage right now, not when everything was coming together. The property had a lot of outdoor work still to do, on the steps down to the black sand beach, on the deck, and in the yard.

Not only that, but the stained glass windows should be here no later than Wednesday, and Alicia would be going to Vermont if they didn't show up as promised. She and Mandie had started to plan the reveal gala, and there simply wasn't a way for Alicia to take a week and return to New York.

Tears pressed into her eyes, and she turned away from the

settled water and headed outside to the RideShare line. The guilt that had been gnawing at her all morning intensified, and she couldn't stop herself from crying.

She should be with them, helping Gray navigate his anxiety about starting at a new school, comforting Lily when she inevitably got overwhelmed by the city's noise and crowds.

She pulled out her phone and typed quickly. *Text me when you get to the apartment safely. Love you all.*

Henry's response came immediately. *We will. Don't work too late tonight. Love you, Lish. This is a good thing, though I know you want to be here.*

That only made her cry harder, because this didn't feel like a good thing. She couldn't stand here with so many people around, especially as a couple of women looked her way with concern in their eyes.

She shook her head and stepped out of line, the summer sun beating down on her as she strode away from the line of cars queueing up to take people to their island destinations.

"Ma'am," someone called, but Alicia kept walking. A woman—one from the RideShare line—came jogging up beside her. "Are you okay? You can ride with us wherever you need to go."

But she couldn't, because she couldn't take a car to New York City. She took a deep breath, which sounded like a sniffle, and tried to smile at the woman. "I'm okay."

"Are you sure?" She reminded Alicia so much of Mandie, and that thought made Alicia stop.

"Yeah," she said with a big breath flowing out of her mouth. "I just sent my kids back to the city with their step-dad, and I just want to be with them."

The woman nodded, her eyes still wide and her mouth

set in a sympathetic stance. "I'm sorry." She didn't try to fix it or offer anything else. She did smile then, everything about her softening. "This sidewalk heads south, and you can walk down the coast for a little bit. It's very calming. I take it in the mornings sometimes, when I just need a little escape."

Alicia nodded. "Thank you."

"You can call a RideShare?" The woman lifted her phone. "They'll come anywhere you are, so you don't have to walk back here or anything."

"I know how to get a ride," Alicia said, a smile coming to her face too. "Thank you." She drew in a big breath and faced the sidewalk. The lighthouse stood tall and proud and stalwart in that direction too, and she exhaled. "I think I'll walk for a little bit."

The woman nodded, and they parted ways. Alicia needed to get to Mandie's to go over a rough schedule for the gala, starting with a date, and they'd have to get that approved by Candace.

They'd put the letters behind them, as Mandie had revealed that she'd spoken to Alice, and she didn't want her father to know about them. Candace had agreed readily, and Suzie had asked to keep them, simply because she liked old things. The handwriting, the speculation, the creation of a person inside her mind.

No one had objected, and Alicia knew she showed up at the jobsite and worked all day as a way to process the letters, her disappointment, her life. It wasn't a bad strategy, in Alicia's opinion.

She walked, her feet eating up a lot of distance as she listened to the birds call greetings to each other, and waves crash against sand and rocks, and the wind whistle while it tried to get where it wanted to go.

Eventually, she told herself she couldn't keep walking down the sidewalk between the water and the highway, and she called for a ride.

Mandie started texting at the same time a sedan pulled onto the shoulder, and Alicia gave the driver her friend's address. *I'm on the way*, she told Mandie. *Rough morning.*

Oh, I'm sorry, Lish. Mandie's response mirrored the woman at the ferry terminal, and it made her smile. *I'll get out the brownies.*

You made brownies?

My mom always had them in the freezer, she said. *She said you never know when you might need them, so I always have a few in the freezer. These are only a few days old, too, so they'll be delicious!*

Alicia smiled, because she'd never heard of someone baking brownies to freeze "just in case." But it so sounded like Mandie, and the driver dropped her off at her friend's house only a few minutes later.

"Here you go," he said, and Alicia quickly tapped to pay him before she got out.

She stood in the driveway for a moment, though she'd been here before. The cottage shone light a bright white beacon in the summer day, and Charlie had painted the shutters and front door blue over the weekend. Mandie had sent pictures, but it looked more vibrant in real life.

The front door opened, and Mandie stepped out onto the steps. "It's cooler in here, I promise."

Alicia smiled and headed her way. She was going to miss Mandie so much when she went back to the city, and she eased into her best friend's arms and hugged her, already crying again.

Mandie simply held her, which Alicia appreciated so

much. She finally managed to draw a breath that didn't enter her lungs as a gasp, and she stepped back, wiping her eyes. "It was so hard to send them back," she said.

"I can't imagine." Mandie led the way inside, where she had her laptop open on the coffee table in the bright living room. She and Charlie owned an orange couch with a chaise, and Alicia just wanted to curl into that corner cushion and take a little nap.

Instead, she sank into the flowered recliner opposite the couch on the other side of the coffee table and all of Mandie's materials.

The work waited exactly where she'd left it, patient and demanding in equal measure. But for the first time all summer, the thought of diving into spreadsheets and vendor contracts felt hollow.

She watched as Mandie sat on the couch, and their eyes met. "You're going to quit once this project is over, aren't you?"

Mandie's face paled and her eyes went wide. Then she swallowed and nodded. "Yes," she said. "I haven't talked to Candace yet, so please don't say anything." She looked down at her hands. "I mean, of course she knows, but I haven't offi-cially said anything."

Alicia started to weep again. "I'm going to miss you so much." She shook her head, feeling foolish. "Do you think Suze knows?"

"She has to," Mandie whispered. "I mean, Charlie has a job here. We bought a house."

Alicia nodded, finally getting control of her emotions. "Yeah."

Their eyes met again, a solid understanding between them. Alicia took another breath, wiped her eyes, and said,

"So you and Charlie will stay with me and Henry when you come to the city."

Mandie grinned and nodded. "We love the city. It's not like we'll never be back."

"I know." She looked down at her purse and plucked a folder from it. "Okay, let's get a date on the calendar."

Because once Alicia had that, she'd know when she could return to her life in New York City.

A COUPLE OF DAYS LATER, ALICIA FOLLOWED SUZIE and Mandie off the ferry, the three of them silent. They'd chatted in line at the ferry terminal on Diamond, but the closer to Rocky Ridge they'd gotten, the less they'd said.

Candace should be at the site already. She'd asked them to come a bit later, because she wanted to go through the property with the construction manager and Flint, and they'd stayed last night to make sure everything could be as perfect as possible.

Of course, Mother Nature could've blown an entire beach full of black sand into the house through the gaping holes in the back wall of the cottage.

She exchanged a glance with Mandie, who said, "It's not too windy this morning."

Alicia nodded and got in the car first. "We're going to the construction site up on Rocky Ridge Road."

"Sure thing," the driver said. "I know it, and it's looking so good."

"Thank you," Suzie said, joining Alicia on the back seat.

"How much does a place like that go for?" he asked as Mandie took the last remaining seat in the car.

Mandie glanced down to Alicia. "We're not sure what our boss will list it for."

"Lots of money on Rocky Ridge," the man said, easing away from the curb. "Folks from Nantucket and the city have second homes here, that kind of thing."

"Yes," Mandie said, and Alicia let them chit-chat about things as he drove them the few minutes to the cove cottage.

She got out just as a couple of men loaded the construction tent into the back of a huge truck. Candace stood on the front porch, talking to Jake and Flint, but her eyes immediately came to Alicia's.

She smiled and lifted her hand in a wave as the others joined her, and then she said, "Here we go," as she took the first step toward the porch.

"What are you going to tell her about the windows?" Suzie hissed, surely without moving her lips. Alicia wasn't sure, because she didn't dare look away from Candace.

The woman was as unreadable as a blank page, and her expression didn't change, nor did she break eye contact with Alicia.

"She's going to fire me," she muttered.

"No," Mandie said softly but with plenty of force. "Because those windows are going to be here today, and we'll have them installed before we leave this place tonight."

Alicia prayed she was right, and she turned as the truck got started and the roar of the engine filled the air. They hadn't finished cleaning up the front yard of all the supply tarps and tools, and they shouldn't be leaving yet.

She watched as the truck left the driveway, and then she saw why.

A bigger truck sat just out of the way of the first, this one with the words *Trucker Transportation* on it.

"The windows," she said, every muscle in her body sagging in relief. "You guys, that's the delivery company who has our windows."

And she meant "ours" in the best way possible. Yes, she'd insisted on the stained glass windows, and each of them had borne some stress over them. She knew they'd make this cottage into a showstopper, and she'd forgotten the excitement and joy of them until this moment.

Mandie squealed and turned to watch the window delivery truck start the turn into the driveway. Alicia joined her, linking one arm through hers and the other through Suzie's as she came to her side.

"I'm going to split the commission on the sale with both of you," Mandie said.

Alicia sucked in a breath and switched her gaze from the slats holding her prized windows to Mandie. "You can't do that."

"I can, and I am." Mandie nodded decisively. "It's one of the things I'm going to talk to Candace about tonight when we meet."

Alicia looked over to her and squeezed her arm. Mandie looked past her to Suzie. "I'm quitting, Suze. This is it for me, and I thought waiting for a baby for over a year was the hardest thing I'd ever done, but this is going to be so much worse."

"Alicia," Candace called behind her, but Alicia didn't look away from Suzie.

Her jaw hardened, and she nodded in curt, little bursts. "I knew it," she said. "I hate it, and I didn't want it to be true, but I knew."

Mandie stepped past her and hugged Suzie. She drew a

deep breath and faced the house, faced Candace. "She has to know too, right?"

"I'm sure she does," Alicia said as she turned and started walking again. "But she'll want to hear it from you, just like she's going to make me account for every penny of this place, and if we can't get that wallpaper to shine like gold...I might not have a job after this either."

Chapter Twenty

Candace smothered the smile threatening to explode onto her face as her team came toward her.

The change in their demeanors after seeing that delivery truck made this trip worth it. One-hundred percent, absolutely.

She'd hoped for exactly that when she'd sent the truck down the lane a half-hour ago, knowing Mandie, Suzie, and Alicia would be arriving together soon enough. She'd wanted to see their expressions when they thought the windows weren't here yet, and she wasn't happy.

And now?

They came forward with grins, laughing, and Mandie herself came jogging up the few steps to the porch first. "So," she said. "What do you think?"

"I think the transformation of this place is nothing short of miraculous." Candace turned and looked up at the ceiling of the overhang above her. "I think I want a cup of coffee here every morning, and I think if that were my reality, I'd never leave."

She reached for Mandie and drew her into a light hug. The moment immediately turned awkward, because when had Candace ever hugged an employee, let alone this one?

But she'd been stepping outside her bounds of normal since Lana had entered her life, and she loved this team. Smiling, she stepped back and drew Alicia to her. "Relieved to see the windows?"

"Yes," she said with a laugh. "You have no idea."

Candace thought she had some idea, but she simply laughed too. When she pulled back this time, she exhaled too. "You have done an amazing job here, Alicia."

"Thank you," she said kindly, and Candace appreciated the strength of their relationship.

She focused on Suzie. "And I hear you're here before Jake and after Jake, and I'm going to *insist* you take all of next week off."

"What?" Suzie asked, and Candace wasn't the only one who laughed as she drew Suzie into a light embrace too. "I can't—"

"You can," Candace said firmly as she stepped back. "In fact, I have something for you." She nodded over to Jake, who grinned like a madman as he handed Suzie an envelope.

Yes, Candace had to get up before the sun to get here and make these arrangements, but every single one of them was worth it.

"What is this?" Suzie demanded.

"Hey, I didn't get a gift," Mandie said. "So I'd just open it and be grateful." She grinned and settled her weight on her back leg as she folded her arms.

Suzie threw a scowl in her direction and then ripped open the envelope. She pulled out a ticket and stared at it. "I'm...going back to the city?"

"Tomorrow morning," Candace said smoothly. Suzie looked at her, those blue eyes filled with surprise. "Daniel is expecting you, and I believe Mandie's mother will be there this weekend to go over a few things for your wedding."

"What?" Suzie asked again, this time the word falling from her mouth in a near-gasp.

"You may return to the site on Monday, August eighteenth," Candace said, turning back to the front door. "Now, I'd like a walk-through and explanation of some of the finer details I don't know about."

Suzie scoffed behind her. "The eighteenth," she said, and since Candace had booked the tickets and contacted both Robin Grover and Daniel, she knew the next twelve days would be taken care of for Suzie.

"I don't believe there are details you don't know about," Mandie said.

"Explain them to Flint, then," Candace said, shooting her a look as she joined her in the living room. "We'll want him to get the specific shots for the gala you need."

"Yes, of course," Alicia said. "In here, we have a wonderful textured wallpaper on the feature wall." She faced the front wall, which held the door and two large windows that overlooked the porch and what would be the lawn beyond.

"It has roses woven throughout, as we learned from Connor that Denise loved roses and grew them here." She moved over to it and ran her fingertips lightly along it. Candace had done the same when she'd arrived earlier. "It has gold thread embedded in the petals, and once we get the stained glass in and the afternoon sun begins to set, this room will be set ablaze."

"I certainly hope so," Candace said. "Tell me about this paint color choice."

"We went with taupe," Mandie said. "To match the wallpaper, of course, but also to mimic the lighter sands found here in the cove. It's meant to represent the beach."

"Taupe is not as popular as gray."

"And the cove cottage is not meant to look like every other house." Mandie pulled in a slight breath a moment later. "It's perfectly aligned with the flooring, which also bears a lighter finish than other modern homes."

"The white pine is classic of coastal communities," Suzie added. "Such as those in Vermont and Maine and even Nantucket."

"As are the white cedar shingles on the exterior," Alicia said, almost as if this trio had orchestrated and practiced this dialogue. Which, Candace would not put past them. In fact, she quite expected it from them.

They paused on the cusp of the kitchen, as the construction crew had brought in the first window and were now lifting it into place. "The carving in the knobs?"

"Suzie?" Alicia prompted.

"Yes, they're horned larks," Suzie said. "They're the only native lark to North America, prominent here in the cove, Nantucket, and Cape Cod. We found a ceramic tile with a lark on it, and Connor said that was a Williams family crest."

She moved a few steps to the first bank of cabinets, where she lovingly touched the knob there. "I found an amazing carver here in the cove, down on Pearl Island, and he had the most intricate saws. He did the larks on all the knobs, which we did in a darker wood to draw out the design and highlight the lark."

"They're stunning," Candace said. "A truly custom piece." She smiled as Suzie lifted her eyes to meet Candace's.

"Thank you," she said. "I think they're one of my favorite things about any house I've worked on."

And Suzie had been with PastForward for fifteen years now. Candace threw a look over to Mandie, as she had a dinner meeting with the woman and her husband that night. She knew what Mandie wanted to talk about—leaving the company—though she hadn't explicitly stated as much.

"We'll have the landscapers here on Monday," Mandie said. "They're still working on the deck and staircase down to the sand, but we fully expect to finish that before our September fifth gala."

"Did that date get approved?" Suzie asked.

"Yes," Mandie said. "Sorry, I thought I texted that out."

"To be fair, I texted her late last night." Candace smiled to her team lead. "As I was on my way here, actually."

"You came in last night?" Alicia asked.

"Show me upstairs," Candace said, though she'd been up there. But it didn't take long to install three windows, and she wanted to see the magnificence of them before she left the site. "And yes, there's no way I could've gotten here ahead of you if I'd flown in this morning."

"You can on the steamer," Mandie said. "It runs from here on Rocky Ridge to New York Harbor."

Candace blinked at her. "And you're just now telling me this?"

Mandie grinned at her. "Would you have ridden a ferry for almost three hours?"

"Daniel's done it once," Suzie said. "He prefers the flight, actually."

Mandie gestured toward her as if to say, *That's why I*

didn't tell you. Then she led the way upstairs, talking about the new location of the steps and how much more open the bottom floor was.

Candace did love the new floorplan and how she could see from front to back and out both sides of the house from the main room. "We can come back to the master suite once those windows are in."

"The view up here is better anyway," Alicia said as she arrived in the loft. Candace loved touring homes, old, new and everywhere in between. In rundown dwellings, she only felt the immense possibilities of a place. Watching her teams pull down the old and renew it, breathe new life into it, brought her so much satisfaction.

And of course, seeing the final product brought a rush like nothing else. It was the whole reason Candace had started PastForward in the first place—that finished product, that culminating experience she could sell to someone ready to make more memories in a place once forgotten.

She stood in the upstairs loft and watched Jake and his crew set the second window. "Talk to me about landscaping out front," she said.

"We're doing coastal gardens," Alicia said. "To match the stained glass, actually."

"Beach roses," Mandie said. "That speak to the wallpaper. Ornamental grasses that also mimic the beach landscape."

"With native shrubs to go with the mature trees here."

Candace nodded at Suzie, the functionality of this team off the charts. They each knew everything, and Candace attributed that to Mandie and her willingness to include everyone as an equal.

She made a mental note of that, because as she continued

training the team leads at PastForward, she wanted them to act like Mandie.

"They're setting the last window," she said. "Let's go see if the hearth can hold four people." She smiled at her team, and this time, she led them down the steps in her heels.

The fireplace sat on the south wall, with gorgeous stone in browns and oranges that would surely flicker with faux-firelight once that sun came into the room.

Candace sat right on the end, and she let the other three women crowd onto the slab of stone too. They did all fit, and she smiled down the row at each of them. "I hope I can invite each of you to Lana's wedding."

"Of course," Alicia said, ever the diplomatic one.

"I'd love that," Mandie gushed in her usual fashion.

Suzie took a moment and nodded. "Yes, that would be great."

Candace acknowledged them. "She's hoping Bradley will be here to walk her down the aisle, but I told her she shouldn't count on him." She sighed and looked at her hands folded in her lap. "She has a real father, and I said she should ask him."

"Oh." Alicia glanced at Mandie. "That's probably best."

"Her dad would want to, wouldn't he?" Mandie asked.

"Of course he does," Candace said. "Lana is a bit... romantic, though. She loves her parents, but she has this excitement over me and Bradley she shouldn't. I'm working on it with her." She nodded, because she didn't always get very personal with her employees. These ladies, though, had carved their way into more than her professional life.

"And, I think you three should know I started a mentoring program at PastForward, and I'd like you to be involved, if possible." She deliberately didn't look at Mandie.

Alicia's sky-high eyebrows were enough.

"A mentoring program?" Suzie asked. "What could I possibly contribute to that?"

"Suze, come on," Mandie said almost under her breath. "You're an amazing worker, and if there's someone who knows more about how to do research than you, I'll...I'll eat my hat."

She nodded, and a beat of silence filled the cottage before Candace burst out laughing. "You'll what?" she asked through her giggles.

Alicia laughed too, and even Suzie smiled.

"It's about helping out some of our newer employees," Candace said after sobering. "Trying to give them situations and examples of how to act on jobsites, decisions that need to be made in high-stress scenarios before they get there, to assess their skills."

She looked down to Suzie on the end. "Your research is impeccable, by the way. And helping someone learn those skills before they're out in the field would be an excellent way to contribute to the mentorship program."

"I'm glad you thought of such a program," Alicia said. "I can help with whatever you need."

Candace watched her for a moment, completely aware of the lines around her eyes and the way she worked seventy hours a week. "I think I'd like to work with you too," she said. "On work-life balance, something I've been really striving for myself in the past year. With Gray and Lily, I don't want you to do more. I want you to do less."

Alicia's eyes filled with tears that Candace didn't quite understand. She nodded, and Mandie took her hand and squeezed it. "She just misses the kids."

"Where are the kids?" Candace asked, surprised.

"In New York," Alicia said. "We're moving in with Henry, and that means the kids will go to a new school this fall. It's registration this week, so Henry took them to the city."

She wiped her eyes quickly and took a deep breath, obviously using it to center herself.

"So you'll be on Suzie's flight tomorrow too," Candace said.

Alicia blinked at her as Mandie's smile widened. "I get the day off too, right?" She grinned at Candace, something powerful moving between them. This understanding that Candace thought she'd never achieve with someone like Mandie.

Someone so unlike herself.

"Yes, everyone is taking the weekend off." She smiled at her team. "And Suzie, back to your research—I had the woman I'm mentoring right now look into Mark Adams and Denise Williams. Anything and everything she could find. Any new people who'd showed up around that time in Massachusetts, New York, Vermont, Maine, or Maryland. New identities. Their social security numbers being used. Any money moving. Anything she could find."

Suzie's face lit up. "And?"

Candace suspected Suzie had done the same, though she'd stayed silent about it at Mandie's request and Candace's endorsement of that request.

"And nothing." Candace lifted her hands and let them fall. "She couldn't find anything to indicate they assumed alternate identities."

Suzie's countenance dimmed. "Yeah, I couldn't either. She probably died in the storm."

"Mark Adams is a very common name," Candace said.

"But we did find a record of him in Toronto. He died in early 2011. Emma believes it's the same Mark Adams."

"But no record of her?"

"No, sadly." Candace offered Suzie a small smile. "Perhaps this story is just as Connor Williams told it."

She nodded. "Yes, it seems so. I still love reading the letters."

Alicia patted her hand. "We know you do, and that's why you're amazing, Suze."

"All right," Jake said. He clapped his hands. "Who wants to come pass off these windows?"

Alicia got to her feet. "That would be me." She went with the construction manager, and Candace enjoyed basking in the sunlight pouring into the house. She too got to her feet and moved over to the entryway of the kitchen.

Three magnificent stained glass panels caught the sunlight, transforming it into rivers of sapphire, emerald, and gold that danced across the interior walls and floor.

Yes, in the afternoon, this would get thrown onto that front wall, and she could already imagine the way the colored light would create a gold symphony of light against the wallpaper and the honey-colored hardwood.

"This is extraordinary," she said as she gazed up at the windows, which bore the blue water of the ocean, the darker, sandy beach, and glorious greens in the dry beach grasses. "The renditions didn't capture the full impact."

With the open floor plan flowing seamlessly from living area to kitchen, and the restored fireplace serving as a natural focal point, those stained glass windows definitely added the crown this jewel of a cottage needed.

"Ladies, if I could get you to vacate the area," Flint said, his camera gear strapped over both shoulders.

"Let's go," Candace said. "I need to get back to my hotel for a meeting, and I believe some of you have some packing to do."

THE SALTWATER TABLE PERCHED ON A BLUFF overlooking Diamond Island's harbor, its deck offering panoramic views of boats bobbing at their moorings. Candace sipped her wine at the corner table that provided privacy while still allowing her to watch the beachgoers from above.

She noted the date of Lana's first dress appointment in the city, and ignored Bradley's text about another business trip. She wasn't his secretary, and he didn't need to account his time to her.

Thankfully, Lana had arranged for her father—the man who loved her and raised her—to walk her down the aisle.

She took another sip of wine, contemplating how some people chose to stay and others chose to leave.

"Yes, that's her."

She looked up as Mandie and Charlie approached the table, their hands linked and their faces wearing matching expressions of nervous determination. Charlie looked exactly like what he was: a devoted husband supporting his wife through a difficult conversation.

"Thank you for meeting us," Mandie said as they settled into their chairs. "This is a lovely table." She glanced out at the water, and Candace smiled at the waves too, then over to Charlie.

"Have you two been here before?"

"No," Charlie said. "There's so many new places in the cove from when we lived here last."

"I'll bet." Candace lifted her wine glass. "Are you drinking?"

"No, thank you," Mandie said, and Charlie shook his head. "I'd take some ginger ale, though."

A waiter appeared at their table, and the two of them put in their drink orders. Candace watched them, noting how Mandie settled into herself fairly quickly and a slip of gladness moved through Candace.

"Should we get the hard stuff out of the way?" Candace asked. "Then we might be able to enjoy the view, the food, and the company."

Mandie met her gaze and nodded, sudden and pure terror entering her expression. "I think you probably know that I'm—the cove cottage is my last project with PastForward." She glanced over to Charlie. "Charlie has an amazing job and we just bought a house here."

Candace nodded, pure resignation settling in her stomach. "I have wondered."

Mandie still looked like she might throw up, and Candace had seen this exact expression on the young woman's face before. "What else?" she asked.

She again glanced at Charlie. "There's—" But she didn't go on to deny there was anything else.

Candace offered her the warmest smile she had. "I know you, Mandie Kelton. You're this fierce woman who marched into my office after asking for a few minutes during a meeting where everyone else looked like you'd just committed career suicide. And you said what was on your mind. You're wearing that same look, so I know there's still something on your mind."

She swallowed, and she and Charlie had a quick conversation without words. Mandie relaxed in every way, her smile soft and beautiful as she said, "Charlie and I are going to have a baby," she whispered.

Tears filled her own eyes, an emotional response that would have terrified her a year ago. Now it felt natural, appropriate, like the only possible reaction to watching someone she cared about step into their future.

"I'm so happy for you," she said, her voice thick with emotion. She didn't need to hide this from either of the people across from her. She wiped her eyes quickly. "Both of you. You've both worked incredibly hard to be here, to create this life that matters, in a place you love."

She reached across the table to cover Mandie's free hand with her own. "When I was your age, I thought success meant choosing career over everything else. I gave up the chance to raise my daughter, because I believed I couldn't have both."

Mandie's tears spilled over, and Charlie passed her a napkin from the dispenser.

"But you're not me," Candace continued. "You're making a different choice, a *better* choice. You're choosing love and family and the kind of life that actually matters."

She nodded and shook her head. "I swear it's just hormones."

"And my wife needs to know that she's making the right choice," Charlie said, watching her.

Candace smiled at her. "You're brilliant, Mandie. You're capable of anything you set your mind to. But right now, you're choosing to focus on growing a family and building a home. That's absolutely the right choice for you."

She nodded and pressed the napkin to her eyes. "I think you're right."

"We haven't told anyone else yet," Charlie said.

"It's still early," Mandie said. "I know you won't say anything to my parents or anything."

Being included touched Candace more deeply than she'd expected. "Of couse not. When are you due?"

"April," Mandie said. "Right around the time the cottage will be featured in all those magazines."

"Perfect timing," Candace said. "You'll be able to see your work celebrated while you're preparing for your next adventure."

Mandie got up and came around the table to hug her. "Thank you for everything. For taking a chance on me, for teaching me so much, for understanding about this."

Candace held her tightly, breathing in the faint scent of her shampoo and committing the moment to memory. "Thank you for showing me what courage looks like."

Some things, Candace had learned—like babies and families and having true friendships, were more important than business.

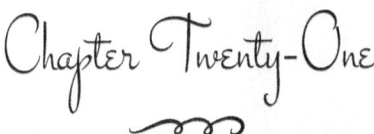

Chapter Twenty-One

S uzie traced her finger along the edge of Daniel's dining table, admiring the way the afternoon light caught the polished mahogany surface. His apartment possessed the kind of understated elegance she'd never thought to want for herself—exposed brick walls, tall windows overlooking a tree-lined street, built-in bookshelves that stretched from floor to ceiling.

The space felt like Daniel himself: thoughtful, warm, substantial without being showy.

"She should be here any minute," Daniel said, emerging from the kitchen with a tray of pastries from the bakery downstairs. The whole place smelled like coffee, as Daniel drank the stuff all day, and especially when expecting guests.

And Robin would be here any minute.

He'd changed into a navy button-down that brought out the color of his eyes, and his hair still held the slight dampness from his shower. "I'll be right back with the milk and sugar."

"Okay." Suzie smoothed her hands down the front of her

dress, one of the few she owned. The soft fabric felt foreign against her skin, but in a good way, like she was trying on a new version of herself and finding it fit better than expected.

"I'm kind of excited," she said, settling into one of the chairs as Daniel returned to the kitchen for the coffee service. "Planning a real wedding, with real flowers, and real people."

He returned and Suzie smiled up at him. "What are we going to do next week?" she asked. She couldn't believe Candace had banned her from the jobsite for twelve full days.

She could admit she'd enjoyed meeting Daniel after coming off the plane, for once, and she'd loved coming home to this apartment with him.

Daniel set the tray down and moved to sit beside her. "Whatever you want. I have the week off too."

Suzie reached over to take his hand in hers. She stroked her fingers down his long ones, this sense of nostalgia and fondness so amazing and becoming less and less strange the more she embraced it.

"I think maybe we could do a little work."

"You're joking."

A grin burst onto her face. "What would you say if I said I wanted to move in with you?"

His hand around hers tightened. "Now I know you're joking."

"I'm not."

He put his other hand under her chin and lifted her face to be level with his. "I would be the happiest man in the world if you moved in with me."

Suzie smiled at him, let her eyes drift closed, and kissed him. "I love you," she whispered.

"I love you too."

Suzie ducked her head again, this time tucking her face

against his chest. "So after we do that—and it'll be a lot of work, because I've lived in my apartment for a long time—we should go by my grandmother's house and see about putting it up for sale."

"You *are* going to work me next week." Daniel put his arms around her and held her within the safety of his embrace. "And I'm here for it."

His buzzer rang, and the moment broke. Suzie let him go get the door, and Robin arrived a few minutes later. Suzie got to her feet to greet her, and Robin smiled for all she was worth as she stepped past Daniel with a, "Hey, you two," as if they were old friends.

She carried a briefcase bag that bulged on the sides, and Daniel took it from her before she stepped into Suzie to hug her.

Suzie had never been a big hugger, but the concept was definitely growing on her. She actually did crave the human touch, and she leaned into Robin and took a deep breath of the woman's cottony, fruity perfume.

"It's great to see you," she said. "Thanks for coming to the city."

"I'm actually scouting a dress for another client," she said. "So this was perfect." She looked at the pastries and coffee on the table, her eyes coming back to Suzie's. "Did you get these at Maughan's?"

"Yes," Daniel said. "I think Suzie wants to move in with me just to be closer to that bakery." He chuckled as he picked up the tray. "We've got their raspberry bread pudding, the mint brownie, and the orange vanilla bean tart."

"I'm going to need one of each," Robin said as she sat in the armchair.

"Coffee?" Suzie asked, this role of hostess almost as natural as others she'd played in her life.

"Absolutely," Robin said as she plucked a brownie from the tray to start. "So you two don't live together right now?"

"Not yet," Suzie said, almost hedging things.

"I find with Suzie," Daniel said, offering her the tray. She took a jar of the bread pudding, though she wouldn't be able to eat it until she'd seen more of what Robin had promised to show them.

Her texts had used words like "spectacular" and "it'll blow your mind," and Suzie didn't like surprises.

"That I have to ask her several times before she believes I'm truly asking for what I want."

She gave him a quick look, though she couldn't argue with him. "I'm moving in here next week, actually," she said.

Robin nodded and reached for a mug. "Where are you now?" She started to pour the coffee.

"I've got a place in Hell's Kitchen," she said. "This place is much nicer, the neighborhood is far quieter, and there is that bakery…" She grinned at Robin as she put a spoonful of sugar in her coffee.

"And then there's the fact that Daniel's here." She took his hand as he sat next to her again.

"Is this SoHo?" Robin asked. "Or Greenwich Village?"

"We're right on the border," Daniel said. "But the building is in SoHo."

"It's a lovely place." She took a sip of her coffee and then set down her mug. "All right. Do you want to see some of my ideas for the dinner and reception?"

Suzie set down her jar of bread pudding. "Yes, please."

Robin reached into her bag and pulled out a folder. She spread photographs across the table like a dealer laying out cards. Images of ceremony spaces with cream fabrics, tall floral arrangements, and elegant table settings bloomed before Suzie's eyes.

"I know you said weren't fussy," Robin said. "But *sophisticated* comes to mind every time we talk about what you want and don't want." She pointed to a picture of a gorgeous staircase draped in ivory fabric, with softly flowing ribbons at each high point.

"There's a beautiful staircase in the museum, and it would make an excellent focal point for the aisle as it flows right into the Grand Hall." She put another picture on top of the first. "We can do fabric and ribbon décor, or something with flowers."

Suzie pulled in a breath and leaned closer, the staircase boasting blooms in ivory, beige, and pale pink absolutely stealing her breath.

"I think I know which one," Robin said, whisking away those pictures. She put another one down. "Now, are you looking for subtle sophistication?"

She let the photo of mostly white and pale-colored flowers enhanced with greenery sit there long enough for Suzie to look at her. "Or statement sophistication?"

Robin put down another picture beside the new one, this one with bright pink, blazing orange, and fabulous ivory flowers. The blooms were bigger, bolder, louder, and wonderful in their own way.

"Number one," Suzie said.

Robin nodded and pointed to the table settings. "Ivory linens, a pale blue charger, and crystal. It's classic, and timeless, and clean."

"She likes clean," Daniel said. "It's beautiful."

"We'll go with that one." Robin removed that photo too.

"I always advocate for tall floral arrangements," she said. "Wedding spaces are so big, and it helps fill them, and you can talk to everyone at the table without having to try to see past the décor."

"I've never seen anything like that," Suzie said.

"The height will be determined by where you want to eat dinner after the ceremony." She put out a few more pictures. "The harbor view room seats up to two hundred guests, with floor-to-ceiling windows overlooking the water. This is a huge room that will feel empty unless we fill it with people."

Suzie shook her head. No way she could fill a room that big with people she wanted at her wedding.

"The ship gallery is more intimate, with a maximum of eighty-nine people, but the backdrop is incredible."

Suzie glanced at Daniel. Eighty-nine seemed like a lot, but he did have parents and siblings, cousins and aunts and uncles.

"What's the third option?" Daniel asked, leaning forward to examine the photographs.

"The rooftop deck." Robin's eyes lit up as she pulled out another set of images. "It's seasonal, obviously, but for a May wedding, it would be available if wanted. You'd have the entire Manhattan skyline as your backdrop, with the harbor stretching out below."

Suzie's breath caught as she looked at the photographs. The deck stretched across the museum's top floor, with glass railings that wouldn't obstruct the view and space for both ceremony and reception. String lights crisscrossed overhead, and planters filled with greenery softened the urban setting.

"That one," she said without hesitation. "That's where I want to get married."

Daniel leaned back and put his arm around her "You're

sure? I think she's just talking about dinner, sweetheart." He raised his eyebrows at Robin.

She nodded. "I suppose you could get married up there, but we'd then need to flip the space if you want dinner served there too, and everything would have to be moved if the weather is bad."

"We want the Grand Hall for the ceremony," Daniel said. "It's got that stained glass you like, Suze."

"Yes," she said. "But I love the idea of having dinner outside."

"It will be more casual," Robin said, and she reached into her bag for another folder. She set out more photos, these with more rustic décor, like lanterns, and unfinished wood slabs, and pampas grass in tall, skinny vases.

Suzie didn't like any of it much at all, and she wrinkled her nose.

"I think you're more classic, traditional elegance than you think," Robin said. She smiled at Suzie and cocked her head. "Tell me I'm wrong."

"I don't think you're wrong," Suzie said, almost confused. "I've just never thought of myself as elegant before."

"It's what you're drawn to, though," Robin said. "I've seen the projects you and Mandie and Alicia work on. They're made of sophistication and elegance. You're *steeped* in it."

"I suppose so," Suzie said. "I guess I'm just not an elegant person."

"You will be in a wedding gown," Robin said. "It's a magical day, Suzie." She tapped the photo of the ship galley. "I think this one. It's smaller and will create that intimacy without losing a single ounce of grandeur."

Suzie looked at Daniel, and he gazed back. "I think she's probably right."

"I think so too," he said, and Robin swept those pictures away.

"Okay," she said. "Now, I want you to look me in the eye and tell me you don't want a wedding cake."

Daniel started to chuckle, but Suzie didn't understand what was so funny. She looked Robin right in the eye and repeated something she'd texted to her previously. "I don't want a wedding cake. I don't even like cake."

"Okay," Robin said without missing a beat. "I just needed to hear you and see you say it. No wedding cake." She made a quick note. "I like that you're so decisive, Suzie. It makes my job so much easier."

Suzie nodded, because making decisions had never been a difficult thing for her. Letting her feelings dictate those decisions...well, she was still working on that.

"Let's talk about the wedding party," she said.

"I'll have three bridesmaids," Suzie said. "Mandie, Alicia, and Daniel's sister, Sarah." She glanced over to Daniel. "Daniel is going to have his brother, Stephen, and his brother-in-law, Carson, and one of his friends from work, Alex."

"Will we be getting them bouquets and boutonnieres?"

Suzie blinked back at her. "Yes?" she guessed.

Robin grinned and made another note. "And the family traditionally wears flowers as well." She glanced over to Daniel. "So any other brothers or in-laws who need a flower? Parents?"

"My mom and dad," he said. "My brother's wife, Teresa." He looked at Suzie while Robin made more notes. "I think my grandmother might come from Buffalo, but I'm not sure. I don't have any other grandparents."

"What about your family, Suzie? Parents, siblings, extended family?"

The familiar tightness settled in Suzie's chest, but it felt different now—acknowledgment rather than pain. "No, no one for me."

"I'm sorry," Robin said, her voice gentle.

"It's okay." Suzie realized she meant it. "I have Daniel's family, and I have friends who've become family."

Daniel squeezed her hand, and she saw understanding in his eyes. He'd never pushed her to talk about her childhood, never tried to fix the parts of her past that couldn't be repaired. Instead, he'd simply loved her as she was and helped her see that family could be chosen as well as inherited.

"All right," Robin said. "The last thing is the menu." She tucked all her photos away and reached back into her bag. A wide binder came out this time, and she held it to her chest. "I don't want you to get overwhelmed, okay?"

Suzie swallowed and looked away from the binder. "Okay."

"We're going to start with you telling me your favorite food. Let's say you were planning the party Mandie is, and you got to serve dinner—anything you wanted. What would it be?"

She glanced over to Daniel. She'd never planned to get married, and hadn't really saved for such an occasion. She did have some inheritance money, and she thought of Mandie's promised to split the commission on the cove cottage.

"Steak and seafood," she said.

Robin opened the binder and took out a small portion of it. "Dessert?"

Suzie looked at her jar of bread pudding. "Something more savory than cloyingly sweet."

Robin shuffled through a few plastic sleeves and extracted three. "One of these will be perfect then."

She placed them on the table, and Daniel picked them up and handed one to Suzie. They said nothing as they switched papers until they'd each read all three of them.

To Suzie, they looked the same. Sure, one had a crab Thermidor while another boasted a lobster tail with compound butter and the third listed shrimp scampi alongside a ribeye.

She handed the sheets back to Robin. "I don't know."

"I'd go with the steak and pasta," Daniel said.

"Great," Suzie said. "That sounds good."

Robin made a few more notes and then let out a sigh. "You guys, this wedding is going to be incredible." She started packing up, and Suzie stood when she did.

"Thank you for your help," she said.

"Of course," Robin said, giving her another hug. She shook Daniel's hand and vacated the apartment.

Suzie stood there, not quite sure what to do with herself now. Then Daniel's hand found hers, and she became anchored to herself, to him, and to reality.

She turned into his arms, breathing in the familiar scent of his cologne mixed with coffee. In a few months, she'd wake up in his apartment every morning, surrounded by his books and his warmth and the life they were building together.

The woman who'd been too scared to set a wedding date had become someone who could plan a future, who could trust in love enough to promise forever, who could choose to build rather than tear down.

"I love you," she said against his chest, the words carrying more weight than usual.

"I love you too." He pulled back to look at her face, his eyes warm with affection and something deeper. "Ready to start the rest of our lives?"

Suzie looked only into his eyes, into the space where she'd learned to believe in herself and in love.

"I'm ready," she said, and she meant it completely.

Chapter Twenty-Two

A licia stood at the back door of the cove cottage, her hand resting on the freshly painted white trim as she gazed out at the completed deck. The honeyed wood shone in the morning light, sealed and ready for its next family of adventures.

"Lish, have you seen these flower beds?" Mandie called from inside the cottage. "Come see how the beach roses look against the new shutters."

Alicia turned back into the kitchen, where Suzie stood running her fingers along the sage green cabinet doors one final time. The carved lark knobs caught the morning light streaming through the stained glass, each tiny bird appearing ready to take flight.

"I can't believe it's actually finished," Suzie said, her voice carrying a note of wonder that Alicia had never heard from her before. "Well, except for the back landscaping, but Jake said that'll be done in time."

"The steps are finished too," Alicia said, actually stepping onto the deck now. A gate at the back led to the new wooden staircase, which wound down to the black sand beach. The railings curved gracefully, following the natural contours of the cliff, and each step had been crafted to weather whatever storms might come. "We should check them out."

"Let me get Mandie. She's enamored with the roses," Suzie said dryly. "As if we've never seen roses before." She walked away, her heavy work boots thudding on the beautiful deck.

Alicia simply smiled out at the water. She hadn't been down to the black sand beach—not one time—and while she'd be back at the cottage before the gala, she wanted to feel the heat of it between her toes.

Behind her, Mandie and Suzie bickered in that endearing way they had, but Alicia just let the beachy breeze play with her hair. Once upon a time, she might have tried to play interference, just to make sure they could stay unified as a team.

She now knew how Suzie and Mandie worked together, and their back-and-forth wasn't malicious or bad.

A few moments later, footsteps came outside again, and Mandie appeared at her side, her tablet tucked under one arm and a measuring tape in her free hand. "We deserve a whole day on the beach, don't we?"

She sighed afterward, and Alicia looked over to her. Her face held plenty of color this morning, though the hottest summer weather in Five Island Cove had already started to wane. Bright patches of red sat in her cheeks, but she looked as beautiful as ever as she smiled at Alicia.

She'd been a little bit all over the map in the past few weeks, but tensions and emotions ran high near the end of a project. Alicia knew that all too well.

"We sure do," Alicia said as she focused on the ocean

again. "In fact, I'm going to tell Candace I'd like more of an office role once I get back o the city."

"You are?" Suzie asked.

Alicia pressed her lips together, the familiar indecision already warring inside her. Perhaps because of the incredulity in Suzie's voice. Perhaps because she'd worked hard and fought for her field team position. Perhaps because life seemed to be one constant back-and-forth about what the right thing was.

"Yes," she said. "I'm married now, and I can't keep dumping my children on Henry."

"You haven't done that," Mandie said. "You're married now, like you said, and raising kids is a shared responsibility."

"They're not Henry's kids."

"He loves them like they are," Suzie said quietly. "But I get it. This work we do...it's not for people who have others who need their time and energy."

"Does that mean—?"

"Let's go down to the beach," Suzie said, cutting off Mandie before she could get the question all the way out.

"All right," Mandie said, her voice pitching up. "Let's go."

Neither Suzie nor Mandie moved, so Alicia reached to open the gate. She started down the steps, the others coming with her.

"How many steps did it end up being?" Suzie asked.

"Fifty-four," Mandie said instantly.

Alicia could've answered the question too, but she didn't feel much like talking today. She wasn't sure why. She loved the ladies descending the cliff with her, and they'd never irritated her too badly.

She simply had her thoughts directing inward. It helped

that she had to truly focus on her steps as she went down, so she didn't stumble or roll an ankle.

The sound of waves grew louder as she approached the beach, and the tang of salt air intensified. The sun glinted off the black sand in a blinding way, and Alicia reached up and flipped her sunglasses down over her eyes from where they'd been resting on her head.

"It's so bright," Suzie complained, which only made Alicia smile.

"But look at this view." Alicia breathed out fully as she stepped off the bottom step and onto the black sand. Heat lifted from it, and it stretched left and right, scattered with smooth stones and pieces of driftwood.

She moved out of the way and turned to look over her shoulder. The cliffs rose straight into the air, a dark gray streaked with white, and the cottage perched above them like a beacon, its white walls and blue shutters a perfect complement to the natural landscape.

"Wow," Suzie said, walking closer to the water. "This is incredible."

Down the beach a ways, a couple of people walked, but otherwise, this beach wasn't filled with tourists or locals.

"It's private property," Mandie said as she came to stand beside Alicia. "You can go to the black sand beach on the south side of the island, near the ferry station. But not up here."

Alicia grinned at her and spread her arms wide. "It's incredible." She let the wind whip through her hair as she tipped her head back and closed her eyes against the sun-filled sky.

"I forgot how different black sand feels," Mandie said. "It holds the heat longer than regular beach sand."

Alicia watched Suzie, who'd kicked off her heavy boots and peeled back her socks. She now stood in the shallow surf where the ocean kissed the sand, and Alicia hastened to join her.

Once her shoes and socks had come off, she eased into the water too, the coolness of it meeting the warmth of the black sand. "This is luxury," she said.

"The gala guests are going to love this," Mandie said from behind them. A few seconds later, she joined them in her bare feet too. "We're going to let them come down here, right?"

"In controlled groups," Alicia said. "We don't want a lot of congestion on the stairs, and we want to keep track of people."

The gala would take place in the evening, and the last thing Alicia needed was losing a VIP guest during the culminating event of this project.

"We've got the caterers scheduled to set up appetizer stations throughout the kitchen and onto the deck, and people can put their name down with a hostess to come down to the beach for photos."

"What about the weather?" Suzie asked, moving to perch on a piece of driftwood that had been worn smooth by years of tides.

"September fifth should still be warm enough for an evening party," Alicia said. Heaven knew she'd checked the forecast every day for the past few days—the very moment Friday had come onto the fourteen-day forecast. "And there's still no indication of rain."

"It's going to be glorious," Mandie said, almost as a proclamation.

Alicia nodded, because they'd been over the details of the

gala a dozen times. She and Mandie had worked closely together to book the services they needed, and she'd spent the most time working on getting invites out to the right people here in the cove.

She drew in a deep breath and released it slowly, reluctant to leave this peaceful moment. In a few hours, she'd be on the ferry back to the city, back to the chaos of preparing Gray and Lily for their first day at a new school. "When do you head back, Suze?"

"The Sunday after the gala," Suzie said. "When I'm back in the office, I'll start working with that new mentee Candace mentioned. Emma? Apparently she's been researching historic preservation techniques, and Candace thinks I can help her understand the practical applications."

"You'll be great at that," Mandie said, looking over to Suzie, their earlier squabble a distant memory. "You have such a gift for seeing the potential in forgotten things."

Alicia watched Suzie's cheeks flush pink at the compliment, and she smiled at how much her friend had changed over the past couple of years. The woman who'd once kept to herself and avoided personal connections now glowed with confidence and purpose.

"What about you, Mandie?" Alicia asked. "Any plans after the gala? Are you going to look for another job here?"

Mandie set her tablet aside and wrapped her arms around her knees. "Charlie and I are going to spend some time getting the house organized. And I need to call my doctor about..." She trailed off, glancing between her friends. Mandie drew a deep breath, her smile becoming radiant. "About my pregnancy. Charlie and I are going to have a baby."

Alicia's heart swelled with joy and something deeper, a

recognition of how much had changed for all of them. "Mandie, that's wonderful news." She stepped over to her best friend and hugged her. "I'm thrilled for you."

"When are you due?" Suzie joined them, wrapping her arms around them both and causing Mandie to stumble slightly.

Alicia started to giggle, and she shifted her feet to make their hug a three-way instead of a Suzie-bear-hold.

"April," Mandie said, her hand moving instinctively to her stomach, which looked normal to Alicia. "I'm just starting to have a little baby bump, and we're going to tell our parents this weekend."

"Amazing," Suzie said.

Alicia knew she thought she was too old to have children, but plenty of women had children in their early forties. With that thought, Alicia realized she and Henry could have a baby together, and she wondered if he even wanted that.

She'd ask him when she got back to the city tonight.

She sat in comfortable silence with Mandie and Suzie, watching the waves roll onto the black sand. Her heart-strings sang as she realized this would likely be their last quiet time together as a team. After the gala, they'd all return to their separate lives, their separate cities, their separate dreams.

"I'm going to miss this," she said finally. "Working with both of you, solving problems together, creating something beautiful from something forgotten."

"We'll stay in touch," Mandie said, though her voice carried the same wistfulness Alicia felt.

"Of course we will," Suzie added. "You're both invited to my wedding, remember? And I expect to meet this baby when he arrives."

"Me too," Alicia said. "I think you've told me it's beautiful in the cove in April."

Mandie grinned, her eyes bright. "It can be," she said. "You're both welcome anytime." She brushed at her eyes. "I didn't think this would be so hard, but it is."

Alicia moved over to her and linked her arm through Mandie's. "You're my favorite team lead I've ever worked for." She reached for Suzie. "And you're my favorite bulldozer-turned-friend I've ever had the pleasure to meet."

Suzie slid her hand into Alicia's, and the three of them looked out at the ocean. It continued to bob and weave, undulate and move, and the whole world seemed open in front of her. Everything felt huge in that moment, and they were just three tiny little figures standing on a black sand beach.

And it felt absolutely beautiful.

YONKERS FELT LIKE HOME IN A WAY ALICIA'S apartment in Queens never had, and it had nothing to do with the dwelling. No, this sense of home had everything to do with the man breathing softly and deeply at her side.

With the quiet stillness in the house before anyone had awakened yet, Alicia let the comfort and peace settle through her. After all, she figured she had only a few more minutes before Lily would burst through the door, all of her first-grade energy accompanying her.

Gray usually didn't have as much enthusiasm for getting up early and sitting in a desk all day, but because he was starting in a new school, Alicia expected him to be a bundle of nerves too.

She'd helped them pick their first-day-of-school clothes last night, and she'd taken the day off work to be able to walk them to school and pick them up afterward. She wanted to make them breakfast, and help them pack their lunches, and hear all about their new friends and teachers over dinner tonight.

She reached for her phone and silenced the alarm set to go off in three minutes. She lay there in the gray darkness for another moment, and then she peeled back the comforter and got up.

After pulling her hair into a messy ponytail, she padded out of the bedroom and down the hall to the kitchen. She flipped on lights and made coffee, then got out the carton of eggs and a gallon of milk.

She glanced at the clock, telling herself not to be too anxious. She and Henry had bought both kids an alarm clock, as they claimed to want to be able to get themselves up for school.

"That'll last about three days," she murmured to herself, and slip of fondness for her children moving through her. She heard footsteps as she cracked the first egg into a bowl.

"Mom," Gray said as he entered the kitchen. He threw his backpack onto the table unceremoniously. "Can we have pancakes?"

"Nope," she said cheerfully. She moved over to him and smoothed her hand over his hair. "We're having toast and eggs, remember?"

He didn't look happy about it, but he nodded. "We can have pancakes tomorrow, right?"

"Yep," she said. "What do you want for dinner tonight?" He'd lost the coin toss to choose first-day breakfast, but the loser got to choose dinner.

"I don't know," Gray said. "I don't know all the places around here yet."

"We can ask Henry," Alicia said.

"What are we asking Henry?" Henry grinned at her as he finished pulling his shirt over his head. He swept her into his arms, making her giggle, and kissed her. "Morning, you."

"Good morning to you too."

"Smells good out here." He moved away from her to pour himself a cup of coffee. "Gray, did you bring down your comb?"

"Yep." He reached into the back pocket of his shorts and pulled it out.

"Did you hear Lily up there?" Alicia asked.

"Yeah, she was in the bathroom." Gray went with Henry into the bathroom just off the kitchen, and she whisked the eggs and a touch of milk together as they talked in low voices.

Gray came out with perfectly combed hair, and Alicia smiled she loved him so much. "Come put your toast down," she said. She set a pan on the stove, put a bit of butter in, and lit the flame.

Then she moved to the bottom of the steps. "Lily-love. Are you coming?"

"Yes!" Lily yelled.

Well, she was awake. Alicia went back to the stove, and she poured the eggs into the pan, where they sizzled against the now-hot butter. She turned the flame to low and started pulling out the things they'd bought for the kids' lunches.

Granola bars. Baby carrots. Chocolate pudding cups. Bread and peanut butter. She turned to the fridge and got out the strawberry jam for Gray, and she set it on the counter at the same time Henry put the honey bear there for Lily.

She shared a glance with him, then her nose picked up

the scent of the eggs, and she spun back to the stove to get them scrambled.

Lily came thundering down the steps, her bright pink backpack on both shoulders. She wore the jean skirt and purple top they'd picked out, and she even had her shoes on already.

"Breakfast first," Alicia said. "We'll make your lunches afterward."

"Mama, I get to go to school all day today," Lily said.

"You sure do, baby." Alicia got down a few plates and set them on the island. Henry herded the kids to the table, where he moved Gray's backpack and got forks for everyone.

Alicia had just pulled the eggs off the flame when Gray's toast popped up, and she moved from one task to the next effortlessly.

Soon enough, she joined everyone at the table with her own piece of toast, noting that Henry had saved enough eggs for her. She knew realistically she wouldn't be able to eat a hot breakfast with the kids every day.

In fact, Alicia didn't normally eat breakfast at all. But this morning, she beamed around at everyone, this sense of feeling...normal descending on her. "Okay," she said. "Give me one thing you're going to do today."

"I'm going to make a new friend," Lily said. She'd probably make ten, and Alicia got up to get the spray bottle and comb so she could do Lily's hair while she ate.

"Gray?" she asked.

"I'm going to try to find someone to play basketball with at recess," he said.

"And you're both going to listen to your teachers, bring home all the papers they give you, and be your best selves."

Alicia finished with Lily's ponytail and moved over to the island to start making lunches. "Right?"

"Yes, Mama," Lily said.

"Yeah," Gray said.

She put together sandwiches and lunches, rushed down the hall to change into something other than pajamas, and soon enough, she tucked their lunchboxes in their backpacks. "It's time to go."

"Yay!" Lily skipped ahead to the front door, and she led the way out of the house and down the block.

Henry came to Alicia's side and took her hand while the kids walked ahead of them. "You didn't eat much."

She shook her head. "No."

"We can go get coffee after we drop them off," he said. "They'll have those lemon scones you like."

She grinned at him and kissed him quickly. He'd taken today off too, and honestly, Alicia wanted to make sure the kids got where they needed to go, get her coffee and lemon scone, and then lay in Henry's arms until school pick-up.

The walk to school took them through tree-lined streets filled with other families making the same journey. Gray's nervousness seemed to ease as he spotted other children his age, and Lily skipped beside them, chattering about whether her new teacher would like the picture she'd drawn.

"There it is," Henry said as they rounded the corner and the brick elementary school came into view. "Your new school."

Alicia's chest tightened with the familiar mixture of pride and anxiety that came with watching her children take their next steps toward independence. Gray squared his shoulders as they approached the building, and Lily bounced on her toes with excitement.

"Come here," she said, crouching down and opening her arms to them. Both Gray and Lily did as she asked, and she looked each of them right in the eyes. "I love you forever." Her voice caught in her throat, and she smiled to try to dislodge it. "We'll be right here to pick you up at three o'clock."

She gathered both of them into her chest at the same time, trying to hold onto the moment for as long as possible.

"Okay, Mom," Gray said, but he hugged her anyway. Tightly too.

"Have an amazing day," she whispered, holding them close for one more moment before letting them join the stream of children flowing through the school doors. She straightened and waved at Lily just before the little girl disappeared, the hallway and other students swallowing her right up.

Henry's arm settled around her waist. "They're going to love it here," he said.

"I know," Alicia said, though she kept watching the doors. She took a breath and turned to face him.

She'd restored more than the cottage over the past months. She'd restored her confidence in her ability to balance competing demands, her faith in the possibility of having both career success and personal fulfillment. Most importantly, she'd restored her belief that she deserved both.

"Henry," she said at the same time he asked, "Should we go get coffee?"

She ducked her head and laced her fingers through his. They took a few steps away from the school, from the crowds, and Alicia cleared her throat.

"Do you want kids?" She turned to watch him, needing to see his reaction.

His eyes widened, but he settled quickly, and Alicia didn't need him to answer verbally.

"Mandie's pregnant," she said. "And I know we're both older than her, but I'm not so old that I can't have another baby."

"I'd love a baby," Henry whispered.

Warmth filled Alicia from top to bottom, and she nodded. "I wouldn't mind either, and I'm not really going to go out in the field anymore, so I'll be able to be a better mom."

"Lish, you're a great mom." He pulled open the door to the coffee shop and out came a roar of chatter and noise. "And great in the field."

Alicia basked in it, this vibrancy of the city she'd missed in Five Island Cove. "Yeah, but Candace has asked me to be the Department Head over the field accountants, and this way, I'll get to wear all my cute skirts and heels *and* be home every morning, evening, and weekend."

She grinned at him. "With you, and with the kids."

The day stretched ahead of her, quiet and unhurried. In a few hours, she'd walk back to the school to collect Gray and Lily, to hear about their first day and sign all of their forms. Tonight, she'd cook dinner in her own kitchen and tuck her children into their beds in their new house. She'd whisper with Henry as they lay in each other's arms, and they'd dream about a future together.

Tomorrow, she'd return to the PastForward office, but as a different person than the one who'd left for the cottage project months ago. She'd return as someone who knew her worth, who understood her priorities, and who'd learned that the most successful restoration of all was the one she'd performed on her own life.

Chapter Twenty-Three

⁓

C andace adjusted the silver bracelet on her wrist and surveyed the transformed cottage from the newly graveled driveway. String lights draped between the mature oak trees cast a warm glow over the gathering crowd, and the white cedar shingles gleamed under the early evening light. The lit windows beckoned guests inside, where soft jazz music drifted through the open front door.

"Candace, this place is absolutely *stunning*." Lana appeared at her side, radiant in a navy dress that complemented her honey-colored hair. She carried herself with the poise of someone comfortable in her own skin, and a surge of pride moved through Candace that had nothing to do with business.

"Thank you for being here," Candace said, touching her daughter's arm. "I'm so glad you and Ted could make the trip."

"Are you kidding?" Lana practically vibrated with energy and smiles. "You create the most beautiful things, and I can't *wait* to go inside."

Ted approached them, his dark hair perfectly styled and his smile genuine. "Candace, congratulations. This restoration is remarkable." He shook her hand warmly. "Hey, sweetheart." He took her in his arms and kissed her quickly. "So it's a mingle-thing at the beginning?"

Candace nodded, her throat tight as yet another car arrived, this one a sleek black sedan that spit out a suited man with silver hair and then the Police Chief.

A dark-haired woman went to meet him, along with a beautiful young woman with sleek, nearly white-silver-blonde hair.

Then Mandie effortlessly moved over to them too, her face filled with radiance. She hugged the younger woman, then the older one. She shook the Chief's hand, and then the other man too.

They turned to face her, and Mandie's eyes found hers after only a moment. Candace knew her role here, and she glided across the pavers in her heels, her silver dress surely catching the light and tossing it around. Gems did that, after all.

"This is Candace," Mandie said. "She's the brains and power behind everything we do at PastForward."

"Good evening," Candace said.

"This is Aaron Sherman," Mandie said. "He's been the Chief of Police for years now. His wife, Eloise, is one of my mother's best friends. Their daughter, Billie, and his father, Greg." Mandie linked her arm through Greg's, and heck, she could be a string of lights for how brightly she glowed.

"Greg was Mayor of Five Island Cove for a while, right?"

"Yes, ma'am." He oozed politician charm, and Candace shook his hand.

"There's drinks and food around the back," she said.

"We're doing an open house until six, when we'll do our presentation."

"It's amazing," Billie gushed. "Look at that porch. We need a porch remodel." She moved off toward the house, taking her parents with her.

"We do?" Chief Sherman grumbled. "You don't even live here anymore."

Mandie giggled and turned to watch the next car arrive. "Oh, this is my parents. Be right back." She bustled off to greet them, and for some reason, a flutter of nerves assaulted Candace's stomach.

The current mayor—Mayor Danielson—laughed, and his big, boisterous voice filled the air. He wore a black suit and his blond hair appropriately windswept. His wife, who looked to be about a decade older than him, stood beside him in a flowing, silk, flowered dress.

They held glasses of rosé and chatted with a couple of other island authorities that Candace had met but forgotten the names of. Mandie knew everyone in the cove, and Candace appreciated her making all the introductions.

Alicia and Henry stood out front too, both of them dressed like the professionals they were. Their children did too, though they looked bored already. Still, they stayed at Alicia's side instead of running around and causing chaos.

She hadn't seen Suzie since arriving, but she'd been wearing a pearly-peachy dress that made her look like a princess, with Daniel her prince at her side in a deep navy suit and a pocket square that matched Suzie's gown.

"Candace, this is my mother," Mandie said. "I believe you've met her, but I can't remember."

"Yes," Candace said diplomatically, her smile stretching

in a professional way. "We've met, but it's lovely to see you again."

Mandie's mother—Robin—smiled too, her blonde hair curled perfectly to match the tip-up of her lips. "You too, Candace." She leaned in for a quick hug, then introduced her husband.

By then, Charlie had arrived with his parents, and Mandie clutched his hand and said, "They have mini beef Wellingtons on the back deck. Will you go get me one?"

"Sure thing, baby." He pressed a kiss to her forehead and took his parents and hers with him. Mandie stayed to keep greeting guests, and she introduced Candace to all of her parents' friends that had known Mandie growing up in the cove, as well as everyone else she and Alicia had curated onto the guest list.

Suzie joined them after a few minutes, and Charlie showed up just as his grandparents emerged from an SUV.

Candace's pulse blipped through its beat, but she fixed her smile onto her face and went to welcome them.

"Hey, Grandpa," Charlie said, giving Connor a quick hug. "Grams."

Mandie did the same, and then Suzie did too. Watching her—the Bulldozer—soften, become feminine, and exhibit such caring made Candace's heart turn to marshmallow too.

At least for a moment.

They had never told Connor or Della about the letters, nor would they. Candace had once buried the past, hoping it would never resurface.

"My daughter, Lana," she said, introducing her to Connor and Della. Her past had come back into her life, and it had been a wonderful thing.

But the letters would only add to Connor's pain, not

lighten it. He and Della went with Mandie and Charlie, leaving Candace with Alicia and Suzie now.

"Where are Henry and Daniel?" she asked.

"Henry took the kids down to the beach," Alicia said.

"How are you two coping with Mandie's departure?" Candace glanced over to Lana, who raised her eyebrows. "Yes?"

"Ted and I are going to get something to drink. Would you like something?"

"Just seltzer," Candace said, for she never drank at company functions like this. She needed her wits about her, after all.

"It feels like the whole cove turned out," Alicia said. "We had an excellent RSVP rate, and I think everyone's here."

Candace nodded, acutely aware that neither of them had answered her question. At least not verbally, but the way they hadn't wanted to say told Candace what she needed to know.

Mandie was a special woman, and she couldn't be replaced.

"Ladies and gentlemen." Mandie's voice carried across the lawn as she stepped onto the front porch, her tablet in hand and her smile radiant. She wore a flowing green dress that complemented her honey-blonde hair, and Charlie stood beside her in a dark brown suit, his hand resting protectively on her lower back.

The crowd quieted, drinks and conversation pausing as all attention focused on the young woman who had led this project with such skill and passion.

"Welcome to the Black Sand Bungalow," Mandie began, her voice strong and clear. "Or, as I like to call it—the Cove Cottage."

A smattering of applause moved through the crowd, and

Mandie smiled politely until it abated. "What you see before you tonight represents months of careful restoration, but more importantly, it represents the preservation of a piece of Five Island Cove history."

Candace watched faces in the crowd, noting how Connor Williams dabbed at his eyes while Della squeezed his hand. These people loved their islands, that was for certain, and Candace had witnessed this kind of deep connection to place before. It was one of the things she loved most about her restoration projects. She got to see how the memory of a place shaped and formed lives.

"This project succeeded because of an incredible team," Mandie said, glancing up from her notes. "Suzie Paxman brought her expertise in historical research and restoration techniques, ensuring every detail honored the cottage's original character while meeting modern standards."

Suzie stood near the rose garden with Daniel, her cheeks pink with pleasure at the recognition.

"And," Mandie said, shooting Suzie a knowing look. "She did it all while engaged and planning her wedding, so we want to acknowledge her fiancé, Daniel, for sharing her with us."

Suzie grinned and shook her head, but she leaned into Daniel, who put a protective arm around her and waved as if he'd single-handedly brought this cottage back to life.

"See, working on a project like this is all-consuming," Mandie said. "Our loved ones sometimes wonder if we'll be eaten alive by the enormity of tasks, how we can't talk about anything but the project, and the sheer number of light switch covers a house needs—or in this case, white pine shingles and lark-carved knobs."

She spoke flawlessly, and she only looked down at her

notes after saying a whole section. Now, she cleared her throat, a flash of emotion crossing her face.

Candace frowned, though she certainly couldn't fire Mandie for letting her emotions show. And was that so bad, anyway?

In the past, Candace would've said yes. But now, she actually appreciated seeing how the project and the people who'd worked on it with her affected Mandie.

"Alicia Swinton managed every financial detail and time-line with precision that kept us on budget and on schedule, no small feat for a project of this scope."

Alicia smiled from her position near the front steps, where Henry held Gray's hand while Lily pressed into her mother's side. The family looked settled and happy, and Candace's gratitude for Alicia's dedication even as she balanced her responsibilities as a mother doubled, and then tripled.

"Not only that, but Alicia is a best friend to everyone who meets her, and she's a mother of two, and she got married a week before this project started. She is the kind of woman you want on speed-dial, and she gladly answers texts in the middle of the night when her team is freaking out over the color of paint that they signed off on just the day before."

Alicia took a few slow steps up to the porch and took the mic from Mandie. It seemed rehearsed, as Mandie didn't wear any surprise on her face.

"I never do this," Alicia said. "But I just have to interrupt."

Mandie stared at her now, and Candace's pulse boomed as she saw Suzie moving toward the porch now too. What in the world was going on? Candace approved every part of the gala, including who said what, and these two were *not* on the agenda.

"I don't know if *gladly* is the word I'd use," Alicia said, beaming at Mandie and then the crowd. "And *Mandie*, as the team lead, chose the paint color and approved it without any team meeting, so if it's awful, that was *not* a team decision."

Suzie arrived on the porch, and she reached for the mic. Alicia relinquished it to her, her surprise melting into her smile.

"The paint color is perfect," she said, her voice a tad brusque. "So there's no chance Mandie will be in any trouble over that." She surveyed the crowd. "Mandie has more to say about the dozens of others who worked with us on this project, but I happen to know she didn't put in anything about herself."

"Suzie," Mandie warned, but she took a step away from the team lead.

"Our construction team, led by Jake Morrison, transformed architectural plans into reality with craftsmanship that will weather storms for generations," she said. "Where are you, Jake? Raise your hand, and everyone on the crew should too."

Jake raised his beer bottle in acknowledgment, his crew scattered throughout the crowd, their faces bearing the satisfaction of work well done as they waved.

"We couldn't have done anything without them," Suzie said. "Or the talented tradesmen here in the cove, from the master carver we discovered on Pearl Island who did the larks in the kitchen, to the woodworkers who did the shingles, flooring, and staircases."

She looked over to Alicia, who nodded.

Suzie faced the crowd again, her features hard and square. But she softened as she said, "This is Mandie's last project with us, and both Alicia and I—" She cleared her throat, and Candace's whole body tingled.

She wouldn't be able to give this speech any better. Mandie stood off to the side now, resigned to whatever Suzie and Alicia wanted to say.

"We are going to be lost without her," Suzie said, her voice a bit raspy and rough. "She has led us on our last three projects, and she has a unique perspective on things that no one else does. She leads us fearlessly and always has, and I can't think of someone I respect and love more than her."

She passed the mic to Alicia and moved around her to hug Mandie. The two women gripped each other, and Candace reached up and wiped her eyes simply watching them.

"Everything Suzie said is true," Alicia said. "If you've been through the cottage, you've seen a piece of Mandie in every item. She has the ability to leave her mark on something in invisible ways, and yes, she's branded herself onto our hears, and we'll miss her greatly."

She twisted, and Mandie took a couple of steps over to her and took the mic. "Thank you," she said, her voice a touch nasally. "I was not planning on anyone saying anything."

She looked down at her tablet and Candace caught the way her chest rose and fell in a long, slow breath.

"And finally." Mandie looked up, her eyes scanning the yard in front of her. "This project exists because Candace Ewing had the vision to see potential where others saw only decay, and she alone had the commitment to invest in preserving our community's history."

Lana squealed, which drew the attention of nearly everyone. Candace didn't want to wave and smile like a Disney princess, but she did anyway. What people didn't understand was that she had done very little here.

In fact, the best thing she'd done was send Mandie, Suzie, and Alicia.

"Thank you for joining us here tonight," Mandie said. "And we hope you'll explore the cove cottage in all her glory, enjoy the refreshments, and experience what happens when a community comes together to honor its past while building its future."

Applause erupted across the lawn, and heat rose through Candace's cheeks. She nodded graciously to those around her, but her focus remained on her team, on the people who had made this transformation possible through their skill and dedication.

The crowd started flowing through the front door and around the deck toward the back of the property. Candace followed the stream of guests inside, eager to see their reactions to the completed interior.

The living room buzzed with conversation as people admired the textured wallpaper with its golden rose pattern. The evening light streaming through the stained glass windows created pools of sapphire, emerald, and amber on the floors and walls, just as Alicia had promised.

Candace moved through the rooms, listening to conversations and watching faces. She heard things like, "Did you see those horned larks in the kitchen?" to "I need a staircase like this." Each comment added to her happiness quota, and she did her best to simply be an observer to those around her, and to the cottage.

The before-and-after video played on a loop on a large

screen in the master bedroom, showing the cottage's transformation from weathered neglect, where nature had tried to reclaim it by putting trees through the roof, to the demo that had reduced it to the studs, to the repairs, to the complete restoration.

Flint had captured every phase of the process, and his videos always created a feast for the eyes and provided an insider view to what it took to do a project like this.

"Incredible," Mayor Danielson said, shaking Candace's hand as the video finished and a countdown timer for the next one began. "This sets a new standard for historic preservation in our community."

"The team deserves all the credit," Candace said, meaning every word. "They brought passion and expertise to every decision."

Connor appeared beside her, his eyes bright with unshed tears. "My wife would have loved seeing her cottage brought back to life like this. The roses, the attention to detail, the way you've honored her memory."

Della nodded, squeezing Connor's arm. "It's beautiful, truly beautiful."

"Thank you." Candace thought of the letters hidden away, the secrets that would remain buried. But looking at Connor's peaceful expression, she knew they had made the right choice. Some truths served no purpose except to cause pain.

"Would you like to see the beach access?" she asked, gesturing toward the back deck.

The group moved outside, where the new wooden staircase curved down the cliff face toward the black sand beach below. The railing caught the evening light, and the sound of waves provided a constant, soothing backdrop.

"Fifty-four steps," Mandie announced, appearing beside them with Charlie.

"May I?" Connor asked, gesturing toward the stairs.

"Of course," Candace said. "That's what they're for."

She watched as Connor and Della began their descent, followed by other guests eager to experience the private beach. The stairs handled the traffic easily, Jake's construction proving as solid as promised.

Lana joined her at the railing, where they both watched the guests explore the beach below. "This is what you do," Lana said softly. "You create spaces where families can make memories."

"It's not what *I* do," Candace said. "It takes a *team* to make something like this happen."

"It's extraordinary," a woman said, and Candace turned to find Alice and Arthur standing hand-in-hand.

"Candace." Alice smiled at her, and the woman reminded Candace so much of herself. Proper. Sophisticated. Perhaps a bit intimidating to others. But Alice had a softness Candace was still learning to develop and then exhibit.

"I wanted to thank you for what you've done here. This cottage holds special meaning for my family, and seeing it restored so beautifully brings me great peace."

"I'm glad we could honor its history." Candace moved into her and gave her a light hug. "Thank you for lending us Mandie for so long. We sure are going to miss her."

"She is one-of-a-kind," Alice said as she stepped back. She wore nothing but love in her expression. "We're glad she's going to stay with us in the cove, though I know what that means for you."

"We'll have to muddle through," Candace said, and Alice

and Arthur nodded and moved over to a table where goat cheese tarts were being served.

She turned back to the railing, and she linked her arm through Lana's. "Where's Ted?"

"He found someone who loves Corvettes as much as she does." Lana beamed at her. "They're speaking English words, but I don't understand what they're saying."

Candace laughed, and it felt so freeing as it left her lungs and flowed out of her mouth. She couldn't wait to see her daughter walk down the aisle and get married.

For that matter, she couldn't wait to watch Suzie do that too, and she couldn't wait to get pictures of Mandie's baby when the time came, and she hoped to cheer Alicia on in any way possible as well.

She thought of Mandie, preparing for motherhood and a new chapter in Five Island Cove. Of Alicia, building a blended family while advancing her career on her own terms. Of Suzie, planning a wedding and learning to trust in love's permanence.

Each of them had grown over the past few years, just as she had. They had become more than colleagues; they had become a chosen family, connected by shared challenges and mutual respect.

The cove cottage would sell quickly, she knew. The restoration was flawless, the location unparalleled, and the story compelling. But the real success of this project lay not in profit margins or market response. It lay in the relationships forged, the skills developed, and the confidence gained by everyone involved.

Candace had owned PastForward for decades, but it wasn't until this year that she'd learned to build more than beautiful spaces. She had learned to build a life that balanced professional achievement with personal connection, and that balance felt like the greatest restoration of all.

"Hey, they just brought out more lobster mac and cheese," Lana said. "Do you—?"

"Yes," Candace said, finally ready to let down her boss persona and have something to eat at one of her parties. "Let's get a glass of wine too. This is a party, right?"

Lana giggled and led the way into the gorgeous kitchen, where most of the food and drink waited for guests. "Yes, Candace, this is a party."

Chapter Twenty-Four

Mandie stood on the sidewalk at the departure gates while Suzie and Alicia got their baggage out of the trunk of the RideShare. Her stomach vibrated, and she couldn't stop her hands from winding around each other.

Her best friends were leaving the cove for good today.

She was no longer employed at PastForward. Tomorrow, a Monday, would dawn with Charlie getting up and going to work as normal, and Mandie would...spend the day doing something.

She actually had plans to go to breakfast with her mom, but after that, Mandie could do whatever she wanted. She'd thought about planting some bulbs that would bloom next spring, or finally going through the last boxes she and Charlie hadn't unpacked yet.

"All right." Suzie slammed the trunk and hefted her big bag up onto the sidewalk. She led the way inside, something Mandie might normally have done. Today, though, she let her friends go first, as they both had tickets back to New York City.

She waited while they checked in and tagged their bags. They dropped them off, and Alicia faced her wearing a sensible black travel suit and a backpack. Suzie came away from the counter a moment later, and she wore her usual jeans and tee, and she too sported a black backpack.

Normally, they'd just head for security, but the three of them stood there and looked at each other. The morning sun streamed in through the windows behind them, warm despite the autumnal chill that had arrived with the first full week of September.

Mandie love, love, *loved* fall in the cove, and that alone buoyed her spirits enough for her to smile. "Come on, you guys. You're just going back to the city. We have working phones."

"I just can't believe this is it." Alicia adjusted her purse strap unnecessarily and looked over her shoulder.

Suzie shifted too, her engagement ring catching the light as she fidgeted with her boarding pass. "It doesn't feel real yet. Going back to the office tomorrow without you there." She exchanged a glance with Alicia. "It's going to be weird."

"Yeah," Alicia said.

"You'll be fine," Mandie said, though her throat tightened around the words. "You have each other, and Candace is going to need you both more than ever." She moved into Suzie and hugged her. "I know we haven't always gotten along, but you're amazing, and I miss you already."

Suzie gripped her hard, as sometimes Suze did way more than she said. Mandie absolutely felt the other woman's love for her, and she squeezed her eyes closed as she hugged Suzie back.

She finally released her, and Mandie moved over to Alicia, her emotions quivering. They broke, and she let the tears stream down her face as she hugged her best friend. "I hate that I'm not going back," she said, her voice tinny and too high. At the same time, she knew she belonged in Five Island Cove.

"Me too," Alicia said.

Mandie stepped back and wiped her eyes, noting that Lish did too. "We're okay." She took a deep breath. "People say goodbye all the time."

"And it's just goodbye for now, anyway," Alicia said.

Mandie nodded, and she glanced over to Suzie.

"I need to say something," Suzie said, her voice carrying that familiar note of determination. "Before I start crying and can't talk."

She turned to face Mandie directly, her blue-green eyes bright and serious. "You taught me how to be part of a team. Before you, I just bulldozed through everything alone. But you showed me that asking for help isn't weakness, and that the best work happens when people trust each other completely."

Mandie's tears started anew, because Suzie had worked at PastForward for a lot longer than Mandie. "Suze—"

"Let me finish." Suzie held up her hand. "You're going to be an incredible mother, because you already know how to bring out the best in people. That baby is *so* lucky."

Alicia stepped forward, wrapping her arms around both of them. "She's right. You have this gift for making everyone feel valued and capable."

The three of them held each other tightly, and Mandie breathed in the familiar scents of Alicia's vanilla perfume and Suzie's practical soap. She wanted to freeze this moment, to hold onto the feeling of being surrounded by people who understood her completely.

They breathed in together and pulled apart, and Suzie swiped almost angrily at her eyes. "I'm going to send a poll for my honeymoon," she said.

"A poll?" Mandie blinked and then started laughing. It felt strange to have hot tears in her eyes and laughter coming out of her mouth, but that was about how their team had always worked.

"We can't agree on where to go," Suzie said in her defense. "So yes, I'm going to poll the people I trust most." She hitched her backpack higher and checked her phone. "We need to get going, Lish."

"Yep." She grabbed onto Mandie again. "Promise me you'll send pictures of everything. The baby bump progress, the nursery, Charlie being ridiculous and not letting you go anywhere alone in the last couple of months."

"I promise." New emotion took the place of the sadness that had been plaguing her since Friday night's gala. Now, only good memories soared through her mind, reminding her of all the amazing experiences she'd had with these women.

She stepped back and looked at Suzie. "And you have to send me wedding planning updates. I want to see every flower arrangement and dress option."

"Deal," Suzie said, then surprised Mandie by initiating another hug. "I love you, my friend."

"I love you too."

Alicia joined them for one final embrace. "The dream team lives on."

Mandie giggled again. Dream team. She distinctly remembered how she'd fought for that first field assignment with Alicia. Suzie had been assigned later, and Mandie had *not* been happy about it.

Now, she couldn't imagine working with anyone but the two of them.

"Okay," she said. "You guys still have to get through security."

"Yep." Alicia sniffled and looked at Suzie. "Let's go." They walked toward the security checkpoint together, but Mandie stayed where she was. She watched as her friends started through the maze of ropes, waving when they both turned back to her one last time.

The entirety of the airport felt empty without them, even though plenty of other travelers moved through the space. Mandie found a seat near the windows of the waiting area and checked her phone. Ginny and Bob's flight from Boston wouldn't arrive for another hour, giving her time to process the goodbye she'd just experienced.

She placed her hand on her still-small belly, imagining the tiny life growing there. "Your Aunt Suzie and Aunt Alicia just left," she whispered. "But don't worry, they'll be back to spoil you rotten."

An hour later, Mandie stood at the baggage claim carousels, scanning the stream of passengers streaming through the wall of glass that separated cleared passengers from those waiting to greet them.

She spotted Ginny's dark hair first, then Bob's tall frame behind her, carrying a diaper bag over his shoulder, a duffle in his hand, and wearing a backpack.

"Ginny!" She raised her hand and bounced on her toes. Oh, how she'd missed Ginny.

"Mandie!" Ginny rushed toward her, baby Caroline nestled against her chest in a soft pink carrier. The baby looked at her with big brown eyes and long lashes, and Mandie fell in love with her instantly.

"Oh, wow," Mandie breathed, reaching out to touch Caroline's impossibly small hand. "She's perfect."

"Isn't she?" Ginny's face glowed with exhaustion and joy. "I can't believe how much she's grown already."

"Look at those cheeks." Mandie grinned at the chubby-cheeked baby and then her best friend. She hugged her, her eyes drifting closed again, this time in bliss. "You're here."

"We made it," Ginny said. "And Caroline didn't howl on the plane for very long."

"She didn't howl at all." Bob grinned at Mandie, and she released Ginny to hug him. "Hey, you."

Mandie took the diaper bag from him. "How was the flight?"

"She slept most of the way," Bob said. "I'm going to go get our bags."

Ginny nodded as she patted Caroline's bottom and swayed. "You're sure we can stay with you?"

"Of course," Mandie said. They hadn't bought any baby furniture or items yet, as she wasn't due for six more months. "If you'd rather—"

"No, we want to," Ginny said. "I just wasn't sure if you wanted to, I don't know, have some quiet time now that you're done with your project."

Mandie did usually need some downtime, but the cove cottage hadn't been as crazy as her other projects. "I think your mom might be a little miffed."

"We're going to be here for a week." Ginny rolled her eyes. "She'll be begging us to leave once she realizes that Caroline only sleeps during the day and screams all night." She grinned at Mandie. "Bob said we can get a hotel if we need to."

Mandie was sure they could, as Bob had been practicing

law with a huge corporation for over five years now. He and Ginny seemed to have plenty of money, and they both loved living in Boston.

Bob reappeared with their luggage, looking from Ginny to Mandie and back. "Ready?"

"Only if we're going to Mort's for lunch. I am *dying* for one of their lobster rolls."

Mandie giggled and turned toward the exit. "As if you can't get a good lobster roll in Boston."

"Is that a no to Mort's?"

"Of course not," Mandie said. "I told Charlie I'd get him something he can take to work tomorrow."

LATER THAT EVENING, MANDIE PULLED BOWLS from the refrigerator, her movements automatic as she began setting out the appetizers she'd planned. Spinach and artichoke dip—already ready to go into the oven—and a fruit salad that would complement the roast Alice was bringing.

The simple act of cooking in her own kitchen filled her with satisfaction. She'd made do in small kitchens in tiny city apartments too, and she simply liked taking a little bit of this and some of that and making something delicious out of all of it together.

In all honesty, her projects at PastForward were the same thing: taking a variety of things—like paint color, a stained glass window, a carved-lark knob—and putting them together in a thoughtful, beautiful way.

She'd just slid the artichoke dip into the oven to get bubbly and brown when the side door opened.

Charlie walked in, laughing, with Bob only a pace behind

him. Ginny brought up the rear, and she passed Caroline to her husband so she could join Mandie in the kitchen. "What are we having for dinner?"

"How was the beach?"

"It's magical." Ginny sighed happily.

"Your mom is bringing pot roast and veggies," Mandie said, naming the classic Sunday dinner. "These are just appetizers, and I'm putting cheddar chive biscuits together next."

"What's your mom bringing?"

"Blueberry cobbler." Mandie's mouth watered just thinking about it. "She's been buying as many as she can for the last month." She grinned at Ginny. "We're lucky she's willing to part with some of them for this."

Ginny giggled. "Is she making her vanilla bean ice cream?"

"Of course." Mandie got out a bowl and then the dry ingredients she needed for the biscuits. "I need eggs and milk."

Ginny moved around the kitchen as if she'd been there for longer than a few hours. Mandie glanced into the living room, where Charlie now held Caroline, his face alight with joy.

Her heart squeezed, the moment absolutely magical—and that wasn't even their baby.

She blinked, so glad she hadn't gotten teary. She focused on final prep for dinner, chit-chatting with Ginny about what they were going to do with Caroline at Halloween—"I already have her costume," Ginny said. "It's this cute little cow onesie."—and if they'd come home for Thanksgiving or Christmas.

Before she knew it, the doorbell rang, followed immediately by her mother's voice calling, "Cobbler incoming."

Mandie's chest tightened, because this was the first big-family dinner she was hosting in her home here in Five Island Cove. Not only that, but she and Charlie had their pregnancy news to share.

"Dad, you can put the ice cream in the freezer in the carport," Mandie said as her father entered the house with a huge ten-gallon container that obviously held ice cream.

"Are we going to enclose that?" Dad asked, coming closer. "I can come help make it a real garage."

"That would be great," Charlie said, getting to his feet.

Mom practically threw the pan of blueberry cobbler on the counter as she said, "Give me that baby. Oh, my word, look how *cute* she is!" She cooed and kissed Caroline, who squealed and flapped one arm.

"We're here too," Alice called, but she came in the side door just as Dad tried to go that way. Things had gotten busy very quickly, but Mandie absolutely loved the energy of having more people in the house.

Dad dodged her and headed outside, while Alice brought in her slow cooker and set it on the counter. The timer on the oven went off, and Mandie slid her hands into a pair of potholders and pulled out the cheddar chive biscuits.

Ginny picked up the pastry brush and started buttering the hot bread, and Mandie followed her with a parmesan-cheese-garlic-salt mixture that melted right into the butter.

"Smells amazing," Mom said, and Mandie smiled at her briefly before resuming her task. She passed Caroline to Alice, and added, "What do you need help with?"

"Setting the table," Mandie said, and her mom dove right in to get that done. Charlie and Bob put the leaf in, and Mande was impressed that Charlie managed to find a tablecloth in the linen closet.

Everything came together quickly after that, and Mandie put the artichoke dip with tortilla chips on the table, along with the fruit salad and the cheddar biscuits. "Everyone come sit down," she called, and in that moment, she realized she sounded exactly like her mother.

She wondered if anyone else heard or saw the same thing, but no one seemed to as they converged on the dining room table and took their seats.

Mandie stood at the corner, her seat in front of her, and looked over to Charlie as he came to her side.

"We have an announcement," she said. Her mother sucked in a breath, and Mandie shot her a glare.

The room fell exceptionally quiet, with Ginny's eyes wide, and Alice watching her with a calculated silence that spoke volumes.

"We're going to have a baby," Charlie said, his voice warm with pride and joy. His arm snaked around her waist and tucked her against his side. "Mandie is due in early April."

It felt like a wave had been sucked back out to sea, and in that pause, nothing moved. Nothing breathed. No one spoke.

Then Mom jumped to her feet. "Congratulations." She let her tears run down her face as she bowled into Mandie and held her tightly. Voices clamored then, offering congrats and asking more questions.

Mandie hugged Ginny next, and then Alice, who smoothed her hand over Mandie's hair and down her face. "You will be a wonderful mother," she said. "We're so happy for you both."

"Thank you, Alice." Mandie sank into her seat, the enormity of this day finally settling onto her shoulders. Her stomach growled, which caused her father to chuckle.

"Let's eat," Charlie said, and he handed Mandie a plate with two biscuits on it.

She got back to her feet and went into the kitchen. "Roast and potatoes in here," she said. "Or you can have dessert first."

"No, the dessert is for later," Mom said. "We're going to take it across the highway to the beach and eat it there."

"We are?" Mandie asked.

"It's the best place to eat blueberry cobbler with vanilla ice cream," she said simply, and Mandie grinned at her.

"I can't believe you didn't tell me about the baby," Ginny said, and Mandie looked over to her. She wore nothing but her usual happy glow. "Our kids will be so close in age."

"Too bad you and Bob can't move back here."

"Or you and Charlie can't move to Boston."

Mandie had just gotten settled here—and she had more to do to truly feel like this was her house—but she grinned at Ginny. "You know what? Anything is possible."

"What are you saying?" Ginny searched her face, her eyes wide and filled with hope. "Would you and Charlie move to Boston?"

"Who would've ever thought we'd come back here?" Mandie smiled and shook her head. "There's only a few pharmacies here."

"Mandie likes to leave doors open," Charlie said.

She smiled at him as he sat down beside her at the table, others still getting food and returning to the table. "Yes, I do," she said. "Because if you close them, you might miss out on an amazing opportunity."

Ginny sat across from her while her mom took the seat

beside her. "Have you thought about names?" she asked, pinching off a piece of biscuit and putting it on the tray of Caroline's highchair.

"We've talked about a few," Mandie said evasively. "It's one of those things I'm sure will hit me like a ton of bricks when it's the right one."

She scooped up a bite of roasted potatoes and carrots, two of her favorite things, and glanced around the table at all of her favorite people. The eastern sun came in the window behind Ginny and Bob, casting their hair in a golden halo as they smiled at one another and Alice asked, "Do you want a boy or a girl?"

Every home she'd restored had started with one thing: vision. And now, this house, her life—this messy, magical, unfinished life—had become her newest project.

One she was building from the inside out, one moment, one memory at a time—starting right now, right here.

I'm so happy for Suzie, Alicia, and Mandie! They overcame so many odds, grew together, grew to love one another, and found their happily-ever-afters!

Books in The Hamptons series

The Hampton House, Book 1: Mandie Kelton, Alicia Halverson, and Suzette Paxman are drawn together by the allure of forgotten elegance and the shadows of the past. They'll have to learn to get along if they have any hope of keeping their jobs, and as they restore an abandoned mansion in The Hamptons, they'll also discover the lost and hidden parts of themselves that make them into the women they're meant to be.

The Yacht Club, Book 2: Mandie Kelton, fresh from the triumphant restoration of the Hampton House, faces a new challenge when her boss, Candace Ewing, reveals their next project: restoring a famous historical yacht once owned by a legendary figure. Tasked with breathing new life into the venerable vessel, Mandie, along with her trusted friends and colleagues—Suzie, Alicia, and the enigmatic Candace—embarks on a journey that will test their skills and uncover long-buried secrets.

The Cove Cottage, Book 3: As the women work together to breathe new life into the Cove Cottage, they realize that the restoration is about more than just bricks and mortar; it's a journey of self-discovery, healing, and the enduring bonds of friendship. With unexpected revelations lurking in the shadows, can they find the courage to uncover the truth and embrace the future?

Books in the Five Island Cove series

The Lighthouse, Book 1: As these 5 best friends work together to find the truth, they learn to let go of what doesn't matter and cling to what does: faith, family, and most of all, friendship.

Secrets, safety, and sisterhood...it all happens at the lighthouse on Five Island Cove.

The Summer Sand Pact, Book 2:

These five best friends made a Summer Sand Pact as teens and have only kept it once or twice—until they reunite decades later and renew their agreement to meet in Five Island Cove every summer.

The Cliffside Inn, Book 3: Spend another month in Five Island Cove and experience an amazing adventure between five best friends, the challenges they face, the secrets threatening to come between them, and their undying support of each other.

Christmas at the Cove, Book 4: Secrets are never discovered during the holidays, right? That's what these five best friends are banking on as they gather once again to Five Island Cove for what they hope will be a Christmas to remember.

The House on Seabreeze Shore, Book 5: Your next trip to Five Island Cove...this time to face a fresh future and leave all the secrets and fears in the past. Join best friends, old and new, as they learn about themselves, strengthen their bonds of friendship, and learn what it truly means to thrive.

Four Weddings and a Baby, Book 6: When disaster strikes, whose wedding will be postponed? Whose dreams will be underwater?

And there's a baby coming too... Best friends, old and new, must learn to work together to clean up after a natural disaster that leaves bouquets and altars, bassinets and baby blankets, in a soggy heap.

The Seafaring Girls, Book 7: Journey to Five Island Cove for a roaring good time with friends old and new, their sons and daughters, and all their new husbands as they navigate the heartaches and celebrations of life and love.

But when someone returns to the Cove that no one ever expected to see again, old wounds open just as they'd started to heal. This group of women will be tested again, both on land and at sea, just as they once were as teens.

Rebuilding Friendship Inn, Book 8: Clara Tanner has lost it all. Her husband is accused in one of the biggest heists on the East Coast, and she relocates her family to Five Island Cove—the hometown she hates.

Clara needs all of their help and support in order to rebuild Friendship Inn, and as all the women pitch in, there's so much more getting fixed up, put in place, and restored.

Then a single phone call changes everything.

Will these women in Five Island Cove rally around one another as they've been doing? Or will this finally be the thing that breaks them?

The Glass Dolphin, Book 9: With new friends in Five Island Cove, has the group grown too big? Is there room for all the different personalities, their problems, and their expanding population?

The Bicycle Book Club, Book 10: Summer is upon Five Island Cove, and that means beach days with friends and family, an explosion of tourism, and summer reading programs! When Tessa decides to look into the past to help shape the future, what she finds in the Five Island Cove library archives could bring them closer together...or splinter them forever.

The Holiday House, Book 11:
Revisit Five Island Cove at Christmastime! Join the women in the cove as they come together for a wedding, the holidays, and new ideals to what it means to be a mother, daughter, sister, aunt, and friend.

The Summer of Weddings, Book 12: In the picturesque setting of Five Island Cove, the bonds of friendship are as enduring as the tides. This summer, the cove is abuzz with wedding bells as Mandie and Charlie, Ginny and Bob, and Julia and Liam prepare to say their vows!

Books in the Nantucket Point series

The Cottage on Nantucket, Book 1: When two sisters arrive at the cottage on Nantucket after their mother's death, they begin down a road filled with the ghosts of their past. And when Tessa finds a final letter addressed only to her in a locked desk drawer, the two sisters will uncover secret after secret that exposes them to danger at their Nantucket cottage.

The Lighthouse Inn, Book 2: The Nantucket Historical Society pairs two women together to begin running a defunct inn, not knowing that they're bitter enemies. When they come face-to-face, Julia and Madelynne are horrified and dumbstruck—and bound together by their future commitment and their obstacles in their pasts...

The Seashell Promise, Book 3: When two sisters arrive at the cottage on Nantucket after their mother's death, they begin down a road filled with the ghosts of their past. And when Tessa finds a final letter addressed only to her in a locked desk drawer, the two sisters will uncover secret after secret that exposes them to danger at their Nantucket cottage.

About Jessie

Jessie Newton is a saleswoman during the day and escapes into romance and women's fiction in the evening, usually with a cat and a cup of tea nearby. She is a Top 30 KU All-Star Author and a USA Today Bestselling Author. She also writes as Elana Johnson and Liz Isaacson as well, with almost 200 books to all of her names. Find out more at www.feelgoodfictionbooks.com.